The Forest Prime Evil

The Forest Prime Evil

Alan Russell

Walker and Company
New York

Sequoia Summer is a fictional movement created by the author and has
no relation to any of the Redwood Summer activities that occurred
in Humboldt County in 1990.
The author has also taken some literary license with the
geography of Humboldt County, creating several nonexistent cities.
The redwoods, amazingly enough, exist. No author would have imagination
enough to create them.

First published in the United States of America in 1992
by Walker Publishing Company, Inc.

Published simultaneously in Canada by Thomas Allen & Son
Canada, Limited, Markham, Ontario

Library of Congress Cataloging-in-Publication Data
Russell, Alan.
The Forest Prime Evil / Alan Russell.
p.   cm.
ISBN 0-8027-3204-6
I. Title.
PS3568.U7654F6   1992
813'.54—dc20   91-37240
CIP

Printed in the United States of America
2 4 6 8 10 9 7 5 3 1

*To the young man and the "old man"—my son,
Luke, and my father, Mark. And to Janet and Barb,
the "other" women in my life.*

The Forest Prime Evil

▽

1

THE STAIRWAY LEADING to my walk-up office on Geary sometimes attracts the homeless, but this was the first squatter I had ever seen in the lotus position. Drawing nearer, I recognized Josh Needleman. It had been five years since I had seen or talked with him. I called his name softly, and he opened his eyes. They were as dark as I remembered them, maybe a shade less brooding than Rasputin's. He rose with a yogi's grace, which probably explained a few years of his disappearance. Josh didn't bother with the conventional handshake, or inquiries about how I had been doing, just acted as if I should have been expecting him. Naturally, he didn't have an appointment. As I remembered, Josh had never been much for appointments. He once told me he never wanted to be a "prisoner of time." By his appearance, it hadn't taken him captive yet.

He was wearing homespun, still apparently believing it wrong to use any leather or animal product for clothing. Josh had once told me that it was not one of "man's higher purposes" to enslave and kill animals. His major quandary, I think, was trying to find what all man's higher purposes are. But, in the course of a sentence or two, I learned that he hadn't yet achieved sainthood. He was still human enough. He wanted revenge.

"We have made a vow," Josh told me, "to find Christopher Shepard's murderer, and exact justice upon those who killed him. This is a sacred pledge, one to which we have bound ourselves."

Christopher Shepard, better known as the Green Man, had thought that planting trees could solve the ills of the world, could cure pollution, end global warming, and help give new life to a tired planet. For twenty years the Green Man had quite literally worked at the grass-roots level, getting down on his hands and knees to plant seeds and seedlings in the earth. A month ago, he himself had been planted in the ground.

Shepard's death had brought more notoriety to Sequoia Summer than three months of active protesting. The summerlong gathering had attracted a small army of mostly young, mostly irreverent protesters to Humboldt County. In an effort to stop old-growth deforestation, the activists had linked arms against bulldozers and defied chain saws by tree sitting. David with a monkey wrench against Goliath.

Shepard was found dead in the middle of a controversial primeval forest he called home, a branch through his skull. One of his favorite quotations had been "He that loves the tree loves the branch." The proverb took on a new, and perverse, meaning in his death.

The death had been ruled accidental, the result of a limb that had fallen from one of the towering redwoods. No landscape is without its inherent dangers. Around the redwood forest are visible reminders of its hazards. When limbs fall several hundred feet, they frequently embed themselves deep in the forest floor. To the uninitiated, these limbs are often mistaken for trees. Over the years, the local folk have had reason to give them a name: widow-makers.

Some creative journalists had suggested that Shepard's body was found in a Christlike pose, supported by the wood. It wasn't like that, but none of the environmentalists had asked for retractions. What they wanted was an investigation. In Humboldt County, "cover-up" was being shouted almost as loudly as "timber."

I had grieved over the Green Man's death but hadn't paid much mind to those who claimed a murder had been committed. These days it's rare for a well-known person to die without an accompanying conspiracy theory, and usually a

TV movie of the week. I had followed the controversy, but I hadn't expected it to show up on my doorstep. Josh's talk of vows and pledging and binding sounded right out of the Middle Ages.

"Who," I asked, "is 'we'?"

"The Committee for Justice," he said.

"That doesn't tell me much."

"The Committee for Justice," Josh said carefully, "is a collective."

I waited patiently. He finally produced. "A collective," he proudly said, "made up of Sequoia Summer campers and members of EverGreen."

I might have told Josh his pride was misplaced. EverGreen wasn't exactly the Junior League. Members described themselves as rebels with a green cause, but others weren't so charitable. Eco-thugs, they said. Mainstream conservation groups were less than enamored with EverGreen's tactics and treated the organization as a pariah. EverGreeners didn't lead nature walks or circulate petitions to save the auk. They advocated ecodefense and justified their tactics by saying that everything they did—including monkey wrenching, tree spiking, sabotaging heavy equipment, and undertaking disinformation campaigns—was for the protection of Mother Earth. One national magazine had described their membership as "postpubescent Girl and Boy Scouts gone anarchic." The EverGreeners didn't sell cookies door to door. But if you had a hankering for smoke bombs, they could deliver faster than Domino's.

"I told them about you," Josh said. "I vouched for you."

Some endorsements you can live without. I had met Josh in a birding class seven years ago. He had been enrolled but only flirting with the idea of being an undergraduate at Berkeley. Even then, Josh's outside interests were more important to him than academics. The ornithology course was one of those Saturday University of California extension classes that attract a lot of older couples looking to share a new hobby. Odd men out find each other, and that's how Josh and I had hooked up.

Over time, I became his sounding board. We continued to see each other after our class was concluded, bird watching being the centerpiece of our relationship. Josh was better at birding than I, could make identifications more surely and quickly. He knew not to chatter out in the field, and he was more at ease there, less tense and vitriolic than elsewhere. But when the binoculars went down, his rigid rectitude and anger always returned. Josh railed against those who had eliminated our wetlands and eradicated the open spaces, the villains who had left the world fit only for "man, rats, ice plant, and pigeons."

I envied Josh his youthful passions, which is another way of saying I thought him naive. Sometimes I argued with him, but mostly I listened. I suppose he took my silence as consent; in most cases it was. But then, as now, I wasn't of the opinion that two wrongs make a right, or that seeking compromise is necessarily wrong. Josh had drawn lines and wasn't about to make any quarter with his many enemies, which seemed to include most of San Francisco, if not the world. I had figured he would ultimately mature and realize that everything isn't black and white, but it seemed he now saw only black and green. He had disappeared five years ago without bothering to tell me where he was going. I had assumed he would turn up sometime. Today was my lucky day.

"Why did you have to vouch for me?"

"We needed someone we could trust," he said. "Someone not in bed with the lumber barons and their political machine. We know they murdered him. It shouldn't be hard for you to prove that."

My mental alarm always goes off when anyone tells me how easy a job is going to be. Normally, you want to run away from cases like that. The rule of thumb in most murder investigations—and Shepard's death hadn't even been ruled a murder—is that if you don't have a pretty good idea who the killer is in the first forty-eight hours, the odds are it will never be solved. I tried to tell this to Josh, but he wasn't inclined to listen.

"The murder hasn't been solved," he said, "because those in power don't want it solved."

The Green Man had died in River Grove, a three-thousand-acre stand of old growth. River Grove was a rallying cry for both lumber interests and conservationists and offered about as much middle ground as abortion. The land was owned by Trans-Mississippi, one of the largest lumber companies in the county. Trans-Miss contended they had a right to "conduct business as usual" on their own property, while the environmentalists were convinced that any business that pursued the "murder of national treasures" was both immoral and illegal. The Green Man had arrived in the middle of the controversy and promptly made his home in the contested forest. Living in a hollowed redwood tree, he had become a notorious and much publicized squatter of River Grove.

Christopher Shepard was usually described as a modern-day Johnny Appleseed, but his pasture far surpassed John Chapman's. From Harlem, New York, to Haarlem, the Netherlands, the Green Man had planted trees. He visited every continent except Antarctica and in his wake left a trail of green. Every day was Arbor Day for him. In his lifetime, he had planted more than 2 million trees. He often said nothing would ever interrupt his life's work, but he forgot that trees are not the only things sometimes cut down in their prime.

"What evidence do you have that the Green Man was murdered?"

Josh shook his head, acted as if he was disappointed by my questions. "Doesn't a head full of wood make you suspicious?"

I refrained from telling him I encountered those every day. "The way he died was not unprecedented, I understand."

"Neither is the rape of the ancient woods. The lumber companies are happy now because they've gotten just what they wanted: a cozy death."

"Whereas you'd prefer a martyr," I said.

For just a moment, I caught that look in his eyes, the one that made me feel unclean, and unenlightened, that spoke of my inferior sensibilities. And maybe, just maybe, threatened me. But the look changed, just as Josh's spiel did.

"Are we supposed to let them get away with murder, Stuart? They do every day, you know. They cut down history. They kill living monuments, trees that were around before Christ, and Socrates, and Buddha, and Aristotle, and Mohammed, trees that predate the major religions and philosophies of this world. Those are the real martyrs, every pre-historic tree that is struck down. They kill these ancient beings, some as big, and every inch as sacred, as the Statue of Liberty. I'd like to bring them to trial for those murders, but they've rigged the laws. I'm told, though, that flesh-and-blood murder still isn't allowed. You aren't supposed to be able to fell what's human and get away with it."

"That's right," I said pointedly. "No one is supposed to profit from murder."

He was a fanatic, but he wasn't stupid. He caught my double meaning and momentarily looked abashed. "Yes," he said, "we want to stop those saws permanently, and maybe we see this as our opportunity to do that, but most of all what we want is justice. They should have to pay for what they have done. And, if they do, the Green Man will not have died in vain."

I preferred a bellicose Josh to one who was sanctimonious. In pursuit of a cause, thinking tends to get colored. But, green flags notwithstanding, I was interested in the case. There was still the matter of proceeding on something other than suspicion and hearsay, though.

"Without violins," I said, "offer me some reasonable evidence that he was murdered."

Josh reached into his shirt and pulled out a rolled-up piece of paper. He removed a rubber band, solemnly unfurled the paper, then silently handed it to me. It was a wanted poster, not exactly the type you see in a post office, but one more closely resembling those that had came out of the Wild West. The Green Man's was the featured portrait. Above and below him, in large print, were the words WANTED: DEAD OR ALIVE!

"Not long after Christopher arrived," Josh said, "we found these plastered all around the county."

"There's no bounty offered," I said.

"None was offered on the spotted owl posters either," he said, "but some of the owls turned up dead anyway, nailed in public places."

I had heard about those posters, and the response to them. The owl impalings harkened back to older times. Hundreds of years ago farmers used to nail birds to their barns. The displays were believed to ward off storms. Maybe that same fearful mind-set had come to the fore again, the desire to stave off storms of change. The possibility of the northern spotted owl being granted protected species status threatened Pacific Northwest logging interests. The presence of the Green Man might have similarly threatened them.

"What else do you have?"

"They've rewritten the dirty tricks manual," Josh said. "They've circulated incendiary communiqués supposedly written by us, letters on Sequoia Summer letterhead detailing plans to abolish the timber industry in its entirety and declaring a need for a complete ban on all logging. They've also been big on creating violent images."

He reached into his shirt for more paperwork and handed it to me. The general theme was environmentalists getting spiked or chain-sawed. Most of the victims were being violated in their anal regions. The majority of the cartoon renderings were crude, but a few of the sketches looked capable, almost professional.

"You think the cartoons incited someone to murder?"

"What you call cartoons, I call hate and pornography. And, yes, I think it's quite possible."

"Beyond indignation, what do you have?"

His lips tightened. With an effort, Josh restrained his anger. "I have the names of those responsible for circulating the posters, and I know where they work."

"Let me guess," I said. "They work for a lumber company."

By the expression on his face, it appeared that even saying the words pained him. "Trans-Mississippi," he spat.

I didn't immediately respond, allowing myself the luxury of a few seconds of thought. The Green Man's death had considerably shortened my twentieth-century-hero list. You'd think with over 5 billion potential applicants, I would have been able to scare up a few more names, but this hasn't been the best century for heroes. We've been pulling the pedestals down faster than we can erect them. I wonder if one day historians will notice the paucity of human statues erected in this area.

I pictured the Green Man in my mind's eye. His mop of hair had generously been described by some as a Prince Valiant cut, but it was apparent his stylist was a kitchen bowl.

He was often portrayed with his crooked smile, which announced his friendliness, and hinted at some touch of mischief. Most symbolic were his trademark bare feet, extremities photographed more than any Madison Avenue model's. Shoeless, he never yielded to the elements but walked through the snow and the cold across earth and hard rock. Shoeless, he was now making his way through the Valley of Death. He had said he remained unshod "so as not to lose contact with Mother Earth." Now she had him in her embrace. His death didn't seem fair; death never does. But murder is the most unfair death of all. I wondered if there was anything to Josh's claims.

"We don't have much money," said Josh, "but we were able to scrape up an eight-hundred-and-twenty-two-dollar retainer for you."

It was madness to consider taking the case. The week before I had turned down an investigation in Palo Alto, claiming it was too far out of the City. Palo Alto is all of thirty miles south. Humboldt County is over two hundred windy miles north of San Francisco. It was away from familiar territory and resources, and the money probably wouldn't even cover expenses. I'd likely be placing myself between a rock and a hard place—no, worse, between a forest and a chain saw.

"We already have your cabin ready," Josh said, "fully stocked with provisions."

Probably a shed, I thought, with tofu.

"I know a place," Josh said softly, "where spotted owls have been seen. I can show you where a marbled murrelet nested."

Threatened species. Ones I didn't have on my life list. Birds that need the ecosystems of old-growth forests to maintain their existence. But, more than the birds even, I could feel the call of the redwood forest, of the towering giants.

"I'll drive up there today," I said. "But that doesn't mean I'll take the case. I'm just going to ask a few questions and do a little looking around."

Josh nodded. He didn't look surprised, didn't even give me the satisfaction of saying "Timber."

$\triangledown$

2

"OFFICES OF STUART Winter. May I help you?"

They say behind every great man there is a woman. No one's bothered to make mention of the fact that behind a lot of mediocre men are great women, which I suspect is a relatively accurate analysis of my relationship with Miss Tuntland. She's my answering service and much more, having handled my calls for the better part of ten years. You'd think in that time we would have met, but our rendezvous have always been talked about, never realized. Miss Tuntland's disabled. She settled on a business where, as she once explained, her "fingers could do the walking." I picture her as a modern-day Emily Dickinson. I know better than to ask how she imagines me.

"I'm leaving town, Miss Tuntland," I said. "Going to the great northern woods."

"Creditors again, Mr. Winter?"

"Nope. I'm branching out."

She sighed, said something about how wooden silence would only encourage me, then demanded a full explanation. I told her what I knew, which, as she was quick to tell me, wasn't much, but it was enough to worry her. Humboldt's logging controversies had drawn heavy media coverage. Miss Tuntland warned me that I was stepping into a modern-day version of a range war.

"Call me Shane," I said.

9

"Did you say 'Lame'?"

I don't like losing arguments, so I usually don't so much debate with Miss Tuntland as attempt end runs. "It will be a little getaway," I said, "an excuse to capture some glimpses of a few rare birds."

"Cuckoos, dodoes, or loons?"

"Grouse."

Miss Tuntland didn't give me a moment to savor my comeback. She never does. "As if investigating a potential murder isn't bad enough, you're mixing it with politics. That smacks of a death wish to me. Proposition One-fifty isn't taking any prisoners."

The election was a month off. Or was that the war? Proposition 150, the Great Trees Initiative, called for the preservation of all old-growth forests in northern California. Proponents said it would save ancient trees. Opponents said it would kill the logging industry. Some said it had already killed the Green Man.

"I'll be careful," I said.

"At the risk of being labeled a codependent or an enabler," she said, "what can I do to help?"

"*Only* if you have some free time," I said, "and *only* if it doesn't inconvenience—"

She'd heard my song and dance before and interrupted me. "What do you need?"

"I'd like to know more about the Green Man: the Kitty Kelley version, if there is one. Personal stuff. I'd also be interested in any scene-of-the-death speculating."

I could hear Miss Tuntland jotting down my requests. The sound of her scratching stopped, and I could sense her pen, and a few of her questions, hanging in the air. Quietly, she asked, "He died in the middle of an ancient forest, didn't he?"

"Yes. About a half mile from his goosepen."

"Goosepen?"

"The early pioneers of redwood country coined the term. It describes a hollowed redwood. Supposedly the settlers kept geese in the gaping redwood crevasses. There's that much room in them."

"And that's where the Green Man lived?"

"Yes."

"I hope yours is a wild goosepen hunt, Mr. Winter."

"So do I."

"Call me every day," she said.

"Do you accept collect calls?" I asked.

"Do you accept wooden nickels?"

As I hung up on her, I reflected that I already had.

I threw my bag into the bed of Rocinante. Her name was twice cribbed. Steinbeck before me bestowed the name of Don Quixote's faithful steed upon his three-quarter-ton mechanical mount. Like Steinbeck, I had painted *Rocinante* in Spanish script on the side of my truck. In the ten years I'd owned her, three people had remembered their Spanish literature. My Rocinante's a 1962 three-quarter-ton Ford pickup. I patted her sides. Metal. These days that's a novelty. A decade earlier I had reluctantly accepted Rocinante as payment in full for a case I had worked on. At the time, I had a car and was in the habit of using the city's public transportation to get around. I had set out to sell her but ended up selling my car instead. She looked the same as when I had gotten her, save for one word I had deleted from the bumper sticker she came with: I'D RATHER EAT SHIT THAN DRIVE A JAPANESE PICKUP. I'd taken a razor blade to the expletive but decided the rest of the ornery message fit the truck. Maybe fit me too. I was willing to let other drivers fill in the blank. My guess was that Vanna didn't need to turn the letters for anyone to solve the riddle.

We started out a little after ten, late enough to miss most of the Marin traffic. The road opened up, and we made good time through Sonoma County, passing by the manicured wineries that have taken over most of the oak-savanna country. The northern stretch of Highway 101 is called the Redwood Highway, and after a time the reminder didn't come only through signs. While in Sonoma County, I spotted the first of many eighteen-wheelers carrying a load of felled redwood. Mills began to appear on both sides of the highway, their stacks of lumber piled high. I saw the by-products before I started to see stands of the real thing.

For 60 million years the Pacific Northwest coniferous forest remained untouched. It wasn't until the mid-1800s that

man started mining the redwoods, *Sequoia sempervirens.*
Since that time, over 95 percent of the ancient redwoods,
the virgin old growth, have been logged. That was what the
activists were rallying about—that last 4 or 5 percent of old
forest.

The redwood vistas started opening up to me from the
road, hints of what was to be, green and living hundred-foot
growth that pointed the way to greater things. The trees
weren't the only roadside attractions. There were billboards,
about one every mile. Most exhorted NO ON 150! There was
only one dissenting message. I was barely able to make out
the wording, but I think it read PRESERVE OLD GROWTH—YES
ON 150. The billboard looked like a termite ad. It was riddled
with holes—had drawn more shotgun and rifle fire than your
average Swiss-cheesed no-hunting sign.

It was midafternoon when I stopped for lunch in Garberville. The town's official main drag was Redwood Drive,
which featured the usual collection of motels, restaurants,
and stores. Its unofficial main drag was marijuana, the cul-
tivation of which went pretty much unimpeded until the
1980s. These days the government uses helicopters, spray-
ing, and infrared sensors in their high-tech campaign against
a high. Informed sources say the enforcement has worked
about as well as prohibition.

It had been almost a dozen years since I'd last been to
Garberville. I was pleased to see it hadn't changed. I remembered the town for its hippies, and rednecks, and trucks, and
dogs, all of which still looked to be around in abundance.
When you land in Garberville, you experience a time warp.
The sixties don't seem to be dead. Long hair abounds, as do
tie-dyed shirts, blue jeans, bandannas, and beards. Even
peace symbols haven't gone extinct.

I grabbed a quick lunch, then Rocinante and I got back
on the road. Our destination was Bayshore and its satellite
Trans-Mississippi shop. Josh had given me three names, or
at least nicknames, of those he said were the wanted poster
perpetrators: Red, Cincy, and Coop. They were co-workers,
and, as the story went, Red was the ringleader. Josh's unim-
peachable source was the girlfriend of another shop worker.
My version of her story was at best fourth hand.

Bayshore proved to be a small town with little in the way of industry besides the tiny mill. The town rested on the banks of the Van Duzen River, hardly a bay, but before we question the nomenclature of our forebears we should look at the names of some of the housing developments being built around us.

The Trans-Miss operation was a specialty shop, a plant that customized wood and created value-added wood products. Logging activists have long decried the "third world" lumber status of the Northwest. They claim the area is nothing but a colony to Japan, supplying raw materials instead of the more lucrative finished wood products. With unemployment running high, many in the area questioned that practice. Exporting lumber was welcomed; exporting jobs wasn't.

The Bayshore shop was probably just large enough to deflect criticism that nothing was being done to ensure jobs for locals. There wasn't a guard or even a receptionist to block my way. I walked inside and saw about a score of men actively at work, most at saw stations. By itself, the name *Red* didn't help me much. Every person in the world with red hair has been called Red at one time or another. I had hoped that some flaming red hair would make it easy for me to spot my man, but I was thwarted in my search. Everyone was wearing protective goggles, and, if that wasn't disguise enough, virtually all the men were also wearing caps. I could identify plenty of beer and liquor logos but little in the way of hair. Rather than try to walk around and peek under cap bands, I approached the man nearest to me.

"Looking for Red," I said.

He pointed off to a corner but was careful about doing so because his band saw was still running. His learning hadn't come without a price. His pointing hand was short a finger.

There were two men working in the corner. They were applying lacquer to some wood. One was wearing a Wild Turkey cap. The other preferred bikes to booze; his headgear identified his kinship to Harley-Davidson, with biker accoutrements to match. Harley had dark, greasy hair that extended over the neckline of his T-shirt. That left me with the Wild Turkey.

Both men watched my approach. Neither offered a greeting. Red was about forty, his partner in priming a decade his junior. Physically they weren't at all alike. Red was small, had light coloring and freckles, while Harley was big and swarthy. What were similar were their mannerisms. It was as if they had studied from the same handbook on how to be a tough case.

Red got a little vigorous with his brushwork and slopped some of the lacquer near my shoes. Harley found that funny. Instead of backing away, I moved closer.

"Better watch it," I said, words that drew their fingers into fists. I pointed to the ground. "You might slip on the floor."

Both of them looked down. I took that moment to push my hand near Red's face. I could have sucker-punched him, and he knew it, but instead I waved my business card under his nose. As he raised his head, I raised the card with it.

"We have some mutual friends, Red. I wonder if we might talk."

"Can't. Can'tcha see I'm working?"

Harley found that funny, which inspired Red to new heights of comic genius. He took his brush and tried to paint the card I was offering him. Harley was beside himself with that one.

"If you can't talk now, how about later?"

"What friends we got in common?"

"How about I tell you that over a beer?"

"You buying?"

I nodded.

"Then I hope we got lots of friends to talk about."

Harley just about split his sides. I asked Red where and when we could meet. He said his shift ended in another hour and suggested we meet at the Blow Hole. He also suggested I bring plenty of cash.

The Blow Hole was a bar in which to get drunk, and not much else. It was a few blocks from the water but didn't have a view. The original owner had attempted a whale motif, but, judging from the graffiti and graphic artistry, the bar was known by a sexual nickname unrelated to a whale's nostril.

The bartendress had a penchant for tattoos, leather, and

black eyeliner. She had the coloring of a spider on a no-blood diet, and the thinness that usually comes from living on cigarettes and booze. Her hair was dyed jet black and stood out all the more because of her paleness. Her lips and nails were also painted black. I expected Dracula to fly in any minute.

The Blow Hole didn't stock Glenfiddich, or any single-malt Scotch for that matter. I ended up ordering a bottle of beer and surreptitiously tried to wipe the lip of the bottle with my sleeve. Spider Lady noticed, though.

"Don't worry," she said. "I only spit in the mixed drinks."

I thanked her for the tip and opined that I'd better stick with beer or wine.

"Beer," she said. "I piss in the wine."

She pulled out a cigarette, and I looked around for matches. I dug through an unemptied ashtray and found a booklet with three strikes left. Someone hadn't wanted to be called out. Or found out. A certain Randi had auto-graphed the matchbook with her name and telephone num-ber. She had also underlined a price of fifty dollars. Matchmaker, matchmaker, make me a match. I closed the cover on Randi, struck a match, and cupped the light with my hands. I navigated through the breezy bar and connected with her cigarette.

She inhaled deeply and a few seconds later exhaled a lot of smoke and a thanks. Then she took another drag, settled in closer to me to be friendly, and in the process emptied her lungs near my face.

"You going to charge me extra for the ambient smoke?" I asked.

She maintained her proximity, and her sassiness. "I don't charge extra for that." The interpretation for anything else was left open.

"If I buy you a drink, will you stop smoking?"

"No. But I'll blow in another direction."

She slowly licked her lips, appeared to be enjoying her little performance. I put a five-dollar bill on the counter. It didn't stay there long. She poured herself a shot of Gold and knocked it down.

"No lime?"

"Do I look like I have scurvy?"

She kept to her part of the bargain and blew the smoke away from me. Even if her dark lips kept coming back close to mine. "Tina," she said.

"Stuart."

"When you came in here, Stu, I didn't think you belonged. Now I'm not so sure."

"I have the same problem. I'm not sure whether I'm a chameleon or a lounge lizard."

"I sort of like squamous things myself."

Tina opened her leather jacket and lifted her tank top up to display a tattoo of a snake corkscrewing downward into her belly button. When she dropped her shirt, I made a mild protest: "I didn't have enough time to identify the species."

"I think you did."

She could afford to be uninhibited because we were the only ones in the bar. I commented on the lack of bodies. "It's early," she said. "We don't get the Chablis sippers in here. We get our regulars, the beer-and-a-shot types."

"Is Red one of those regulars?"

Tina looked surprised. "You know him?"

"He's supposed to meet me here in a couple of minutes."

"You didn't answer my question."

If she was sharp enough to pick up on my evasiveness, I wondered what else she had noticed over the past few months. "I met him about an hour ago. I'm a private investigator looking into the death of the Green Man."

I passed her my card. Tina gave it a careful look. "Why do you want to talk with Red?"

I pulled out the wanted poster, attached a twenty with it. "Ring a bell?"

The money interested her more than the poster. She pocketed the president and pushed the rest of the paper back my way. "Coupla' months ago Red didn't have any problems buying himself, or no one else, a drink."

"That all?"

"Shouldn't it be? Red's here more than he's home. He's an asshole who hangs around with two other assholes."

"Cincy and Coop," I said, remembering Josh's names. She nodded.

"I think I met one of them today. A wanna-be biker type."

"That would be Cincy—which isn't short for Cincinnati—it's short for sinsemilla. Coop dresses even stupider."

"Their fashion statements don't exactly interest me," I said, tapping the poster.

"Why don't you save my lips some wear," she said, "and tell me what you know first?"

"I know that the posters were circulated around Humboldt County. I know that Red and his friends were behind them."

"And that's all you know?"

I shrugged.

She laughed, mostly to herself. "Maybe that's all there is to know."

"What do you mean?"

"I mean Red's full of shit. He talks big, but that's probably all it is. He's been acting like he's a vigilante. He's gone out of his way to make people think that he's been putting them EverGroaners in their place. My guess is that he hasn't done much more than drive by their camp a few times, throw some beer cans, and yell 'fuck you.' To Red, that would be a major campaign."

"But he's indicated differently? Implied he's done more?"

"He's all but announced himself as C.I.FuckingA."

"In what ways?"

"Like the dough he got. Like how he got the money to print the posters. He told people he has friends in high places. I told him we all know pot farmers. He didn't think that was funny."

"He's so much hot air?"

"You got a real nice way of saying bullshit, mister."

"I bet you say that to everybody."

"No. Just mostly to bullshit artists."

Tina winked, gave me an eye of darkness. Then she poured another shot of Gold and drank it in a gulp. "He did tell one story, though, that sounded more true than not. Cincy and Coop had about the same version."

She took a long, last drag on her cigarette and spoke with the smoke coming out her nose. "They were liquored up here one night, talking big, and they announced they were going to pay the Green Man a visit, said they were going to go to River Grove to mess him up.

"Next night the three of them were back here. They weren't talking so big in the beginning of the evening, but then they got their wind back with a few drinks in them. Seems your Green man was doing some entertaining in the woods. He had himself a wild woman. A real screamer. 'Course you got to take that with a margarita of salt. These guys are mostly acquainted with women that inflate."

"When was this?"

"I couldn't tell you."

"Sure?"

She thought for about half a minute, snapped her fingers. "The night of that big summer storm. They were there before the rain. They said it was damn windy when they made their visit, but that she was screaming even louder than the wind."

"And they just walked away from the coupling?"

"Doesn't sound like them, does it? Course when they talked about it they were full of 'should ofs' and 'could ofs.' If you had to listen to them every night like I do, you'd know that was the story of their life."

I tried to get Tina to remember what else was said, but she couldn't add much more.

"Their favorite line was that they should have done a train on the bitch. That she would have liked it. That she was screaming for more and they should have given it to her. They said that for a couple of weeks. Those bozos got two topics of conversation: sex and getting wasted. And while I don't have anything against either one of those things, sometimes I kinda like to discuss the weather too."

"Did they identify the woman?"

"Yeah. The way they identify all ladies they're not scamming on: bitch and fucking bitch."

"They didn't know her?"

"No."

"They didn't describe her?"

"Let's say they had a generic description that fits all women."

A customer walked in, and we stopped talking. Tina

started making small talk with the regular and continued that pattern as more and more men walked in. Before long the whole place was filled up. Tina was right: it wasn't a Chablis crowd. Everyone knew everyone else. I was the joker in the deck that no one seemed pleased to see. The few times I tried to look around, I got granite stares. It was easier, and wiser, to look straight ahead. Tina knew better than to act friendly toward me. She approached three times to ask if I needed a new beer. Twice, I didn't. Once, I did.

Red was the better part of an hour late for our appointment. He hadn't changed clothes, and he hadn't showered. The bar stool next to me was the only vacant seat. Red sat down, then announced for the entire bar to hear, "Give me an amber shower, honey. A double. Over my rocks, of course."

Tina pretended deafness but eventually came over and filled a glass with ice and Wild Turkey, then dropped it in front of him. He reached for her, but she knew that move and easily escaped his hands.

"Tina," he said, "you're getting more irresistible every day."

She responded by asking to be paid. Red didn't look at me, just said, "Pay her."

I did. Then I opened my mouth to speak, but Red spoke first. "This isn't the time to talk," he said.

But apparently it was the time to drink. Red ordered another double. And about ten minutes later, another. He talked with other people, but no one appeared anxious to converse with him. Except me. When he finally looked at me, he didn't try to hide his disdain.

"When you tried to pick my nose this afternoon with your business card, I noticed it said you're from San Francisco. I hear only faggots live in San Francisco."

"Is that so?"

"That's what I've been told. And I don't see anything to make me think different."

I guess I was supposed to take offense. I noticed that Red's brave and loud words coincided with the appearance of Harley, a.k.a. Cincy, and a third bovine-looking companion who I assumed was Coop. I'd seen the scene in a lot of bad westerns. In real life it didn't play any better.

Draw, pardner. Or, better yet, show what was drawn. I pulled the poster out of my pants pocket and unfolded it in front of Red. "Wonder what you could tell me about this," I said.

Everyone was watching us. Cincy and Coop had moved behind me and were doing some heavy breathing on my neck.

"I can tell you to go to hell."

"Anything else?"

"Eat shit and die."

"Thanks, but I've already eaten," I said, standing up. Cincy and Coop didn't budge. All I had to do was inhale and we'd be bumping chests. I was about to push by, which was what they wanted me to do, when a loud nose caused everyone in the place to jump. There was a sudden opening in the blockade. I walked straight for the door and, when I reached it, glanced back. Tina looked at home wielding an ax handle. The bar counter was still shaking.

Red waved to me from his bar stool, remembering my departure with the shout of "Goody-bye, Mr. Private Dickhead!"

The laughter followed me outside, but Red and Cincy and Coop didn't.

$\triangledown$

3

IN ANIMALS THERE IS the instinct to flee or to fight. Man is supposed to be more complex than that. I had walked out of the bar knowing it wasn't in my best interests to stay. But I wasn't the kind of animal to flee. Walking away from the bar was one thing, walking away from the case was quite another. Now, I wanted to fight.

The investigation I had suddenly committed to didn't promise to be easy. The territory in question was spread out over eighty miles, from Garberville to Arcata, and those were the highway miles. The backwoods roads would be much slower navigating.

What was left of Sequoia Summer was sequestered in Sweetwater, an area in the southwest part of Humboldt County not far from the Lost Coast. Josh had told me there were currently fewer than a hundred true believers who remained to carry the redwood flag. The surprise wasn't that there were so few but that there were still so many. For students, the bell had already sounded for fall semester. For the rest, life's responsibilities were calling. Those who had stayed believed there was no greater duty than protecting the tall trees and remembering the Green Man. Undoubtedly fanatics every one. Oh, joy.

My drive south along 101 paralleled the Avenue of the Giants. Even from the highway, the redwoods dominated the landscape. The sun hadn't yet set, but in redwood country that's a moot point. There were long stretches where the redwoods blocked out the sky, where I'd look above and expect to see clouds but be treated instead to vast canopies of red and green.

Logging has long been Humboldt County's biggest industry and employer. It wasn't hard to see the motivation behind old-growth deforestation. The larger, older trees are worth more. To a bank holding a note, the redwoods aren't history, they're a commodity. Logging companies look at ancient redwoods not in terms of their years but their board feet. A very large redwood translates to around 125,000 board feet. At today's retail prices, that means a single tree can be worth a quarter of a million dollars. Big bounty on big trees. And big business. I passed fleets of eighteen-wheelers carrying enormous logs. I didn't try to calculate their worth, only knew that when it came to money trees weren't the only things that got cut down.

The summer had seen tree sittings, passive resistance campaigns, bulldozer blockades, and rallies. At the height of the demonstrations, there had been upward of a thousand protesters. That isn't the kind of number that usually captures national attention, but, considering that there were no major urban areas around, no television sets and Jacuzzis to go home to after chanting in some park, the figures weren't negligible either. The protesters had to camp, had to be willing to rough it. Under conditions like that, even the best of causes lose their luster, usually more quickly than not. Ask George Washington about the high dropout rate in his Continental army.

The last scheduled demonstration had been set for early September. The plan had been for the protesters to pack up and go home, their cause to be remembered and organized during the year from "central command posts," which translated to a few cubicles in a few big cities. The death of the Green Man had changed all that. Not all of the tents had folded up, even though the nights were getting colder and longer.

I traveled west on the Mattole Road through the Humboldt Redwoods State Park. The road was windy, and slow, and shrouded, and for all of that I was grateful. I had a chance to cool down, and think, and observe. Josh had told me the camp was off a dirt road near the Mattole River. He had been vague with landmarks, had just given me a blanket assurance that I couldn't miss the turnoff. I could and did. After giving up on several other dirt roads, I finally connected with the right one and arrived at camp just as the sun was setting.

The Sequoia Summer-cum-Autumn camp looked like a mini–tent city, something like old black-and-white pictures of logging camps. There was little in the way of conveniences or modern equipment; a primitive, solar-powered kitchen, a potter's wheel, and a propane kiln were about the only exceptions.

When I stepped out of Rocinante, the green welcome mat wasn't immediately forthcoming. It was almost déjà vu of my reception at the Blow Hole. Heads turned and stared. No one said anything, and I didn't know what the password was. It was dinnertime, and there was a line making its way forward to an immense metal caldron filled with spaghetti. The eyes of the campers were dark circled, making them look older than their years.

I was about to announce, "I come in peace," when Josh stepped out of his tent and did that for me. "Don't worry," he said, "he's not a narc. His name is Stuart, and he'll be assisting us in our quest for justice."

The eyes looked a little friendlier now. Some heads nodded, and several voices called out greetings. I did my imitation of being neighborly, hoping a few of them might learn something from it.

"Have you eaten?" Josh asked.

"I had a late lunch in Garberville," I said.

"Better have some spaghetti anyway," he said. "Your next meal won't be until morning.

"Oatmeal," he added, announcing the word like it was the special of the day.

"What happened to my stocked cabin?" I asked.

"It's been commandeered," Josh said, not bothering to offer an apology. "Ashe arrived unexpectedly today. She's meeting with Teller and a few of the others right now. We always give her the cabin when she's here. But don't worry, she'll blow out in three days tops. In the meantime, we've got a tent for you. Better that way anyway. It will be easier to direct you."

He didn't wait for my reaction, just joined the chow line

and expected me to follow him. Sotto voce I announced, "I don't do investigation by committee."

Josh turned halfway around. "But we'll need to review your progress every day in order to—"

"No," I said.

Now he was all the way around. "What do you mean?"

"I work by myself," I said.

"But we're a collective here," said Josh. "Everyone makes decisions together."

My experience is that when groups of people come together to root out evil, they become like the Spanish Inquisition, or the House Committee on Un-American Activities. "Not this time."

"This isn't what we expected," Josh said.

"Life's full of surprises."

"You won't be reimbursed for the motels," Josh threatened, "or any of the expenses."

I shrugged. If the spaghetti and tent were supposed to be inducements, they weren't doing the job.

Josh faced front once more. He would have preferred to continue the argument but realized that everyone around us was listening. Two minutes later he broke his silence to ask for a large serving of spaghetti. I wasn't that brave. Blood might be thicker than water, but I wouldn't have taken any bets on the spaghetti sauce.

"Hungry?" the pasta slinger asked with a smile. Her dirty blond hair was tied back in a red bandanna. She had bracelets that stretched from her wrists almost to her elbows. When she moved, it sounded like castanets clacking. Earth mother type, heavy, but she carried her weight lightly, easily, as if it belonged.

I returned her smile but not her enthusiasm. "Not too," I said.

She measured accordingly, and I thanked her. Most people were seated at large, communal tables, but Josh picked a spot for us away from everyone else. Several lanterns were already turned on, and we were on the periphery of their light. It was getting dark fast. When you live in a city, you forget about darkness. There are always lights, illumination enough to see in front of you, to watch your feet connecting with the ground instead of being disembodied from you. But I don't usually worry about losing my feet. Just my head.

"Stuart," said Josh in an aggrieved tone, "I put my ass on the line for you. There were a lot of people who didn't want you here. They're suspicious of any investigators, private or otherwise. They assume a fascist mind-set. But I convinced them you were different."

"Who didn't want me on the case?"

He didn't like the question. "Why do you ask?"

"I'd like to know who was afraid of being investigated."

Josh signed. "There you go again. See, you're asking the wrong questions, and jumping to the wrong conclusions. We're not the bad guys."

"But you'll be glad to point out all the bad guys to me?"

"Yes," said Josh, either not hearing my sarcasm or not wanting to.

"Fine. Now who didn't want me on the case?"

He sighed again. "About half the people here. Everyone gets a vote. That's how we decide things."

"And of that group, was anyone particularly vehement about not wanting to hire me?"

"Why are you making me feel like a snitch?" he asked, his voice rising. "Why don't you ask me about the politics of lumber money? Why don't you let me tell you how the tallest trees in the world are being sacrificed to help pay for junk bonds?"

"Because usually it does more good to ask people what they don't want to talk about, as opposed to what they do."

Josh shoveled an enormous amount of spaghetti into his mouth. It gave him a reprieve from having to say anything. Then he filled his fork and mouth again. I sat and watched, admiring his fortitude. I was prepared to wait out the rest of his plate, but he never finished. The sound of an approaching vehicle brought him to his feet. A moving dust cloud encircled an old Jeep Wagoneer, the motes magnified in its headlights.

"Ashe and Teller," Josh said.

Seven people got out of the Jeep, three women and four men. Their mood was light, their conversation pleasant and full of laughs. Teller and Ashe were easily identified, he because of his age and white Saint Nick beard, and she because some people stand out in any crowd.

Ashe O'Connor was lissome and tall, about five foot nine. Someone had written of her: "She could have been a model but chose to be a role model instead." She had thick, dark hair. It was held up by several barrettes, and made me think of Rapunzel, and made me wish she'd let it down.

Her good looks hadn't hurt her cause. Ashe was the much photographed force behind Proposition 150. The opposition had deridingly labeled her the Green Goddess, but that strategy seemed to be backfiring on them. Though the Great Trees Initiative had been outspent by lumber interests by about a ten-to-one ratio, the latest polls showed that public opinion was evenly divided. The estimated buyout cost for the old-growth groves was well over a billion dollars. If Ashe could get the citizens of California to shoulder that kind of debt willingly, her current tag as a miracle worker wouldn't be far off the mark.

Some people have substance, a gravity immediately felt by others. I watched the satellites orbiting around her. Even though I was standing in the shadows, she noticed my scrutiny. Her attention made Josh remember me. "This is Stuart Winter," he said. "He's—"

Ashe knew who I was. And knew what was politically correct to be announced and what wasn't. "Ashe O'Connor," she said, extending her hand. "It's a pleasure."

She shook hands like a politician, making contact but not touching, then quietly told me we'd have to talk later. Her admirers were gathering already, and she went to them.

My next introduction was to Thomas Teller. He was in his sixties but carried himself with the vigor of a much younger man. His long, white hair was bunched into a ponytail, and his cotton beard probably hadn't been cut in forty years. His shoulders were broad, and his handshake callused and robust, almost to the point of being challenging. He had gained notoriety over the years by being one of those people who never stop beating the drums. Teller had been with the beats when they demanded their rights to free speech, had been antiwar(s), and antinukes, and antiapartheid. Old growth was his latest bugaboo and was now his full-time protest. He hadn't left Humboldt for almost three years, had endured the isolation of the last two winters to be the conscience of the old forests.

Some leftover spaghetti was brought out for the late-comers. They sat down at a table, and spectators began to settle around them on the ground. The scene reminded me too much of dogs waiting for scraps of food, or a word of praise. I thought about walking down to the river, but Josh reappeared with someone else in tow.

He was a small man, probably a shade over five feet, but he didn't come across as short so much as compact. He was well built, his arms thick, reminiscent of Popeye, his legs so heavily muscled they looked bowed. He looked to be about thirty, had longish dark hair and intent brown eyes.

"Stuart, I wanted you to meet Doc. Doc, this is Stuart."

We shook hands. His hands were out of proportion to his frame, almost as large as mine, and his grip was firm.

"Doc," I said. I couldn't help but wonder whether his nickname was university earned or whether it had come from one of Disney's dwarfs.

"Born MacArthur Witt," he said, as if reading my thoughts or, more likely, having faced the situation many times before. "I was called half-Witt before getting my Ph.D. I gladly traded in on nicknames."

Josh spread his arms to take in the expanse. "Doc is our expert out here."

"I like your laboratory," I said.

"Depends on where you're looking," he said. "My postdoc was a study of the effect of clear-cuts on the environment."

"Past tense?"

He attempted nonchalance, but I detected some professional pique. "The funding ran out earlier this year," he said, "but my questions didn't."

"When the other side tells their lies," said Josh, "Doc sets the record straight."

Doc bowed and appeared not a little pleased. "I look bigger in print," he said.

Josh didn't stay to chat. He deserted us "to help get things going."

"Almost show-and-tell time," Doc said.

"What do you mean?"

"It's called Circle. I find it one of the few good endorsements for watching television."

I gave him a questioning look, and he answered it with a little smile. "You must excuse my outlook," he said. "Nature assigned me the role of court jester, and I do my best to play the part."

He was adept at self-deprecating remarks, but I didn't sense that he really believed them. He pointed to a circle of rocks. A few people were already seated outside the stones. "Circle is the nightly drama that goes on around the campfire," he said. "Teller is the Circle master. He weaves tales, and tells stories. Everyone is supposed to leave heartened and renewed. The strange thing is, it usually works."

"Do you attend every night?"

"No. Just often enough to remember why I'm a misanthrope." The little smile emerged again.

"How long have you been living in the area?"

"Eighteen months, the last six unofficially."

"Any chance of more funding?"

"I doubt it. What I've been studying wouldn't benefit anything except the trees. If you're not feeding the maw of some entity or organization, you're not likely to get a free ride.

"But," he added, tapping the aluminum mess plate he was holding, "I have found a tin lining to my cloud. There's always this wonderful meal line for my spaghetti, or beans, or gruel."

"Want to make a hundred bucks?"

"Who am I supposed to kill?" His smile again.

"Take me on a tenderfoot tour," I said. "An hour or two. I need to know about the redwoods."

Doc sniffed for a moment, reminding me of a predator testing the scent of another's kill. "Sure."

"Tomorrow morning?"

He nodded.

"Nine o'clock? At Founders Grove?"

He nodded again, his head suddenly accented in a beam of light. Stabs from sweeping flashlights crisscrossed the grounds. The lights were turned on and off, the outdoor theater apparently being called to session.

"Show time," Doc said. "And the last thing this short fellow needs is another dose of Longfellow."

I watched him walk across the clearing. His short legs gave the appearance of awkwardness, not unlike a penguin's walk, but he still managed to move swiftly. He vaulted onto a motorcycle, an off-trail bike, but his acrobatics weren't for show. He would have had to climb up the vehicle otherwise. Doc must have known the path well, that or he just liked speed. In a few moments he was lost to sight, and sound, the trees swallowing him up.

Night is excuse enough for people to move closer, to hunker together against the unknown and the darkness. It's instinctual, still a part of us despite twenty-four-hour Denny's. I moved toward the fire, even if its appearance violated my every camping instinct. I expected a bonfire with blazing flames. I expected a cord of wood to be piled high, the stacked logs ready to be tossed into the inferno. I expected man to do what he has always done, to deny the dying of the light in as rebellious a manner as possible. But the campfire for the night was apparently going to revolve around two ersatz logs, the kind that consist of pressed sawdust and wax and copper coloring.

The wrappered logs were set in the middle of the circle of rocks. I'd endured their kind of fire before. They didn't give off the sounds or smells of real wood. No sharp pops, no woody perfume. These were logs meant to expire in some sedate suburban condominium fireplace, to burn predictably and uninterestingly; logs for double-income no-kid types to sip white zinfandel in front of. I couldn't see why, on the border of one of the great forestlands in the world, real wood hadn't been gathered.

I took a seat by myself near the so-called fire, but the spots were filling rapidly. A jingle and jangle announced a neighbor, the plump spaghetti server. "My name's Sasha," she said, extending her hand toward mine, a movement that caused massive bracelet collisions.

"Stuart," I said, shaking out a tune on her arm. Then I pointed to the counterfeit wood. The logs had an unnatural blue glow, looked more like pilot lights than a blazing fire. "Why the fake campfire?"

"We didn't want to be hypocrites," she said. "We keep talking about the benefits of old growth. Since cannibalizing the forest, even its floor, isn't in keeping with our thinking, we decided Circle should be conducted with the store logs."

A neighbor joined me to my left, another young woman. Our circle became complete, and a second formed behind us. There was a town hall atmosphere, but without the tension of taxes and bond issues. When Teller stepped into the center of his rock ring, the conversations hushed.

"Let the Circle be joined," he said.

My neighbors extended their hands toward me. Self-consciously, I accepted them. Some of us work hard to create shells we don't like breached. Holding hands with strangers was hard for me. I've always found it easier to reach out to help than just to reach out. My hand-holding doubts came on fast. Was I holding on to the other hands firmly enough? Or too tight? Was I really perspiring that much? Or were we jointly creating bodily fluids? Were my hands clammy? Odd how I was challenged simply to hold the hands of strangers. More complicated than sex, I thought.

Teller looked around. His eyes seemed to hold mine, to carry on a silent conversation. Some people have that power. They can look through a crowd and seem to stare at everyone. Teller reminded me of an Old Testament prophet. All he needed was a robe and a voice of grim prediction.

Then he spoke, and I decided he didn't need that robe.

"This is the forest primeval. The murmuring pines and the hemlocks,
    Bearded with moss, and in garments green, indistinct in the twilight,
    Stand like Druids of eld, with voices sad and prophetic,
    Stand like harpers hoar, with beards that rest on their bosoms.
    Loud from its rocky caverns, the deep-voiced neighboring ocean
    Speaks, and in accents disconsolate answers the wail of the forest.
    This is the forest primeval."

Teller knew that wail of the forest. He had a voice that challenged Stentor's, a presence that erected the dead hairs on the backs of my arms. He was a Druid of eld speaking for

30

his holy forest. After his opening address, there was a quiet to the woods, as if they were listening. The silence added to the expectation. I could hear the echo of Teller's words in my mind, the loud, mournful syllables working their way through my head. So that was what Doc had meant about Longfellow; Circle's nightly convocation evidently began with Longfellow's "Evangeline." I wondered if he'd conclude with Allen Ginsberg's "Howl."

"I don't have a story tonight," said Teller, his voice suddenly congenial, airy. His announcement caused clucks of disapproval around the circle. They say storytelling is coming back into vogue, but I'm still dubious. That would mean listening's making a comeback too.

Teller smiled, pleased at their disappointment. "But I do have a memory," he said, "one that many of us share."

He had a lot of voices. Now it was soft and gentle, giving off a warmth that the fire didn't have.

"Like all of you," he said, "I've been thinking about the Green Man. Everyone has their own memories of him, but what I like to remember most is that first day he came among us.

"He arrived unannounced, which made his presence all the more exciting. We knew he would be coming sometime in the summer, but he hadn't told anyone when, for he had many groves to attend to. When he walked into camp, all of us cheered. An impromptu celebration began, but the merriment didn't last long. Within an hour of his arrival, terrible news came to us. Another virgin grove had been clear-cut."

Teller's face was a map of pain for all to see. "Old and virgin," he said. "Usually the words don't go together. But we use them interchangeably. Old growth. Virgin forest. Trans-Mississippi showed no respect for the elderly. They raped a virgin stand."

He was trembling, and his voice cracked.

"We came too late. We gathered at the scene of the desolation, and all of us felt the terrible loss. I think I can almost understand a mother's pain at losing her child. We experienced that emptiness, that awful void. We stumbled around the man-cut barrens, the victims of a war. I remember some of you counted the tree rings, and cried out for the slaughter of the ancients.

"We had forgotten about our Green Man. But amidst all our lamentation, his voice was heard, a cry in the vanished wilderness. He called us to a great tree stump, as wide as a kitchen table.

"When we gathered to him, we heard what the movement now calls the 'Sermon on the Stump.' We didn't call it that then. We gave no title to what he said. I suppose that we knew his words were special, for with them our hopes were renewed. But how many people know when they are a part of a historic moment?

"Later, we dwelt on what he said. Later, we remembered his words. Now, I think, would be a good time to reflect on them again.

"From his stump, this is what he said:

'Blessed are the trees, for they provide us air.
Blessed are the leaves, for they give us shelter.
Blessed are the roots, for they hold together the earth.
Blessed are those who plant the trees, for they bring life to the plant.
Blessed are those who would be stewards, for they tend the gardens of the gods.' "

Teller stopped his recitation, looked solemn. "He had only been with us for a few hours," he said, "and yet he already had an understanding that surpassed our own. He took away our pain, and gave us hope. He told us to hate neither the ax nor the axman, said we should love our enemies. We found this forgiving hard, but in the days that followed he gave to us a balm: he showed us how to plant redwood seedlings. For every one they took, he told us to plant a dozen. 'We will win that way,' he said."

Teller's concluding words were uplifting, but I sensed he believed in that victory about as much as a politician who's behind a few thousand votes at midnight. When Teller left his stage and walked away, I excused myself from the hand-holding and followed him.

$\triangledown$

4

TWENTY STEPS AWAY from the lanterns and campfire, and I was walking like one blind. There were clouds obscuring the moon and a mist coming up from the Mattole River. I felt along for a path, progressing like a tightrope walker. I took a turn, and it wasn't long before I figured out I hadn't found a major trail, or maybe hadn't found a trail at all. I listened for Teller's footsteps but only heard the flow of the river, its passage marked by whispers and sighs. It wasn't with my ears but with my nose that I picked up Teller's trail. The scent of cannabis, a brimstone beckoning, tugged me along.

I pushed through scrub. Belatedly, I remembered having seen poison oak all around the area. If the river hadn't been so close, and the smell of pot so near, I might have ceased forging my own trail. I fought through a final patch of brambles and stumbled into a clearing at the water's edge.

"There's a path, you know."

I turned toward the voice, but it was too dark to make out a figure. He revealed himself with the hiss of his pulling lungs, snakelike and hungry, and the flaring ember of his smoke stick. The light from his joint momentarily silhouetted Teller's white hair and beard.

"I missed it," I said.

I moved closer to him, marking the space by the burning end of his cigarette. When I got close, he extended the light toward me, offering it with the words "Peace pipe?"

"I didn't know we were at war," I said but accepted the joint and made a show of inhaling without doing too much damage to my lungs, then handed it back to him.

"I'm breaking camp rules again," Teller explained, "but then I stopped bucking for sainthood a long time ago. The Sequoia Summer movement is supposed to be above reproach: no alcohol, no drugs, no antics. But I'm too old to reprimand. They know I come down to the river every night to smoke my reefer, but they pretend ignorance."

He took another long drag, then passed the cigarette my way again. I waved it away. "Eighty-six proof is my vice of choice," I said.

"You're not supporting the local economy," Teller said. "But don't feel guilty. Of late I've personally helped it along quite a bit." As if to emphasize his point, and his joint, he inhaled deeply.

"Why?"

The words came out in a protracted billow of smoke. "Anesthetizing myself to failure."

"If I'm to believe Sequoia Summer's press releases, you're on the threshold of victory."

"If you believe any press releases, you're a fool."

"What if Proposition One-fifty passes?"

"I will be very, very happy. But I will still be mindful of the price."

"The Green Man?"

"To quote the government, which I don't very often, 'He paid the ultimate price.' "

"Do you think he was murdered?"

Teller thought about that for a few moments. "He died under suspicious circumstances," he finally said.

"Did you like him?"

"I paved the way for him. Like John the Baptist, I shouted to the world that a messiah was coming along. I was the voice in the wilderness."

I wondered which was the more attractive diet for a martyr: locusts and honey or the camp spaghetti.

"You prepared the way for Shepard to be the savior of this forest?"

"That was the script."

"Did he change his part?"

"To my way of thinking, yes. To his, probably not." Teller sucked at his cannabis, and in its glow I caught the thoughtful look on his face. When he spoke, he only used the upper part of his diaphragm, retaining the smoke in his lungs. His words sounded gravelly, constricted.

"Did you hear my eulogizing tonight?"

"Yes."

"Since Shepard's death, I've spent many nights thinking about him. He said that victory would be ours if we planted many saplings for every tree that was lost. He believed that, held to that view even after I argued that we could not afford such Pyrrhic victories.

"He didn't know the reference, so I explained about King Pyrrhus of Epirus, and how his army had fought the Romans in a bloody, terrible battle."

He paused for breath, and I took up the recitation: "And when Pyrrhus was congratulated on his victory, he looked out to the battlefield, and saw all of his dead, and said: 'One more such victory, and we are lost.' "

It was a favorite story of mine, and apparently of Teller's. I could hear him nod, hear his long beard rubbing against his shirt. "I told Shepard that whenever any old growth was lost, I felt like Pyrrhus looking upon his too many dead."

"And what did he say?"

"He smiled and nodded, but he didn't fathom my meaning. He was the Green Man. To him, growth was life. He preferred the role of creator to that of sustainer."

"Tell me about him."

Teller liked to use his hands when he talked. I watched the ember pathway of his joint. It moved up, and down, and around. I was reminded of a magician's conjuring and wondered what rabbits were being pulled out of the hat.

"He was many things, and many people."

"What do you mean?"

"Shepard wasn't the first Green Man, just the latest. He knew his history, and tried to live up to it."

Teller took a final drag on his joint. It burned down almost to nothing. I listened to him roll the remaining paper between his large fingers.

35

"The historic Green Man has been with us for a very long time. You can find him in old paintings and statues. Sculptors and artists often displayed his body in tree trunks and branches, and made much of his leafy smile. Sometimes the Green Man even had antlers. He was depicted with attributes of man, and the woods, and animals. And the gods. I shouldn't forget the gods.

"For many centuries he endured, whether as Green George, or Father May, or the Little Leaf Man, or Jack-in-the-Green. Apparently, chlorophyll, and the blood royal, and ichor, ran through the Green Man's veins. He was revered as the Leaf King, the Grass King, the King of the May, and the King of the Wood. As Pan and Sylvanus, even as the Green Knight and Robin Hood, the Green Man was acknowledged as the ruler of the woods and the forests. That was the legacy that Christopher Shepard knew. That was the background he accepted, and the mantle he wanted to assume."

"Did he succeed in becoming that Green Man of legend?"

"To some degree. But the fit wasn't perfect. The Green Man disappeared from this world when groves stopped being sacred, when Druids and dryads were forgotten, and when oracles were no longer heard in the rattle of trees. Shepard tried to resurrect a myth."

"You don't sound as if you approve."

"The legends of one time are difficult to translate to another."

"But he tried?"

"Shepard took his role seriously. He studied. And he cast a shadow that wasn't only his. If you knew the histories of other renowned tree planters, you'd see how Shepard grafted their characters onto his own."

"You mean like Johnny Appleseed?"

"Not only John Chapman but a number of others."

"How did he copy them?"

"Outlooks. Philosophies. Actions. The mythology of Chapman-Appleseed was that he was slightly touched and went around barefoot planting apple trees. There is something in that image that appeals, something gentle, and harmless, and beautiful. Shepard knew that. So he went around unshod and captured the public's imagination. But,

36

much like Chapman, he had ulterior motives."

I sounded skeptical. "I never imagined apple-tree planting as being fraught with intrigue."

"Apples were commerce, especially in a new world which had few apple trees. One scholar documented Chapman's life through a trail of deeds and records and found out that he either owned or leased more than twenty properties in his lifetime. When he was doing his planting in the early eighteen hundreds, apples weren't only the fruit of pies. Apple vinegar was the favored pioneer preservative, and apple butter could stand the rigors of winter, and applejack brandy was the drink of the day. Chapman wasn't some romantic. He was a pragmatist."

I thought about that. Something still didn't ring true. "The Green Man wasn't selling apples on street corners," I said.

"He was selling the philosophy of trees," said Teller.

"Which is?"

"A treeless world is a barren world. He liked to quote Julius Sterling Morton, who said that no vista is complete without a tree in sight."

"Morton?"

"The founder of Arbor Day. When Morton settled in Nebraska, he looked out to the treeless plains and saw an inhospitable country. He planted thousands of trees in the belief that human roots are aided by tree roots. To his way of thinking, trees bring communities."

I found myself arguing. "The Green Man was an activist," I said, "not some Jaycees booster. He planted trees because in them he saw good, and knew how they benefited mankind. He said they are the lungs of the world—"

Teller interrupted. "A line he borrowed from Richard St. Barbe Baker, another tree planter."

"I don't know the name."

"If millions of trees could talk, they would tell you about him. He was the first international tree planter, even had the nickname Man of the Trees. St. Barbe Baker was a philosopher, a writer, and, most of all, a tree planter. He had a daily ritual of hugging a tree, not with some timid embrace, but with wide, sweeping arms, the grasp of one friend to another. St. Barbe Baker said it was his way of gathering energy and recharging his batteries. Shepard adopted that ritual as well, and promoted the practice, although I could never tell if he was charging his batteries or his libido."

"What do you mean by that?"

Teller rubbed his eyes and sighed. "St. Barbe Baker's hugging wasn't a spectacle. Shepard's was."

"Did he hug more than trees?"

"How am I supposed to answer that question?"

"Did he have a girlfriend? Anyone sharing his goosepen?"

"I couldn't tell you."

"You didn't hear anything?"

"No."

"Were you jealous of him? Or should I say green with envy?"

"Not that I was aware. Do I sound that way?"

"Not exactly. But you've painted an almost Machiavellian picture of him."

"That wasn't my intention. I doubt whether anyone was ever so committed to planting trees. But I always thought of the Green Man as a redwood: great, but lacking in roots. There wasn't much depth to him."

"What do you mean by lacking in roots?"

"For all their height, redwoods have very shallow root systems. They don't even have a taproot. Some redwoods stand over three hundred feet high, yet their roots don't even go six feet into the ground.

"The Green Man was magnificent like the redwoods. You could stand in awe of his presence. But he wasn't deep."

I listened as Teller stretched out on the ground and found a willow for a backrest. He gently chided me when I tried to press him with yet another question. "Shhh," he said. "Let's listen to the river talk for a while."

Even the rivers in Humboldt County don't flow as expected. Most of them travel northward to the ocean, in direct contradiction to the accepted theory that such rivers are supposed to flow south. A few lone crickets sounded, making brave music against the coming cold.

I did my eavesdropping on the currents and found my thoughts tumbling along with the white water and riffles. What was truth, and what was invention? Supposedly the

Green Man had first made his name in southern California, had turned up at one of those housing developments where stucco houses and fast-food franchises appear before the trees. The developers had promised parks and delivered some rectangular lots of sod and sand; they had promised greenery, and their word was ice plant.

Shoeless, Shepard had arrived upon the urban wasteland. At first he wasn't noticed. Residents figured him for another gardener seeding ice plant. But then he started showing up with his saplings in backyards where there was only hard pack and clay, and maybe a Weber Barbeque. And when people ran out to him and asked him what he was doing, Shepard told them he was "planting dreams."

A few residents called the police. Some expressed disappointment that he wasn't there planting the palms that the developer had promised. But a surprising number ended up helping him in his labors. He explained to them his vision of what could be, said how "tall oaks from little acorns grow." I wondered if tall tales grew the same way. As the story went, a community had grown around his plantings. Neighbors shared in his dream, and his trees brought a bonding of individuals and spirits.

"There was a movie that won an Oscar a few years back," I said, breaking the silence, "an animated picture that—"

"*The Man Who Planted Trees,*" said Teller.

The story line revolved around a hermit who brought back a world. It was a modern parable of reforestation. Over the course of forty years the hermit planted trees that healed a despoiled land. It all seemed so simple and yet so wise; the hermit tirelessly and selflessly planting, the world renewing itself.

"People think of the Green Man when they watch that film," I said. There was biography in my remark and maybe a little plea too. I was beginning to feel self-conscious about my hero worship. And a little betrayed. I wanted reassurance.

"I know," said Teller, "and I think that's how he thought of himself."

"Was he a fraud?"

"No. But he couldn't see the forest for the trees. He couldn't even see the redwoods for the giant Leucæna."

▽

5

I ASKED TELLER what he meant, but either he chose not to hear me or he had already drifted into his cannabis dreams. I lingered for a few minutes, feeling oddly content sitting in the dark listening to a stranger snore and the river run, before setting out to find the trail. This time the elusive path didn't escape me. I went slowly but progressed up the grade in about half the time it had taken me to get down. As I approached the camp I heard voices and realized that circle was still in session.

I stayed on the outskirts of the campfire and found a place to listen and not be seen. Ashe O'Connor was speaking to a rapt audience. She told the campers how much their presence meant to the cause, said the eyes of the state, no, of the world, were upon them. They were the front line of the movement, the necessary catalyst for change. They were tangible proof to all, a visible commitment that could be seen and felt and remembered.

Ashe was a good speaker. They drank in her words, had a need for them. She put nobility into their day-to-day drudgery, squared all to their purpose for being there. The formal part of Circle concluded with her talk. Hands broke apart, but most of the campers were not quick to leave. Some guitars were brought out, and the circle grew tighter, bodies moving closer to the still flickering store logs.

An admiring throng formed around Ashe. I waited for the

crowd to break up, but my patience gave out before the well-wishers. Josh was among the pack, and I tapped on his shoulder to get his attention.

"I'd like to talk with the queen," I said.

"I don't know if that's a good idea," he said.

"Tell her that. She suggested it to me earlier."

That changed matters. Josh worked his way to her ear, and after their short conference he came back to me with two words: "Big Top."

I followed him to a large tent, not Ringling Bros. and Barnum & Bailey large, but giant enough to dwarf the pup tents around it. At first I saw its interior only in glimpses of the flashlight, but then Josh fired up a lantern. The tent could comfortably sleep at least a dozen, but the space wasn't devoted to any sleeping arrangements. There were two desks with typewriters, a hand-operated mimeograph machine, and about a dozen boxes stuffed full of papers.

There was a mustiness pervading the tent. It was an antique model made of canvas that looked to be army surplus. Only generals had ranked tents that large. I wondered what other campaigns had been waged from inside its flaps.

I started sifting through one of the boxes. There were announcements for marches, some piecemeal press kits, and assorted public awareness literature detailing old-growth deforestation. The more I poked around, the more nervous Josh appeared. After finishing with the box, I took a step over to the nearest desk.

"What are you doing, Stuart?"

"Making myself comfortable."

"You have a strange way of doing that."

I didn't answer him. A nail had been hammered into the desk and a length of twine secured to it. I pulled up the twine and landed a clipboard that was marked "Methuselah's Mounties." At first glance I thought it was just another petition to save the old trees. But there were more than signatures on the page. The week was marked out, with each day divided into three eight-hour blocks and signatures affixed to what looked to be work shifts.

"What is this?" I asked.

"Methuselah is a magnificent thousand-year-old redwood," said Josh. "We're trying to protect him from Trans-Mississippi."

"And how are you doing that?"

"By putting our bodies on the line. We're tree-sitting. Our sentries protect him twenty-four hours a day. If the loggers want to get to him, they'll have to go through us first."

"George Pope Morris alive and well," I mused.

Josh looked to me for an explanation, and I resorted to Morris's verse:

> Woodman, spare that tree!
> Touch not a single bough!
> In youth it sheltered me,
> And I'll protect it now.

Josh didn't ask me to continue, and I didn't remember the rest of the words anyway. I returned my attention to the clipboard, backtracked through some of its pages to the night of September 2.

"If I read this correctly," I said, "B shift is from three to eleven, and C shift would be the graveyard hours."

Josh was stiffer than ever. "That's right."

"So on September the second you had Barry somebody working the first shift, Sasha on the second, and Teller closed out on C shift."

He nodded, then cautiously asked, "Why your curiosity about those times, and that date?"

"Because the coroner said that was the night the Green Man died. He figured the time of death to be between eight P.M. and two A.M. I find those hours particularly interesting."

Josh didn't say anything.

"Do you remember that night?"

"No."

I didn't like the quickness in his answer. "You should," I said. "He died the night of the summer storm. It doesn't rain around here much that time of year. The storm caught a lot of people by surprise. Surely you remember the wind and the thunder?"

Tersely, he answered, "Vaguely."

"I'm told the woods aren't the best place to walk around in

42

a storm," I said. "Maybe the Green Man was tempting fate."

"Or maybe the lumber companies were waiting for a stormy night to kill him."

"I have a report that the Green Man might have been entertaining that night. Did he have a girlfriend?"

Josh shook his head. "Not that I know of."

"No camp romance?"

"I wasn't in the habit of doing sleeping-bag checks."

"No talk about one of the campers making nocturnal visits to River Grove?"

"No."

Josh's darkening face was an interesting study in colors, but I turned away from it to study the clipboard once more. The sentry duty for the rest of the week had already been assigned. It must have been Teller's turn again; he had the seven-to-three shift the next morning. I tapped on the clipboard reflectively. The noise apparently didn't settle Josh's nerves.

"Why are you snooping around here, Stuart? What are you looking for?"

"Enlightenment," I said. "Did you know that Buddha became enlightened while sitting under the bodhi tree?"

"And don't forget," said a voice from outside the tent, "that Newton started thinking about gravity while sitting under a tree and watching an apple fall."

The tent flap opened, and Ashe stepped inside. I wondered how long she had been listening. "Amazing what thoughts trees inspire," she said.

"And deeds," I added, perhaps a bit darkly.

"I'm sorry I was delayed," she said, then touched Josh lightly on the shoulder. "Thanks for helping, Josh."

He hesitated at her gentle dismissal, gave me a not altogether charitable look, and conveyed that glance to Ashe. But he did accede to her silent request for him to leave. Then it was Ashe's turn to look at me.

"Try reading the fourth line," I said.

She had full eyebrows, and they came together almost as one. "What do you mean?"

"That kind of scrutiny is usually reserved for an eye chart."

She didn't lower her eyes. "I wasn't happy to hear that you were hired, Mr. Winter. Had I been around during the debate, I would have spoken against your being employed. But, now that you are here, I'm trying to decide whether to trust you."

"My Boy Scout oath is a little rusty."

She frowned. "I consider this a serious matter."

"So do I. It's jumping through your hoops that I don't take seriously."

She still didn't give up her staring. "Josh recommended you, but apparently he's having second thoughts now."

"That's because he's learned I don't come with puppet strings."

"I hope I don't have to remind you that we're in the middle of a political campaign, and the last thing we need is a bull in a china shop."

"Understood. But there's one thing I don't understand."

"What's that?"

"Why you're up here taking time off from that all-important political campaign."

Ashe allowed her chin an imperial tilt. "I came back to be in the woods," she said. "It renews me, helps me to remember what I'm fighting for."

Her words sounded noble, but that didn't make them believable. I wish I could say I stared at her only to discern the truth. It wasn't polite to keep looking at her, but I found it difficult to refrain. She moved several strands of fallen hair from her forehead. The barrettes couldn't keep all of her tresses in place. Some locks had escaped and went halfway down her back. A shadow reached out and touched them, moving where I dared not. Ashe started, as if I was the one who had reached for her.

"A moth," I said.

She followed its fluttering. "It's so large."

The moth seemed torn between the light and Ashe, flittered around both. "You don't see as many large moths anymore," I said. "They've declined in numbers."

Ashe held her finger out, but the moth didn't alight. It began to show more interest in the lantern.

"What's happened to them?" she asked.

"Decimated range, ravaged breeding grounds, diminished

feeding terrain, and too many bright, attractive lights."

It was flying around Ashe's head again, as interested in her hair as I was. "And probably too many people trying to stick pins in them," she said.

I had left that observation to her. The moth flew back toward the lantern. "I don't want it to get burned," she said.

I turned off the lantern, left us in darkness. Ashe didn't immediately flee, and neither did I.

"How do you know about moths?"

"I hang around lampposts."

"Really."

She didn't allow me any escape, captured me in one word. Pinned me. In the darkness it was easier to talk. "I've read an article or two," I said. "You know how it is: send a moth-eaten check to a noble cause and your guilt money earns you a subscription to a glossy magazine that demonstrates in wonderful color pictures how the world is going to hell in a handbasket."

"Some people don't read the articles," Ashe said.

"I can't resist picking scabs either."

It wasn't the usual adult show-and-tell time with the lights off, but there was something personal about our being together. We could both feel it. For long seconds we stood in the darkness, almost close enough to touch. Ashe broke the silence. "Maybe we ought to let the moth out."

"You lead the way, and I'm sure he'll follow."

She felt along the canvas, found the opening, and stepped outside. Then we propped the tent flap open just to make sure the moth found its freedom. There was still singing going on around the campfire. The clouds weren't as thick, and the moon was shining through, which made it easier for us to walk back. When we reached the campsite proper, Ashe turned to me and said good night.

"Where are you going?"

"To get Teller."

"I'll go with you."

"No need," she said.

I didn't push it. Maybe Ashe didn't want me to know about the cannabis. She went one way, and I went the other. I can't say I liked that. I didn't muse for long, though. A singer with a lot of lung, and a lot of soul, stepped in on my thoughts. She knew her Joni Mitchell, and she knew her cause; words for a forest primeval. I listened to the lament of paradise lost, and the erecting of parking lots.

There was an encore last verse, and everyone joined in. Even me.

$\triangledown$

6

At 11:00 P.M. only one motel in Garberville had a front desk clerk on duty. At that hour, all the other motels were ring-the-doorbell operations, and since I felt like doing neither a price comparison nor an "Avon calling" routine, it was easy selecting my home for the night.

My only demand of the clerk was to give me a room with a working telephone. After ascertaining that my credit was good, he did. Miss Tuntland was used to me calling late, even seemed to prefer our talking in the quiet hours when we didn't have to juggle our sentences between her other business calls.

"Mr. Winter, I presume?" she said.

"Dr. Livingstone to you," I said.

"That's right," she said. "You're calling from the Heart of Darkness, aren't you?"

"No. The forest primeval."

"Same thing, isn't it?"

I wanted to discount her words as mere flippancy, but her inquiry had an edge of seriousness I couldn't just slide by. There was some truth to her literary allusion, something Conradesque about Humboldt County. Heart of Greeness, maybe. Northern Humboldt County is reputed to be home to Bigfoot. Sasquatch legends are not the tales of the urban East, or the rural Midwest, or even the Badlands. In Marin or in Hollywood no one looks in the backyard almost expecting to sight a monster, or at least a nonhuman monster. The northern woods, with its big trees and wide spaces and rugged terrain, offers the illusion of still being largely unconquered, a landscape of the unknown.

"Tell me about Mistah Kurtz."

My cases were more than vicarious sleuthing for Miss Tuntland. She wasn't so much my switchboard as an answering board. People think I work alone. Maybe I even promote that impression. But I know that's not true. So does she.

"There's been plenty written about the Green Man," Miss Tuntland said, the slightest bit of satisfaction in her voice, "but most of the pieces read like public relations releases. Shepard usually orchestrated his talking to the media while he was out planting. He always involved the reporters in his work, made them toil at his side. It was a brilliant tactic: they gained an appreciation for his labors, and invariably their copy was sympathetic."

"No dirt on him?"

"Only the kind shoveled. He talked a lot about trees, but not much about himself. Even most of his quotes weren't his own."

"What do you mean?"

"He always had some homily or proverb appropriate to a situation, a stock body of passages all having to do with trees. It was difficult getting a quote out of him that wasn't someone else's. While looking for the Green Man, I had to keep sweeping away other people's leaves."

That was in keeping with what Teller had said, I thought, Shepard emulating other tree planters and trying to live up to the historical image of the Green Man.

"Anything stand out in his background? Upbringing? Love interests?"

"He came out of the middle class, from the Midwest, and a middle-of-the-road family. Those who've traced his roots have scared up the usual anecdotal stories: how he tended to fallen birds and was helpful and considerate. I even read one account that seemed to be the exact opposite of the George Washington myth: instead of young George telling his father, I cannot tell a lie, I chopped down the cherry tree, in the Green Man story there's some fable about young Christopher confessing to his father that it was he who had dug up the front lawn and planted a tree."

"Maybe the story's true."

"That from the man who's been coaching my cynicism for a decade?"

I told her about his proclivity for imitation. Maybe he had decided to duplicate the George Washington story but with his own twist.

Although Miss Tuntland was in no way satisfied she had gotten "to the roots" of the Green Man, she had managed to document his two decades of tree planting. His work had kept him crisscrossing continents. He typically stayed with a project from six months to a year and in the last three years had done plantings in the Sahara, and Kenya, and China, and Poland.

"Where did he plan to go next?" I asked.

"To work on his Green Belt," she said. "Shepard envisioned a forest extending around the world, from Portland, Maine to Portland, Oregon, and from Dublin to Vladivostok."

I whistled. "He didn't think small."

"No," Miss Tuntland said, "he didn't."

We talked about Sequoia Summer, its participants, and all the emotions it had stirred up. In the small quiet that followed, Miss Tuntland divined my need for more help.

"What now?"

"Ashe O'Conner," I said.

"The Green Goddess," said Miss Tuntland.

"The same," I said. "I'm curious as to how frequently Ashe has visited Humboldt County in the last few months. Unless redwoods have been given the right to vote, I don't know why she'd be spending so much time here."

"I'll check on that," she said. "And, Mr. Winter?"

"Yes?"

"I would remind you what invariably happens to mortals when they consort with the gods."

She didn't give me a chance to respond; she chose that moment to pass on my messages. Miss Tuntland said she had hinted to my callers that I was attending a Boy Scout jamboree. To me, though, she wasn't quite so nonchalant. I told her good-bye and heard that little pause from her, the one I've come to know is significant.

"Watch your ax," she said, then hung up.

I was awake before the sun and went down to the front desk to ask for a breakfast recommendation. The switchboard was beeping, and the clerk kept smiling and holding his finger up, my signal to wait for him to clear the PBX of calls.

"Breakfast?" I asked, just getting the word in before the interruptions started anew.

"Woodrow's," he said apologetically and raised his finger once more, this time to point south.

The morning was cold. I hugged my brown Harris tweed to my body, and walked uptown. Garberville doesn't have that many restaurants, but I still managed to miss the one I was looking for, and had to backtrack. I had been looking for Woodrow's, figuring some male proprietor had immortalized a greasy spoon with his first name. But two words had gone into the restaurant's naming, not one: Wood Rose.

The Wood Rose was a funky little restaurant with good smells, and good wood, and what looked to be good food. There wasn't any hostess, but a waitress smiled and signaled for me to take an open chair at an already occupied table.

I hesitated for a moment. The table was meant for a deuce. In San Francisco I would have waited for a table to vacate, or a spot at the counter to open. But when in Garberville . . . I walked over to the table and cleared my throat. A paper came down, and big glasses looked up. He was about forty-five, had a large nose, a bemused expression, and the ubiquitous town beard. He was slouched back into the vinyl, using his denim jacket as a pillow. Tricolored sneakers pointed out from under the table's edge.

"The waitress suggested," I said, pointing to the chair, not finishing my thought.

He looked to the chair, and so did I. Then, with his red, white, and blue footwear, he eased the chair out from under the table. "Property is theft," he said. "Sit."

"These days," I said, taking the chair, "I wonder if Marx wouldn't say the same thing about property taxes."

He smiled, continued to hold his newspaper for a moment, then slowly put it down, apparently in favor of me.

"Not so loud," he said. "The only things I know about Marx, I learned in here. This is where the Trots, and the Marxists, and the anarchists, and the socialists, and the revisionists, all like to rehash the ills of the world."

"And which *ist* are you?"

"Art-ist," he said, laughing.

I gave him a disbelieving look, and he held up his right hand. "What kind of artist?" I asked.

"Glass, mostly," he said, running his hand through his beard. "Large pieces."

"Your stuff shown in town?"

He gave a little laugh. "No," he said. "Artists live where they can afford the rent, and those are usually places that don't have art galleries. Oxymoronic truth. Or maybe just moronic. My work mostly sells in San Francisco. People have money there."

I identified myself as a San Franciscan, but not one with money. We exchanged names. His was Randall Maroney, but he said everyone called him Maroon. Colorful nickname. Maroon recommended the cheese-and-mushroom omelet with the home fries, which saved me from having to look at the menu.

"You an *ist*?" he asked, a gentle enough way of inquiring about what I was doing in town.

"A nonexhibitionist."

He laughed and didn't pry any further. Privacy was respected in Humboldt. With its tradition of marijuana farmers, people had learned to ask no questions and hear no lies.

I gradually steered the conversation over to the Green Man. Maroon seemed more than happy with the topic. "Lots of talk after his death," he said. "For two, three mornings here, he was what went down with my coffee."

I tried to draw him out. "A lot of loggers cheering, I guess?"

He shook his head. "Not really. Some of the Paul Bunyan posers were glad to see him go, but it's not like the lumber companies declared a holiday or anything."

"That's how it is with death," I said. "Everyone is suddenly willing to let bygones by bygones."

51

Maroon shook his head slightly. "It wasn't quite that way," he said.

"Then how was it?"

He looked at me for a second and wondered who the hell I was to be asking these kinds of questions, and where my curiosity was leading. I hadn't exactly finessed the interview and had the feeling I wouldn't be getting much more in the way of answers without giving something in return.

"Answer to your *ist* question," I said. "Free-lance journalist. In search of Deep Throat. Or Sawdust Mouth. Or something. I'm wondering if there isn't a story here."

Maroon relaxed a little. "I'm not your best source," he said.

"I'm not your best reporter," I said. "If I do a piece, I'll cite you as an 'uninformed source.' "

That drew a little chuckle. "It's probably nothing," said Maroon, discounting the story with both his voice and his hands, "but I heard someone say that the Green Man had been getting cozy with Trans-Miss."

I looked properly skeptical. Reportorial, I hoped. "Who told you that?" I asked. "A fantas-*ist*?"

His beard didn't hide Maroon's smile. "No, I don't think so. Environmentalist, yes. He said that Shepard was a real loose cannon, that he didn't understand the politics of old growth, and that the only thing he knew how to do was plant trees."

"So how did that put him in bed with Trans-Miss?"

"I'm not saying it did. But there was some guilt by association. What I've heard is that the Green Man visited the offices of Trans-Mississippi a few days before his death. Went there and asked for a tour, if you can believe that. He wanted to see their tree-planting operation."

I was still playing hard to convince. "Maybe he wanted to better know the enemy."

"Maybe," said Maroon. "Most people in the movement will tell you that Shepard was an environmental martyr and that he gave his life to the cause. This decade's Chico Mendes."

I'd heard that analogy. Mendes had died in Brazil. He had been trying to organize the rubber tappers and, in his own way, to halt the deforestation of the Amazon. In that case, justice had been as slow as deforestation was quick.

"I'm a little dubious about martyr-of-the-month flavors," I said, still playing the cynic. "Doesn't anyone die of natural causes anymore?"

"A branch through the head isn't exactly old age," said Maroon, "but I know what you mean. Lots of theories. Some say the Green Man was killed by the FBI, and some say he was a CIA plant killed by a cabal of extreme Greens."

"I suppose it's just a matter of time before someone says little green men were in on the killing of the big Green Man," I said.

I was warming up to the curmudgeon role. As long as I kept the conversation light, and not threatening, I figured Maroon would keep talking.

My food arrived. I took a bite; then my fork took on a life of its own. I was hungry, and the food was good. Between bites, I continued to ask questions. "Wasn't there some group that claimed divine intervention?" I said. "Thought the hand of God was behind the spearing?"

Maroon nodded. "The Third Day," he said, "and the Right Reverend Reginald Sawyer. You know about them and him?"

"Genesis," I said. "On the third day God created among other things trees. Same God said man should have dominion over the earth. Thus, The Third Day."

"Also known as Three-D," said Maroon. "Those kind of glasses are even better than rose-colored."

"Conservative, huh?"

Maroon whistled. "Conservative understates him by about a century or two. We're talking about a frontier mindset, a real atavist."

Another *ist* for my list. I took a bite of the home fries and was glad I didn't have to interrupt my eating with more questioning. Maroon was on a roll, and I had an appetite.

"Sawyer seems to have a personal vendetta against the forest," he said. "His God, he likes to say, abhors pantheism. He thinks old growth is a new age plot designed to draw the young and impressionable away from the true faith back to the days of tree worship."

I chewed a little more, and chewed on what Sawyer sermonized. I'd heard an idle mind is the devil's playground. But now I was being told it was old growth.

$\triangledown$

7

SEVEN MILES NORTH of Garberville I exited at Sylvandale and started on a stretch of road called the Avenue of the Giants. Physically, the road isn't far from 101. But there are special places along its thirty-three-mile expanse that call for you to stop and linger, that allow you escape into another world.

"The redwoods," wrote John Steinbeck in *Travels with Charley,* "once seen, leave a mark or create a vision that stays with you always. No one has ever successfully painted or photographed a redwood tree. The feeling they produce is not transferable. From them comes silence and awe. It's not only their unbelievable stature, nor the color which seems to shift and vary under your eyes, no, they are not like any trees we know, they are ambassadors from another time. . . . The vainest, most slap-happy and irreverent of men, in the presence of redwoods, goes under a spell of wonder and respect. Respect—that's the word. One feels the need to bow to unquestioned sovereigns."

Steinbeck devoted a number of his travel pages to the *Sequoia sempervirens,* gave more words to those trees than he did to most states. He assumed that the redwoods would be the high point of the trip for his French poodle, Charley. What dog, he reasoned, wouldn't see a waiting redwood as a heavenly vision? What greater deed could a canine aspire to than to sprinkle at the foot of the granddaddy of all trees?

Scouting for just the right tree, Steinbeck finally found one to his liking, a three-hundred-foot giant. He let Charley out of his Rocinante, expecting a historic moment. But Charley didn't respond as expected. It took all of Steinbeck's urging and guile to get Charley to do his oblations at the foot of the redwood. You can lead a dog to the brink, but you can't make him make water.

Sixty-five million years ago the dinosaurs disappeared. Redwoods are almost that old. Their ancient grandeur speaks of that prehistoric legacy. They are eldritch presences, out of proportion to human sensibilities. But it is more than their gargantuan appearance that people find disquieting; their aura of anomaly and mystery make them stand out as much as their height. The oldest known coast redwood was estimated to be 2,200 years old when it was chopped down in 1932. But even that figure might be misleading. Some contend that redwoods are immortals.

It is not simple to kill a redwood. Early settlers were frustrated by the trees. They cut them down while clearing fields, only to have them rise from their stumps again. These were trees that refused to die, trees unlike any the farmers had dealt with before. Their stump sprouting wasn't new life but a continuation of the old. To the dramatic, there was a measure of resurrection in these trees. Determining the life and death of a redwood almost becomes a moot point, even if that notion is not agreeable to the human psyche. Immortality, long the psychological domain of *Homo sapiens*, is encroached upon by the physical reality of these tall trees. Counting their rings and years tells only a part of the story. Within the circles, a sylvanist might discern the climatic events of a thousand years, while a poet might read the history of the ages.

And what of the Green Man? I thought. How would I count his rings?

I took the Dyerville Loop and pulled over into a parking area at Founders Grove. There were only two other cars in the parking lot. The morning was cool. Sequoias contribute to their own microclimate. The canopy of the forest helps them to retain the foggy ocean moisture, insulating the trees from any temperature extremes.

It was eight-thirty. Doc wasn't due to arrive for another half hour. Rather than sit around, I decided to take a walk on my own. Trail guides were offered from a display box at the head of the path. The way was flat and well marked, but, even in this much-traveled area, I had only to take a few steps off the trail to feel alone—and overwhelmed. You give up your shadow when you walk among the redwoods, and a bit of human arrogance as well. I stepped through the Walk-Thru Tree and felt a little bit like Alice through the looking-glass. You're not supposed to be able to pass through a tree in much the same manner you would a tunnel.

There were other varieties of trees in the grove, including red elderberries, tanbark oaks, and California laurels, but at first glance hills always get overlooked against the backdrop of great mountains. For a long time I stood at the base of the downed Dyerville Giant. It had been the second largest tree in the world until its fall in 1991. In redwood time, the race is not to the swift.

I continued my walk among the titans. When standing underneath the trees, I tried to take my mental measures, even though I couldn't see their tops. To get that perspective, I had to move back, had to look up at monuments longer than a football field. And me, a cheering section of one. With optimum growing conditions, redwoods can shoot up more than a foot a year. I thought about that. You do a lot of silent thinking and neck contorting around such giants. I was Steinbeck's vain, irreverent man, caught in a spell of wonder and respect. I tried to identify my feelings, to think of what I would tell Miss Tuntland later. I felt as short of words as I did of stature. Any description, I knew, would be inappropriate. Our language is suited to describe poplars, and birches, and aspens but fails these leafy leviathans.

Interpretive guide in hand, I made my way along the trail. Ironically, Trail Marker 13 designated a widow-maker. Unlucky 13. I wondered if the number was portentous, if the Green Man's number had just come up. I read from the trail guide: "Though the limbs you see in front of you seem to be growing, they broke from one of the surrounding redwood trees and, falling several hundred feet, became embedded in the ground— a fairly common occurrence during storms and high winds.

You can see why they were given the name 'widow-makers.' "

I examined the widow-makers. As advertised, they did look like trees. Usually, I don't violate park rules, but I was compelled to try an experiment. I put two hands on one of the widow-makers and pulled. There was some give to it. With an Arthurian yank, I might have been able to unearth the widow-maker, but in my own mind I was satisfied that such a falling limb could impale a human skull.

The trail ended too soon for me. The woods had imparted a special sensation, a balm. I had trouble identifying the feeling. I felt renewed. Invigorated. And something else, something more. I searched for the word, the impression. It was new to me, or at least forgotten. And then I knew: I felt young. That was it. Young.

Younger than springtime.

"Making do without me, I see."

I awoke from my reverie. Doc looked amused. "I've seen that look before," he said. "I call it 'lost in the woods.' "

"You ever suffer from that malady?"

"Sometimes."

"What's the cure?"

"A clear-cut."

Doc led me away from the paths. "Trailblazing is the best way to walk in the woods," he prescribed, a philosophy the rangers probably would not have endorsed, but we practiced what he preached. As we walked, Doc lectured. "Touch that redwood bark," he insisted. I tentatively reached out. "No," he said, "really touch it." I did as he said, ran my hand along it.

"Redwoods can stand up to almost anything but saws," he said. "The high tannin content of their wood, and their thick bark, gives them amazing resistance to everything from insect infestations to fires."

He patted the bark. "We're talking major water retention here, thousands of gallons."

The figure surprised me. "I've been told their root structure isn't very deep," I said. "I suppose that means it rains a lot around here."

"Some winters it's biblical," he said. "Forty days and forty nights. Average rainfall in these parts is over sixty inches, though more than a hundred and twenty have been recorded.

Everyone still talks about the great flood of nineteen sixty-four. The Eel overflowed and washed away a few towns around here. Course the fact of the matter is there wasn't an inordinate amount of rain that year. People learned the hard way what happens when you cut down trees indiscriminately, and how fast runoff and silt from logging can combine for disaster."

The farther we walked into the woods, the more it felt like we were venturing into a lake, swimming underwater. The light filtered down, green and diffused. Even trekking along the forest floor felt different, dreamlike. I commented on the spongy surface. Doc came to a stop and insisted I dig. I scooped up several inches of decomposing matter and had to go through lots of humus before I found earth.

"Part of the old in old growth," he said. "The forest perpetuates itself through the past. Nowhere in the world is there a greater accumulation of plant mass than in these primeval forests. An acre of old growth can contain over two hundred tons of dead wood. Nurse logs, we call 'em. Those snags and downed logs are the bank account of the forest, nutrients for it to call upon."

"Let sleeping logs lie," I said.

Doc allowed a grimace before lecturing again. "A fallen redwood can take up to five centuries to decompose," he said. "The cellulose and lignin can only be broken down by bacteria, and fungi, and microorganisms. But, if you can't remember that, just think of these downed trees as time-release vitamins."

As we continued our walk, I directed the conversation to my favorite pastime. "Seen any spotted owls around here?"

"A few. Not many. There's really not that much room for them out here."

I gave him a questioning glance. All I could see was room. Doc explained. "Nesting pairs need about three thousand acres of old growth to raise their young," he said. "Their needs have run into a lot of vested interests."

"The new snail darter," I said, remembering the little fish that held up a dam. That held up progress, some insisted.

"That's what the lumber interests say."

"What do you say?"

"That self-interest runs the world. People don't wear 'If It's Hootin', I'm Shootin' ' shirts because they hate spotted owls. They wear them because they're scared the owl might be designated a threatened species. If your way of life was jeopardized by a bird, I daresay you might have an itchy trigger finger."

"The law of the jungle, huh?"

"Close enough."

"And you accept that?"

"I don't like it that the owls have been portrayed as the enemies, and that the timber industry has pictured them as preying on humans. If asked, I would state that the owls feed on wood rats and tree mice."

"But only if asked?"

"I'm not as adept at soapbox speeches as others."

"You don't seem very emotionally involved."

"I am a scientist."

"Some scientists are also advocates. Some scientists liken the spotted owl to a miner's canary. They see it as an indicator species, a portent for a dying forest."

"I think that's somewhat simplistic," said Doc. "Less than one percent of all organisms that ever lived are on earth today. Extinction is nothing new."

"Isn't that kind of resignation defeatist?"

"The study of ecology is the study of the interrelationship of organisms and their environment. There is no such thing as a static environment. I can't be romantic about the woods. That's not how I've been trained."

I was curious about how he had been trained, and motioned all around us. "What do you see out here?"

"Interrelationships mostly," he said. "Neutralism, and parasitism, and commensalism, and mutualism. They're all here."

I understood his *isms* about as well as I did *ists* and looked to him for a better explanation.

"Everyone thinks the woods are so bucolic," Doc said. "They're not at all. Around us is competition, and predation, and decay, and death."

His words sounded bitter. In them I could almost hear Mr. Kurtz's "The horror! The horror!"

59

"You paint a bleak picture."

"That wasn't my intention. But then I'm not one to walk around the woods reciting Joyce Kilmer poetry either."

He made me laugh, and I think he liked that.

"You wouldn't be laughing if you had been forced to listen to innumerable recitals," he said. In a mocking falsetto, he recounted, "I think that I shall never see / A poem lovely as a tree."

"Who was forcing you to listen?"

Doc sighed. "Force wasn't exactly the right word. Her name was Jane. She was a Sequoia Summer camper for six or seven weeks. I think most of her wood lore came from *Bambi.* Maybe I liked that she was naive. Or maybe I just liked how she looked in her cut-off shorts. She repeated that poem incessantly, and one time I challenged her. I said, 'Kilmer didn't write his poem on water. He used paper. A tree was sacrificed for his poem. A tree, according to him, that was superior to his words.' Jane didn't like that."

"Why'd she leave?"

"She became disillusioned."

"With the woods?"

"No." He smiled at that thought. "The trees remained beautiful to her. It was people that ruined them for her."

"Which people?"

"People with an ax to grind." This time he gave me the questioning look. "I thought you came out here to learn about the woods."

I motioned for him to lead on. It didn't take Doc many steps before he started lecturing again—about food webs, and nutrient cycles, and heartwood, and sapwood. Doc pointed out other trees and plants, kept up a running commentary on what there was around us. I stopped him in front of a little tree that looked familiar to me, then recognized that it wasn't a tree.

"A widow-maker," I said.

He nodded.

"How do you think he died?"

Doc shrugged. "Freak accidents happen. He was the victim of one. You hear plenty of conspiracy theories. But Shepard wasn't the first to die from a widow-maker, and he probably won't be the last."

I looked up. The redwoods blotted out the sky. I wondered if death was lurking up in the heavens. "In the words of Chicken Little, should I be worried that 'the sky is falling'?"

Doc shook his head. "You might as well be watching out for meteorites."

Doesn't that contradict what you just said about the Green Man's death?"

"I wouldn't advise walking around the forest when it's windy or storming. He shouldn't have been out under those conditions. Everybody knows that."

"Did you know him?"

"I saw him, but I didn't know him."

We started walking again. Doc had a primeval forest for his lecture hall, and he put it to good use. He knew his way around the woods and didn't need a compass or any markers to finish up our hike right where we started.

"What brought you to the redwoods?" I asked.

His enigmatic smile returned. "Do you remember that old line about how a dwarf sees farther than the giant when he rides on giants' shoulders?"

I nodded.

"Well, I wondered what I'd be able to see from a redwood."

"Like the view?"

Maybe he didn't hear. Or maybe he just didn't want to answer. I remembered his pecuniary state, reached into my pocket, and pulled out some bills. "Not a grant exactly," I said, "but thank you."

Doc was proud. For a moment he looked like he might not take the money, but then he accepted it with a shrug. "The root of all evil," he said.

"Not all," I said. "I've found evil has plenty of other roots."

▽

8

I DROVE AS FAR north as I could along the Avenue of the Giants before returning to the freeway. I was getting used to the open country, enjoying the absence of fast-food eateries and convenience stores. The only major forms of hucksterism were the gift shops, each trying to outkitsch the other. Most of the come-ons were tree oriented; there were drive-through trees, one-log gift shops, living hollow trees, tree homes, tree houses, and trees that had survived lightning, floods, fires, and logger's axes (and one which had supposedly taken on all those calamities and was in the process of celebrating its thousandth year on the planet). Large redwood carvings abounded, most of them awful. Some roadside attractions promised mysteries of nature; others had Bigfoot come-ons. All had burls of every shape and size for sale.

Getting off 101, I crossed the Fern Bridge, an old concrete arch bridge the likes of which you don't see anymore. My destination was Ferndale, and the Reverend Reginald Sawyer. I had heard from some of the Green Man's friends and was curious about what his enemies had to say about him. The road leading southwest was flat and rustic, providing scenery of green pastures, and very fat and contented cows.

The entire village of Ferndale is a state historical landmark. The town touts itself as "the Victorian Village," and for good reason. Its early settlers, grown rich from dairying, moved into Ferndale in the mid-1800s and built their Victorian houses, what the locals called Butterfat Palaces. While driving through town, I got to see some of them. You'd expect a San Franciscan to be a snob about things Victorian, but even I had to admit that Ferndale's houses were worth a long look.

Ferndale was another one-road town, but it was two coats of paint and one coat of primer removed from Garberville. More than that, it exuded a much more conservative air. The village looked like a set for Thornton Wilder's *Our Town*, but it didn't come across as a tourist trap. While inquiring about directions, I heard a young man lectured to by a passerby. Apparently the boy had dropped a candy wrapper. Red-faced, he retrieved and then disposed of his litter. No wonder the streets were spotless.

The Truth Evangelical Church was several miles south of town. My direction giver, a salty old man with a dour expression, described it as "out there." I wasn't sure if "out there" signified a different town, or a different sensibility, or both. Most of the in-town churches were established in the 1800s, and looked it. Sawyer's house of worship was apparently less staid. My navigator mentioned, with some disdain, that at night it was lit up "like the Star of Bethlehem." Then I thought he mumbled something about frankincense. But it could have been Frankenstein.

Most of the countryside around Ferndale is cutover floodplain, the trees harvested over a century ago. With the ocean only five miles west, and the Eel River Delta meandering not far from town, the area offers both fresh- and saltwater marshes. Over a short drive I went from conifer forests to tidal flats to upland meadows.

The Truth Evangelical Church was situated atop a rise, about the only significant elevation to be seen for miles around. The church was modern, at odds with the Gothic revival style of most of Ferndale's other churches. Its steeple was high and proud. Affixed to it was a sign which read: A CITY THAT IS SET ON AN HILL CANNOT BE HID. In smaller letters, it credited Matthew 5:14.

The large parking lot contained only three cars and a church bus. Behind the parking area was a fenced playing field with a jungle gym, swings, and a merry-go-round. Everything looked new.

I had the choice of a winding path or stairs, and I took the dozen upward steps. The church wasn't as large as it appeared from below. Exterior ornamentation was minimal, but someone had taken great pains with the rose garden which lined the path. The splash of colors welcomed like nothing else on the grounds, the sole display of warmth and lightness. A long row of floodlights stretched along the grass and took aim at the church. Let there be light, and lots of it.

The church was attenuated, long but thin. A stand of pines tried to flesh the structure out. There was a corridor that led from the church to a vestry, and farther down the path was a parsonage. The house was a Cape Cod design, with wide bay windows that looked out to the valley below. The only architectural cliché missing was a white picket fence.

I tried the house first. Like the playground, it didn't look as if it had been broken in enough. I rang the doorbell once, waited thirty seconds, then rang it a second time. The door was finally opened by a small woman in a rather severe frock that made her look older than she was—thirty going on fifty.

"I'm sorry, I didn't hear you," she said, her green eyes looking everywhere but at me. "Sounds don't carry very far in the house. My vanity, I suppose. I asked for lots of insulation."

She didn't need to make the apology, but I sensed she was used to offering her shortcomings to others, and undoubtedly the Lord. Her self-proclaimed vanity interested me. What would be a sin? I wondered. Probably a hot tub.

"Stuart Winter," I said, extending my hand.

She took time from wringing her thin hands to shake mine briefly, then went back to twisting at her thin gold wedding band. "I'm the Reverend Reginald Sawyer's wife," she said.

"I lost your name somewhere in that title," I said.

Very softly, she answered, "Ruth."

I had expected someone older. I'd seen her husband on the news a few times, and he had to be in his fifties. Maybe she dressed as she did to impart more years to her person. A makeover artist could have easily made her a different woman. Her brown hair was resigned to a lifeless bun, and her face was pale, without color.

"I was hoping I could have a few minutes of your husband's time," I said.

"You'll probably find him in church," she said, "practicing his sermon."

It wasn't exactly the manner in which she said it, but I sensed a reason behind her wanting plenty of insulation in the house. Hearing sermons rehearsed on a daily basis, I imagined, would make a little quiet a precious thing.

"Thank you," I said.

She nodded, and her eyes caught mine for a moment, but then she looked down, embarrassed. Without raising her head, she closed the door.

The church was open. I walked inside and called out greetings, but no one answered. Redwood motif dominated, a lot of John Muir's "nature's cathedrals" having gone into the making of one of man's. Redwood paneling and stained glass lined the walls, each enhancing the glow of the other. The altar at the front of the church, and the dramatic cross that hung on the far wall, were made from burls. Redwood burls are likened to benign human tumors, the difference being that the sequoia tumors have been known to be as much as eight feet thick. The consistency of burl wood is different from that of redwood, usually darker, heavier, and harder, with a much more pronounced grain. The burls of worship were striking pieces of wood. The cross was muscular, about five feet high and three feet wide. It was awash in lights and cast a blood red gleam. If you didn't genuflect, you at least took notice.

I walked up the aisle and saw there were no prayer cushions for the faithful. Knees had to face up to hardwood floors. I investigated the vestibules on both sides of the church, but neither was occupied. The only thing out of the ordinary was a tape recorder atop the pulpit. Usually you see a Bible. Curious, I went to it and pushed the play button.

There was static for a few moments, then a voice that didn't lack for wind, or lungs, or passion. The tiny speaker in the recorder muted the orator's bass, made it a bit tinny, but it was still loud enough to be heard throughout the church. I lowered the volume.

"We're going to talk about miracles today," announced a voice I assumed was Reverend Sawyer's. "Now you know that the Bible, the living word of God, is full of miracles, hundreds of them.

"Observe Mark, chapter eight, beginning at verse twenty-two: 'And Jesus cometh to Bethsaida; and they bring a blind man unto him, and besought him to touch him.

" 'And he took the blind man by the hand, and led him out of the town; and when he had spit on his eyes, and put his hands upon him, he asked him if he saw ought.

" 'And he looked up, and said, I see men as trees, walking.

" 'After that he put his hands again upon his eyes, and made him look up: and he was restored, and saw every man clearly.'

"Some of you, I fear, are like that blind man. You don't see, or don't want to see, the miracles going on in your life.

"Others of you can only partially see. Though the Lord has put his hand on you, your eyesight is but half restored. You only see men as trees.

"I offer you the miracle of seeing clearly, I offer you the touch of Jesus. Thank the Lord . . ."

I thanked him for the fast-forward button, using it to jump through the rest of the tape. There didn't seem to be much continuity to Sawyer's talk. His dialogue jumped between miracles and angels. Sawyer seemed to think there was an army of angels waiting to be called upon, all ready to come to the aid of the faithful.

The rambling tenor of his sermon surprised me. Sawyer was known for his conservative political tirades, which usually had an agenda that centered more on the tangible than on the ecclesiastical.

I rewound the tape, brought it back to its genesis. Or Leviticus. Or whatever. Then I went looking for Sawyer again, searched the vestry but found it empty. There was a lingering smell of coffee and doughnuts, and fried chicken, the aroma of church socials. On the far wall was a mosaic, Christ and his twelve disciples sitting down to his last meal. I hunted out Judas's expression and wasn't surprised to see he had a poker face.

I walked back to the parsonage, pushed the bell again, and waited. Mrs. Sawyer was faster this time—she must have been working on her vanity.

66

"I'm sorry to bother you again, Mrs. Sawyer," I said, "but I couldn't find your husband in the church or in the vestry."

She didn't say anything, waiting for me to continue the conversation. "Perhaps he slipped back inside," I said, "and you didn't hear him."

"The Reverend," she said, "isn't the kind of person who slips anywhere."

She made it sound as if I had used the word *slither*.

"Well, maybe he *walked* inside," I said, "and is quietly resting somewhere."

She shook her head.

"Any other ideas where he could be? I very much want to ask him some questions."

She didn't rise to the bait, didn't ask me about the questions, and didn't ask me in to wait for him over a cup of coffee. Usually preachers' wives are hospitable. It comes with the territory. But maybe she sensed a wolf in sheep's clothing.

"He might be out walking," she finally said.

"Does he often go for walks?"

"Of late, yes."

"Any particular path?"

"The Lord's," she said.

I couldn't tell if she was making a little joke and looked at her for some giveaway. She didn't like being examined closely and blushed a little. The color added to her features, gave hint that if Ruth Sawyer allowed herself to be other than serious she could look considerably prettier. "I will tell my husband you called, Mr. Winter."

"But he won't know what I was here for," I said, still trying to draw her into further conversation.

"You don't strike me as someone easily dissuaded," she said. "I am sure you will acquaint him with your purpose."

She hadn't made a move to close the door, but she clearly wanted to retreat back into her silent house. "Please give him my business card," I said, handing it to her in such a way that she couldn't help but read it and take note of my occupation.

I've had doors shut on me faster, but not too many.

9

MY BUSINESS CARD hadn't gained me the extra five minutes of conversation I desired, but I still wasn't ready to leave. A good investigator knows when to wait. And how to wait. I grabbed my Leitz binoculars out of my truck. They led me like a divining rod, pulling me to a promising spot. No water, but something better, a splendid view. Ostensibly, I was going to be looking for the wandering Reverend Mr. Sawyer, but I hoped for plenty of secondary diversions.

At first I found only the expected and commonplace, plenty of sparrows and finches and starlings, and a few horned larks and meadowlarks. I did my desultory viewing, and for ten minutes overlooked the obvious. The great blue heron had remained motionless, but I still should have noticed four feet of bird. My ready excuse was that I hadn't expected the heron to be in the field. It's easy to miss things when you don't think they belong. With all the bodies of water nearby, I would have expected the heron to be hunting for fish instead of working the field below me. But this heron evidently had a taste for pocket gophers. He was standing ready at a hole, his long, sharp bill primed for a spearing. I waited for him to strike, but his patience was greater than mine, and I finally looked elsewhere.

Working my binoculars across the clearing, I noticed that the same field looked very different than it had just minutes before. Something was missing. Some things. The many small birds had vanished. I looked around for the reason and discovered it: a loggerhead shrike. Shrikes are frequently referred to as butcher birds, a nickname deriving from their habit of impaling their larger prey on any available spike. Victims have been found hanging from barbed wire, branches, thorns, from virtually any small spear capable of suspending the shrike's prey.

Because of the way they dispatch their game, shrikes have been painted as insatiable killers, bloody hunters that impale victim after victim on a crucifix row. But studies have shown that shrikes kill no more than they can eat. They have an infallible memory for where they have hung their victims and always return to finish off their larder.

What is ironic is that these butcher birds are songbirds, the only truly predatory songbirds. They're not as operatic as most songbirds, but they do have a very respectable warble. Lady Death singing. They're deceptive birds. To the casual glance, they're innocuous, eight inches of innocence; the size of a robin, the coloring of a mockingbird, and the soul of an eagle. Shrikes weigh only about two ounces but will take on prey much larger than themselves, including birds, rodents, amphibians, and snakes.

My shrike was hunting insects, which make up the bulk of their diet, vampire reputation notwithstanding. I saw it catch, then devour, what looked like a bee, then watched it go after other quarry. Twice, a grasshopper escaped capture, then it was caught. I watched the shrike transfer the grasshopper from beak to foot. Shrikes aren't like other birds of prey. They don't have talons. But even without some of the weapons associated with other feathered hunters, they're every bit as effective. I followed the shrike and his victim as far as a blackberry patch; then they were lost to me. I wondered whether the grasshopper would end up spiked on the end of a blackberry thorn or just eaten in the shade.

Humans are drawn to the macabre; maybe that's why so many birders get excited by shrikes. Death by so-called natural causes doesn't interest us. But an impaled figure is another matter altogether. I wondered if that was what had drawn me to the investigation of the Green Man's death, and wondered also whether I was on a shrike hunt or a snipe hunt.

"Mr. Winter?"

I visibly started. Some hunter of hunters. I put down the binoculars and turned around. The Reverend Reginald Sawyer was standing behind me. He was holding my business card. My reaction seemed to satisfy the minister. Maybe it gave him pleasure to see people squirming.

Sawyer had curly hair, which was more black than gray. His wire-rim glasses covered very dark eyes and rested upon a ski-jump nose, one with a long downhill and good takeoff. An expert's jump. His face was well fleshed, his jowls prominent. He wasn't wearing the vestments of the clergy, just a dark suit. But some people can look pontifical in the most basic of outfits. Sawyer was one of those.

He was looking suspiciously at my binoculars. "I'm a bird-watcher," I explained. "You've got a nice spot for viewing up here. Hope you don't mind."

"No," he said, but he left a lot of room for interpretation in his answer.

I tried to make conversation—and make him less skeptical. "God's country for birding," I said. "Everything is so close, and so abundant—wetlands, and fields, and deltas, and woodlands, and meadows. A birder's paradise."

Conversationally, I had gone one short step beyond the weather. Maybe that was my mistake. "It was not for birds that the Lord created this earth," said Sawyer in a pedantic voice. "In Genesis one, verse twenty-six, we are told that God made man in his image, with dominion over the fish of the sea, and the fowl of the air."

Unbeknownst to him, I had already heard one of his sermons, and I wasn't in the mood for another. "Silly me," I said. "Here I was under the impression that we no longer had to sacrifice birds to God."

There wasn't much Christian charity in Sawyer's eyes. "You didn't travel from San Francisco just to look at birds," he said, "and it's apparent you didn't come to me to hear about God."

"No," I said. "I came to you to hear about the Green Man."

He shook his jowls, said, "I can't help you," then started to walk away.

I followed him. "I'm doing background," I explained. "I've been hired to look into his death."

"Why?" asked Sawyer. "He is in God's hands."

"And on the way to those hands," I said, "some suggest a commandment or two might have been broken."

The Reverend Mr. Sawyer stopped walking, took a long moment to read my face. "What are you saying?"

"I'm not saying anything. I'm investigating a death."

"And what's this talk of broken commandments?"

"The sixth," I said. Sawyer didn't comment, but he didn't move either. He looked a little puzzled, or perhaps relieved. I wondered whether I had identified the wrong commandment. Quite possible. I made sure of my reference. "Thou shalt not kill."

If looks could break that commandment . . . Sawyer glared at me, made it quite clear I didn't need to explain the Bible to him, then once more started walking away. I dogged his steps.

"I can't help you," he told me a second time.

"Why not?"

"I know what they're trying to do. I know what you're trying to do. To make him more than he was. I think that was his plan all along."

"I'm not following you."

"I've seen his image on T-shirts and sweatshirts. Idolatry. His words are repeated as if they were holy. They're not. And he wasn't."

"Then why don't you tell me about him? Why not clarify the misconceptions? I'm not on a holy crusade. I'm just trying to understand him. You were his rival. The last thing I want from you is platitudes."

I've found that the best way to get an earful of someone's faults is to sing their praises in front of those who know them. But that only works with the living. To learn about the dead you have to be more inventive.

We stopped walking again, this time in front of the vestry. Something I had said evidently rankled Sawyer. "What do you mean by 'rival'?" he asked.

"The media," I told him, "painted the two of you as being at loggerheads. I wondered how much of that was point-counterpoint, and how much of it was personal."

"We didn't debate on street corners," said Sawyer.

"But your paths did cross?"

"Once," he conceded.

"Where?"

"A public forum."

"What were the circumstances?"

"I was speaking for The Third Day. He was supposed to give a talk on the woods."

"But he didn't?"

Sawyer shook his head.

"What did he talk about?"

"He profaned the word of God."

"In what way?"

"I don't wish to discuss it."

Sawyer looked human, if bedeviled is the true countenance of humanity. It was clearly a painful memory. I tried to draw it from him in a roundabout way.

"When did this happen?"

"In June."

"Not long after he arrived?"

Sawyer took off his glasses, rubbed them, and nodded.

"He often liked to use the words of others," I said, "to make his point."

"He used the Bible," whispered Sawyer.

"To say what?"

Almost choking, he said, "To read from the Song of Solomon."

The faithful explain the Song of Solomon by saying it's an allegorical representation of God's love for his people. Others just see it as biblical erotica.

"Why did he do that?"

Sawyer's face went blank. "To mock me. To make a joke of the Bible. To confuse its holy message."

"But to what purpose?"

Sawyer couldn't, or didn't, answer.

"How many people witnessed this?"

Painfully: "I don't know. A hundred, two hundred."

"How long did he read?"

"I didn't stay to hear him finish. And I can't stay to talk to you. The deacons will be here shortly . . ."

"Five minutes," I said.

Sawyer looked up the path to his house, considered, then

motioned for me to enter the vestry. We sat at the nearest table, our backs to the mosaic. He made a point of looking at his watch. The stopwatch was running.

"Did you ever talk with him personally?" I asked.

"No."

"So you didn't know the man?"

"I knew him well enough."

"Well enough?"

"I knew him well enough to stay my distance. 'He that toucheth pitch shall be defiled therewith.' Ecclesiasticus."

"The Green Man was pitch?"

"I don't like that name. It gives him a title. It makes him special. That's what he wanted."

"Shepard was pitch?"

"He was worse than pitch. He blackened the hearts of many, set them on the path of evil."

"He planted trees."

"He murdered souls. Ask your same questions of those who have hired you. Make them speak honestly. They'll tell you of his practices."

"Why don't you tell me?"

"I wouldn't profane holy ground."

Before coming to America, my Scottish grandfather preached in the highlands. In his dotage, he preached to his grandchildren. We were the tougher audience, I think, but he persisted. Through repetition alone, some of his words sank into the hard ground of our heads. Whenever I wouldn't own up to mischief, my grandfather always confronted me with a quotation from Luke. It usually worked for him, so I gave it a try.

"For nothing is secret," I said, a little of grandfather's lilt in my voice, "that shall not be made manifest; neither any thing hid, that shall not be known and come abroad."

The Reverend Mr. Sawyer grew visibly perturbed. The faithful don't like their own ammunition used against them.

"He called himself a pantheist," he said, "but he was worse than that. He was an abomination.

"He led the children into temptations, set up ceremonies. Under his shameful guidance, they worshiped tree spirits, and invoked false gods."

I was skeptical, but I tried not to show it. "How come I haven't heard of this?" I asked.

"Because it was a secret society," he said. "And not something *they* like to talk about."

"Who is they?"

"EverGreen and their ilk. They have hidden his deeds, downplayed them."

"How is it that the media never caught on?"

"Because the ceremonies were done in darkness!" White flecks of froth appeared at the corners of his mouth. "Because they were hidden!"

"And how did you hear of all this?"

"I have my sources," he said, after which he firmed his jaw and sucked at his jowls, making it clear he wasn't about to give those sources up.

"Tell me about the ceremonies." I said.

He didn't say anything.

"Everyone has different standards," I said. "A dentist might find the roasting of marshmallows the worst sin of the woods, while . . ."

"This isn't about roasting marshmallows. It's about ritualism. It's about tree worship and sick rites."

"What kind of rites?"

"He called it a return to the old, a return to the sacred. He encouraged couples to dance around trees, couples proclaimed as the king and queen of the woods, and members of the royal court. He taught them their dance steps, the steps to hell. The couples held a stick between them, were admonished not to let go. Eventually they dropped to the ground, exhausted. And there, under their tree, they could only release that stick for the arms of each other."

It was the same voice I had heard on the tape, intense and fanatical. But I didn't need a fast-forward button. Sawyer was speaking quickly, frenziedly. "He conducted perversions called candlelight services. In them he called for the woodland sprites to appear, asked that they visit and show themselves. He offered prayers to these dryads, set out feasts of fruit and wine and ale, and encouraged all to sin.

"His blasphemies were many. He aped the ceremonies of

Druid priests, and, when the moon was full, he shed his clothes and walked around naked, and encouraged his followers to do the same. He singled out certain trees as Maypoles and perverted a child's game, encouraging ribaldry and carnal displays. He told everyone he was the spirit of Pan and acted out that fantasy, strutting about like a satyr in rut. That was your Green Man!"

Sawyer was convinced of what he said. But conviction is one thing, knowing what you're saying another. I didn't believe him, or didn't want to believe him.

"Things get exaggerated," I said. "Hide-and-go-seek suddenly becomes an evil pastime of the night. Ring-around-the-rosy is imbued with sensual aspects."

Sawyer shook his head. He almost looked sad. "I have not overstated his perversions."

Part of the Green Man's appeal was his innocence. His homilies about trees. His bare feet. Saturnalian revelries weren't in keeping with his gentle image. Or with what I expected, or wanted.

"Did you hear this from his enemies?" I asked.

"I heard it from his friends," hissed Sawyer.

I leaned back, caught myself looking at Judas again. With friends like that . . .

"How do you think he died?"

Sawyer exhaled, then breathed in deeply. He took a few seconds to gain control of himself again, then quietly responded: "A widow-maker."

It wasn't the answer I expected. It wasn't the answer she expected either. Ruth Sawyer threw the door open. Her face was contorted. "That's not how he died," she said, her voice hysterical. "God smote him!"

I wondered how long she had been listening. Her husband's voice tended to carry, and mine wasn't in the whisper league either.

"He was a sinner, and God took his right hand, and cast his judgment. The storm that night was his breath, the thunder his anger!"

The Reverend Sawyer went to his wife. They reversed the roles I had already come to expect of them. She was agitated and loud, and he was quiet and calm. "There, there," he said, touching her lightly on the shoulder. "Let's go back to the house."

Like a windup toy finally running down, Mrs. Sawyer stopped her railing and let herself be led away. They slowly made their way up the path, then entered the parsonage. There, she would be safe. What she called vanity others call peace and quiet. She obviously needed that.

$\triangledown$

10

The English historian Thomas Macaulay wrote, "The Puritan hated bear-baiting, not because it gave pain to the bear, but because it gave pleasure to the spectators." I suspected Reginald Sawyer of having that kind of mentality. He was suspicious of what gave pleasure to others, probably considered suffering the normal state of humanity. I didn't know what kind of nocturnal activities, if any, the Green Man had organized, only that the Reverend Mr. Sawyer would have considered laughter and levity sins enough, and anything else an outright affront to God. Still, his accusations merited investigation. At this juncture, everything did.

The Humboldt County Sheriff's Department had investigated the Green Man's death and had stood by the findings of their sheriff's coroner's office. Under California law, coroners are supposed to determine the manner, cause, and circumstance of death. But what the forensic scientists had concluded about Shepard's death was less than definitive. They stated that they could find nothing "substantive" which indicated foul play and that his death was "likely an act of God." That kind of hedging is usually reserved for politicians.

It wasn't a politician I wanted to talk to, but a sheriff's deputy named Rod Evans. My original plan had been to go to the Fortuna sheriff's station and introduce myself to Evans, but, while driving through town, I reconsidered that strategy.

Evans had found the Green Man's body. Shepard hadn't been seen for almost a week, but that hadn't been cause for any alarm. Those involved with Sequoia Summer were used to his irregular appearances. Since he had no phone, and had settled almost forty miles from the Sweetwater camp, he wasn't an everyday visitor. The Green Man lived in his goose-pen in the virgin woods of River Grove. He had settled there, the story went, to watch for any signs of Trans-Mississippi encroachment.

I had gleaned Evans's name from the early news reports. River Grove was about five miles east of Fortuna, accessible only by a logging road. Evans's discovery had given him his moment of fame. He hadn't appeared in the newspapers since having surrendered the investigation to others. Cops aren't different from anyone else. Patrol officers can't help but resent being brushed aside by a homicide team. You wouldn't think people would get proprietary over a body, but it happens all the time.

Not that many corpses turn up in Humboldt County, especially celebrity corpses. I knew better than to try to get anyone from the homicide investigation to talk with me. Cops tend to get downright hostile when PI's start asking them questions about their cases. Officially, Rod Evans hadn't worked on the case. But I knew he would have had more than a passing interest in the investigation. I was betting that he might be pleased someone remembered his name beyond that first day of glory. Or, if not pleased, at least willing to talk.

I pulled over to a gas station, found a phone booth and an intact telephone book. I invested a quarter, dialed the sheriff's number, and asked for Deputy Rod Evans. The connection went through. History in the making. Not only was there a cop around when I needed one, but it was the very cop I wanted.

"Evans."

I identified myself, my location, and my purpose for wanting to talk to him. I did that in less than half a minute. It took him a few seconds to digest everything I had said. Then he asked me why I hadn't presented myself at the station.

"Figured I'd make it easier on you," I said. "I have about ten minutes' worth of questions. I know how things work, though. Those ten minutes could cost you ten hours of grief. Thought I'd save you the hassle."

It's hard to hang up on someone, or tell them to go to hell, when they've just shown themselves to be considerate. I pushed on with that accommodating theme.

"Everything will be off the record," I said. "It's just that you're the one who found the body. That makes you the one person I would really like to talk with."

Where did I learn to ooze and schmooze like that? I wondered. Sometimes investigating is about as straightforward as selling used cars.

"Okay," he said. Then, in a lower voice: "You know where the airport is?"

I didn't even know Fortuna had an airport. "Yes," I said.

"I'll meet you there in about half an hour."

The Rohnerville Airport was on the south end of town. There wasn't much going on there. A number of idle planes belonging to the California Department of Forestry sat on the edge of the runway. It was that time of year, after another long, hot summer, and California in its umpteenth year of drought. The combustible forest, and human sparks aplenty.

A black-and-white came into view, cruised by me, and gradually looped back. I didn't flag him down, just nodded. The deputy didn't respond. It reminded me of how sharks usually approach divers. They like to glide by, seemingly uninterested on their first run, then, with each pass, they move closer and closer. The black-and-white passed me a second time. And I nodded once more. Cops don't believe in turning their heads when looking at something. I'm not sure whether it's taught at the academy, but they rival lizards in their mastery of peripheral gazing. And they do it with dark sunglasses, no less.

I was humming the theme song to *Jaws* on the third pass. This time Evans stopped and slowly rolled down his window. "Winter?"

Discontinuing my humming, I nodded for the third time, then approached the car. Evans left the engine running. I produced my ID before he asked. He took his time looking at my credentials. Didn't even take off his aviator's sunglasses. Something else police learn.

79

Evans was about thirty. He looked like a high school football star a dozen years later. Some of his brawn was going south. He had slicked back, dark hair and a jaw like Fearless Fosdick's. His hands were huge, not the kind you'd want to get on the bad side of. He wore the largest wedding ring I had ever seen. On a smaller hand it might have served for brass knuckles.

I got back my ID and a declaration of independence as well. "Don't usually go in for this James Bond stuff," he said.

"Like I said . . ."

I know what you said. Who are you working for?"

"Sequoia Summer."

"And they hired you to investigate the death of Christopher Shepard?"

"That's right."

"Lot of people already done that."

"I know."

"And you think you can do better?'

"I'm being paid to try."

Evans didn't say anything. But he finally did turn off his engine. I took that as my turn to ask the questions.

"How was it that you discovered his body?" I asked.

"Just patrolling," he said. "Can't say I was looking for him, even though everyone knew he was camped up there in River Grove. Trans-Miss owns the road; hell, they own the whole area, unless the courts decide different. They were the ones who come to us an asked us to patrol regular and arrest anyone driving on that stretch."

"Why didn't they just ask you to arrest the Green Man?"

"Probably didn't want the publicity. Probably figured he would get tired of his Boy Scout trip."

"If the road was closed, how'd he get back and forth to Sweetwater?"

"Road wasn't closed. People were just subject to arrest. But I understand he usually walked into Fortuna and got a ride from there."

I found that hard to believe. "Just to get to town he had to walk, what, five miles?"

" 'Bout that. They said he was one for walking."

"And you found his body where?"

"Just off the logging road. In plain sight."

"Which was about a half mile from his goosepen?"

"About."

It wasn't adding up for me. "Why was he walking around so far away from his tree so late, especially on a stormy night?"

Evans didn't immediately respond. He looked at his large fingers, picked a little at his thumb, then teased me along. "There's more to it than that, even," he said.

"Such as?"

Evans thumped his ring on the steering wheel several times. "We've been holding back on the press with this poker hand, so this better not come back to me."

"It won't."

He deliberated a moment. "The man was buck naked when he died."

I didn't say anything. But the Reverend Mr. Sawyer's words came back to me, how Shepard had walked about naked in the woods, strutting like a satyr in rut.

"Course we learned that wasn't too unusual," he said.

"What do you mean?"

"Supposedly your Green Man didn't much like to wear clothes in the woods. Didn't much like to wear clothes at all."

"What else didn't you tell the press?"

"The condition of his body. Lots of critters in the woods. They had themselves a feast, and in so doing they impacted the forensics."

"In what way?"

"Made the body, and the widow-maker, hard to read. They chewed the hell out of that branch. Guess they were attracted to the blood."

These days we're used to having science provide all the answers with the evidence of fibers or dirt samples. Revenge of the mice.

"No other bruises on his body? No sign of any other trauma?"

There was the slightest hesitation. "No."

"Nothing?"

Again the pause. "Nothing official. But the way he was laid out in the woods made it look like he was some kind of sacrifice. They tell me his insides were pulled out by birds and things, but I just don't know."

"Are you saying his death looked ceremonial?"

"I'm saying it looked weird."

"Did forensics pick up on that?"

"No. They said he died from the impact and penetration of the branch into his skull."

"Could someone plunging a branch into his head have caused that penetration?"

"The lab boys don't think so."

"What do they think?"

"That time and gravity caused a branch to drop off natural, and come to rest after falling a coupla' hundred feet in the Green Man's skull."

"And what do you think?"

"I think I don't want to answer that question."

Sometimes I know when to shut up and let the silence ask its own questions. Eventually, Evans did want to answer.

"It was spooky when I found him," he said. "There he was, sort of propped up. Looked like a scarecrow. Scared the hell out of me, I can tell you that. Like I said, he looked like he was a warning, or a sacrifice. His eyes had been pecked out. His flesh was bloated and stripped. He smelled. Ain't no dignity in death."

"What about the widow-maker itself? No hairs or particles of skin?"

"It was out there almost a week in the open," said Evans. "There was that rainstorm, and enough birds and animals visiting to make the area read like a goddamn zoo. Add to that a widow-maker split and chewed up, and old man redwood being a tough read in the first place, and you have a very unhappy forensics crew."

"Did you stay around for the walk-through?"

He nodded.

"Did they do it by the book?"

Evans didn't spare me his scowl. "We got police procedures out here too, Winter. The photographer did his thing, then the physical evidence man went over everything. Lots of tracks, all animal. Most of the area had been washed out from the storm. Rained all night, you know. There were rivulets and gullies. Didn't please the hell out of anyone."

A plane circled the field, approached for the landing. Both of us watched it.

"Any foul-play theories?" I asked.

"Lots of them. They all had their hour. Malaysian hawk was maybe good for an hour and a half."

"Malaysian hawk?"

"Some of them pot growers have gotten real good at protecting their crops. With all his traipsing about, someone figured Shepard might have walked into the wrong field, found a Malaysian hawk, and then got his body brought back to River Grove."

"I take it a Malaysian hawk is a booby trap," I said.

"You got it," he said. "Trip stick and swinging branch. Swoops down from above. Swing low, sweet chariot time."

"But you say that theory didn't pan out?"

"No," he said. "No rope fiber on the widow-maker. And everyone figured the branch was too light anyway. To make a Malaysian hawk that means business, you got to use at least a thousand-pound log. That widow-maker only weighed a couple of pounds."

"Have you seen any of those Malaysian hawks firsthand?"

"Just one. Mean-looking bastard. Around here if you stumble on a pot field, you back out careful and then get the proper reinforcements. We got what we call our mine field experts. They know how to look for the pit traps, and spike traps, and snares. Not to mention the all-time favorite: the wire-triggered shotguns."

In the tradition of this country, I thought. But now it wasn't hillbillies guarding their moonshine from revenuers. It was pot farmers standing like Ma and Pa Kettle with their Uzis.

"Since murder was never ruled out," I asked, "were any suspects interrogated?"

The deputy shook his head. "Not that some EverGreen committee didn't supply us with a list of their murder candidates," he said. "But their number-one suspect was Bull Dozier, the CEO of Trans-Miss. There were plenty of people who disliked your Green Man. But there wasn't anything to show that anyone disliked him enough to kill him."

I pulled out the wanted poster. "What about this?"

Evans didn't look very interested. "That was a joke. Some mill hands made those up. Buster bluster time."

I put away the poster. "Did Shepard have a girlfriend?"

"Not that I heard."

"Did you hear any talk of cults? Secret societies?"

Evans shook his head, gave me a look of interest. "That a possibility?"

I shrugged. "It's just a story for now."

The sound from the plane grew louder. It was committed to land. We watched it touch down on the runway, bounce once, then settle on a straight path.

"What's the back-room talk?" I asked.

"Almost to a man the investigators think he died of natural causes, if you can call a widow-maker a natural cause. If he had been murdered, why didn't someone just hide his body? We're talking about thousands of acres of woods up there, nothing human for miles around. Wouldn't take a genius to find a burial spot that would never be found. And I do mean never."

"Still doesn't make sense," I said.

"What doesn't?"

"Where he died."

Evans gave a little laugh. "Most people were more concerned with how he died."

"Near a road late at night," I said, "about half a mile from where he was living."

"Near a logging road. Not the same thing. You'd have to see the area."

"I'd like to," I said. "Would you consider taking me there?"

Evans didn't say anything. He finally took off his aviator's dark glasses, rubbed them absently, then looked at me. He had brown, bearlike eyes. Like an ursine's, they were small for his large head, soulful but at the same time distrusting. Within them was the promise that they could be dangerous. Very dangerous.

"Come to think of it," he said, "that ol' Green Man probably wasn't out there waiting for a bus, was he?"

▽

11

I HAD A FEW hours to call my own before Evans could play tour guide. He drew a map of where I was to meet him, a spot just off Highway 36, and while he was drawing I asked for him to add to his map and show me where I could find Methuselah. Evans didn't have to think on it, using his big right hand to add on a few lines and landmarks. As he drew, he volunteered that he had made almost daily visits to the tree throughout June and July.

"Media circus back then," he explained. "Guess they kept hoping that Trans-Miss would move in and cut the thing down with a sitter in it. That's what your campers wanted, too. They egged T-M on. But them lumber companies aren't stupid. Trans-Miss just waited out the media, and now they're going to wait out the sitters. It's that time of year when everybody's beginning to air out their down comforters. Cold and rain are coming soon. It's going to give a lot of people pleasure to know that, as the weather turns nastier and nastier, there'll still be some fools sitting up a tree."

Evans chuckled and shook his head. His small eyes scanned the horizon hopefully. There were clouds, but none had a hint of rain in it. With a sigh, he put his dark glasses back on. "See you in a few," he said, then drove off.

Methuselah was a rarity: an old-growth redwood easily accessible by road in a nonpark setting. One of the mysteries of Methuselah's longevity was that the tree stood in the midst of second growth. Why it hadn't been felled sixty years back with the rest of its redwood neighbors no one could be sure. Trans-Miss considered Methuselah an oversight that needed to be rectified.

Three signs told me I had come to the right place. I ignored the two that read NO ENTRY and PRIVATE LOGGING ROAD. The third simply read METHUSELAH and directed me forward with an arrow.

Evans had told me I'd have to drive along for a mile or so, then leave my eyes open for a path that had been tramped to Methuselah's grove. I had driven that mile, was inching along and looking at both sides of the road when I saw a familiar motorcycle. I parked Rocinante and walked over to the bike. Its engine was only slightly warm.

I wondered what had brought Doc to these woods, pondering that question as I looked around. Conservationists sometimes deridingly refer to lumber company acreage as "Christmas Tree plantations," but even though there was only the much maligned second and third growth around me, the area didn't strike me as sterile. A variety of birds flittered by, and a Douglas squirrel took me to task for trespassing. The grove was lighter and less dense than the one I had walked through that morning, the light not having to fight through a storied canopy of giants. Most of the trees were less than sixty feet high. Tall enough for you to tilt your head but not the kind of heights that keep the north woods chiropractors busy realigning strained vertebræ.

I heard a sound not in keeping with the woods—not even a second-growth forest—and tried to locate its source. It wasn't a sound with which I was familiar, and more's the pity. Most of my friends don't climb trees any more.

Doc was descending from a redwood. He wasn't exactly rappeling down, but his arms and legs were working in tandem in what resembled a hopping motion. I walked over to his tree and met him as he landed. He was winded but looked proud.

"Aerobics of the woods," he said, panting.

"People usually take a stroll in the woods," I said, "not a climb."

86

"I'm in training," Doc said. "If I'm lucky, I might get some grant money for a canopy study I've proposed."

"A what?"

"Canopy study."

He took a few more breaths, then explained further. "Most canopy studies have been done in South America. Scientists set themselves up in observational posts aboveground. They look down from the treetops instead of up at them."

"Why the nosebleed seats?"

"Gives them a totally different perspective. It's hard to believe, but there are diverse biotic communities that change over the course of just a single tree. New species of insects have been discovered on the upper levels of trees, insects which live out their entire lives there."

"And you think the potential for those kinds of discoveries exists in these woods?"

"I don't know. There are enough redwood decks around for many to simply assume the trees are among the most studied anywhere. I'm sure there will also be those who claim redwoods wouldn't be conducive to a canopy study."

"Why is that?"

"Their trunks rise up forever, and they don't have the same kind of understory, and canopy, and emergent layers as do other trees that have been studied.

"But," he said, patting a tree trunk, "there are still secrets in these woods."

"Yes," I said, "there are."

Doc ignored my dark agreement. "Just a few years ago someone discovered the first marbled murrelet nest in the old woods. Who would have figured that?"

I nodded. No one had expected seabirds to be making their nests inland among the high limbs of evergreen trees.

"I'm just getting my climbing legs," said Doc. "Fifty feet's about my limit. But I think it's going to get real interesting when I get a couple of hundred feet up. Already birds are flying beneath me, not even noticing me. It's a kick."

"You'll get that view you wanted from the giant's shoulder."

It was his turn to nod, then he turned away to fiddle with his equipment, loosening latches from his waist and shoulders. The climbing gear didn't look state of the art. It was old, the leather worn and cracked.

"Sure that's safe?"

"Hasn't killed anyone yet," said Doc.

He looked like he was about to say more, but then he stopped talking and went back to removing the belt.

"Where'd you get it?"

"Borrowed it."

"From whom?"

His answer came reluctantly: "Teller." An explanation followed. "He's worked about a million jobs. Half a century ago he was a lumberjack. They still called them that back then. You get him talking, and he can tell you about the days before mechanical tree harvesters, when they had fallers, and buckers, and swampers, and teamsters, when toppers were sent up to climb trees."

There was the slightest tone of Luddite nostalgia in Doc's voice. It was also clear that he greatly admired Teller. He awoke from his musing.

"You came for the lecture this morning," he said. "I doubt whether you planned on one this afternoon as well."

"I actually came looking for Teller," I said. "Figured he could answer the little riddle he left in my head last night."

"What riddle?"

"Just before he fell asleep, Teller was talking about the Green Man, and he said that Shepard couldn't see the forest for the trees. Then he said he couldn't even see the redwoods for the giant Leucæna. I was curious as to what he meant."

"I can help you with that," said Doc. "The giant Leucæna is a species of tree. It's being touted as the wonder tree of this century."

Whenever the word *wonder* precedes something, there's invariably the downside explanation afterward, be it cost, or side effects, or warning. "What's its drawback?"

"The drawback of any introduced plant or tree: they usually don't belong. Teller's big on Aldo Leopold. Every other circle he gives Leopold's catechism: 'A thing is right when it tends to preserve the integrity, stability, and beauty of the biotic community. It is wrong when it tends otherwise.' "

"Did Teller ever repeat that to the Green Man?"

"He would have had to."

"But Shepard still couldn't see the redwoods for the giant Leucæna?"

"After planting Leucæna around the globe? Hardly. He talked up its virtues right here in redwood country."

"In what way?"

"He thought the lumber companies should plant giant Leucæna instead of redwoods. Said they should learn about the miracle tree. That didn't sit well with Teller. To him, the miracle of the redwoods was more than miracle enough."

"Did they argue?"

"Not that I heard. But Teller was upset that the Green Man couldn't understand the importance of indigenous trees and plants. Shepard's done other tree planting in California, and apparently he's been pretty indiscriminate, not attending to the bioregions or prevailing ecosystems. He's used Norway pines, and eucalyptus, and Afghan pines. To the purists like Teller, that's bad. They think those trees are well and fine in Norway, or Australia, or Afghanistan, but not in California, not in areas where birds, and plants, and animals have built relationships with native trees and need them for their survival."

"Is Teller right?"

"More right than wrong. But California is such a mishmash of imports, be it plant, tree, or animal, that I don't think it really matters. Even before man got blamed for every environmental ill, nature was doing a pretty good job of dispersing species."

"You don't sound very concerned."

"I'm a scientist."

"You said the same thing this morning. You make it sound like that absolves you from being human."

Doc smiled. "I didn't mean it that way. What I should have said is that I try and be objective. In these woods, I think that makes me the rarest species of them all."

"Better watch out for the cross fire," I said, then looked around, but not for rifles. "Which way to Methuselah?"

Doc pointed east.

"Far?"

"Just down the slope, then a hundred yards or so."

"Where did Teller park?"

"He didn't. The Green Queen dropped him off. She had some large items she needed to pick up for her mother, so Teller loaned her the Jeep. He'll be piggybacking back to camp on my bike."

"Her mother lives around here?"

Doc shrugged. "Guess so."

He didn't meet my glance, instead looked at a nearby tree and tugged at his climbing rig. "Want to take a go at a tree?" he asked. "Get above the armpits of humanity? Get a real view?"

"You go ahead," I said, not a little wistfully. "I have my own six-foot-under viewing to keep me occupied."

I walked where Doc had pointed and found the path. Methuselah stood out from the other redwoods even at a distance. They looked skinny, adolescent. Methuselah was much broader and taller, a powerful man among little boys. The platform had been built about thirty feet up. Teller was sitting there, motionless.

"Ahoy, the tree."

Owl-like, Teller moved his white head, took note of my appearance, but didn't bother to wave. As I approached the tree, I sniffed the air. No smell of cannabis. When I got to its base, I cupped my hands over my mouth. "How do I get up?"

His voice drifted down to me. "What reason is there for your ascending?"

"None. Except that you'll probably get damn tired of me shouting questions."

Teller sighed louder than he had spoken, then he lowered the drawbridge, a chain ladder that came within inches of braining me. I started climbing up, trepidatious at first, then remembering childhood fun. Tree forts had been serious business back in my youth. We had kept a cache of acorns in our big coast live oak and defended our fort from all challengers. I made it to the top but didn't see any acorns, just a few air horns.

"In case the enemy breaches the defenses?" I asked.

Teller was drawing in the ladder but looked over to where I was pointing. "That was the original idea," he said.

"But now?"

"We have a sympathizer who lives within hearing range. Sometimes campers forget their shifts. If we signal, he'll come and see what's going on, maybe even assume the post if it's an emergency."

There was a weariness to Teller's words. I was reminded of disc jockeys who had gone up to sit in towers, vowing not to come down until their sporting team had won, then been forced to remain on their perch for half a season. Sometimes an idea that seems wonderful when conceived becomes more and more of a millstone over time.

"You think the sentries are keeping Methuselah standing?" I asked.

Teller shook his head, his beard waving more than his chin. "It's the lawsuit we filed," he said.

"So why keep doing this?"

"Because we said we would."

"When does it stop?"

"When the battle is won."

"Or until election day?"

Teller allowed himself a little smile. "Unofficially, there has been talk of that. The media still show up now and again, and they always find a sentry. We'll certainly have to keep up our presence until November."

"Don't you find it boring?"

"No. I was a fire watcher once. Lived high up in the world. I could see fifty, a hundred miles, in all directions. I miss those days. I don't believe I ever thought so deeply."

"Is that why you volunteer to sit here so frequently? So that you can think?"

He nodded. Then he smiled, albeit a little ruefully. "And I can't deny that I like to get away. The young invigorate me. Their enthusiasm is infectious. But I need a rest from their questions, from being the patriarch."

"Do they ask you about your other fights? Your other causes?"

Teller shook his head. "People section redwoods, and look at the stories there, but we're not adept at reading the wrinkles in humans. I tell them stories in Circle, mine and others, but I don't know what makes an impression, or what they remember."

91

"You've been in Humboldt County for more than two years now."

"I want to die here," he said.

I gave him a look, and he held up his hands. "Not soon," he said. "I'm just beginning to know what it's like to settle roots."

"Have you made friends?"

"A few."

"Doc must be one of them?"

"Yes. He needed a mentor. Or maybe he needed a father."

"I left him climbing a tree."

Teller beamed. "He's getting better at that. He needed some direction. I told him he should get used to the climbing."

His words suggested he was talking about more than trees. "Think his canopy study will get him anywhere?"

"Off the ground at least." Teller snorted. "That's an important step for Doc. He's still learning about the real world."

"Aren't we all?"

"Doc's had it different than most. His father died when he was young. He didn't have any brothers or sisters, just a well-off mother who thought the sun rose and set around him. Doc was indulged. He never thought about money, just kept going to school. That was their deal, I think: as long as he told her he was studying something or other, she was content. He never worked. Then, a few years ago, his mother died. Doc was left with a good sum of money, but not as much as he must have expected. His broker set him up in some investments that went south, and suddenly Doc was just another graduate student struggling along. Difference is, Doc never expected that. Now he's still coming to terms with the fact that he's going to have to work for a living and not be a gentleman scientist."

"He told me you'd held down quite a few jobs."

Teller nodded. "I used to get on a bus," he said, "sometimes with no more than five dollars in my pocket, and I'd go off to a town I didn't know anything about. It never took me more than a day to find a job, and I didn't get on that bus again until I had a hundred dollars in my pocket."

"Then another town?"

"That, or another cause."

"Tempted to hop a bus these days?"

"Not really. I've finally found a place I call home."

"What do you do when you're not hugging trees?"

"You're asking for a lot of secrets," he said, but he wasn't looking at me. He was looking inside and smiling. "I read an awful lot," he said, "and I square dance. Every Thursday. My Circle talk is always abbreviated that night, and no one knows why. I guess everyone thinks I have a date. To most in the movement, that's acceptable."

"But do-si-doing in the woods wouldn't be?"

"Questionable, maybe."

"What about other ceremonies in the woods?"

"What do you mean?"

"I heard the Green Man was trying to bring back the old ways, trying to resurrect more than his name. Any truth to that?"

"He was exuberant," said Teller.

"Interesting description," I said. "Something like calling a clear-cut 'forest enhancement.' "

That was hitting below the timber line. Teller flinched. He wasn't good at obfuscating. For too long he had railed for truth.

"I don't know if even he knew what he was doing," he said. "For a great man, he was incredibly naive."

"Was he a great man?"

Teller nodded, long and seriously. "Oh, yes. I think to be a great man you have to have one vision, a singleness of purpose. Most of us are diverted by other interests. The fever in us bursts. It never did with him."

"Along with his fever," I said, "he spread his passions."

Teller didn't say anything. He made me tell him what I knew. I did. Teller didn't say anything back for a while, just contemplated what I had told him.

"I'd heard talk," he finally admitted. "But I preferred to think it was just that."

"You never participated in the ceremonies?"

"No."

"Let's assume it's true," I said. "Why was Shepard playing the bongos to a bunch of young, racing hormones?"

"To help further his dream," said Teller. "I guess he

thought that by indoctrinating followers into the secrets of the woods, he would gather disciples. The Green Belt drove him to such deeds, the thought of billions and billions of trees surrounding the globe. I don't know if any pharaoh or king ever dreamed so grandly."

"Forest rituals seem rather extreme."

"So was his goal."

"You sound supportive."

"Of the concept, not his practices. We've cut down billions of trees, and look at the results: global warming, loss of humus and topsoil, wind and rain erosion, increasing severity of drought and floods, and spreading deserts."

"Pagan practices don't exactly answer those problems."

"There are truths in what you call pagan practices. When the missionaries sought to cut the sacred groves in Lithuania, many prevailed upon their prince to protect the trees, saying that it was wrong to destroy the house of the god from which they received rain and sunshine.

"Instinctively people know it's wrong to cut down their woods. When a forest is cleared, the humus is destroyed, and the earth is laid open to the elements. Without tree cover, temperatures rise. Without shade, moisture is not retained. We start a vicious cycle, and we don't know where it stops."

"But I understand that you believe irresponsible tree planting is far worse than no tree planting at all."

"True. Which isn't to say I didn't believe in reforesting. I do—when it's done wisely. History tells us we must. When the trees were cut down in the Midwest, there were no roots to hold the soil, and there was the Dust Bowl. In the north of England, there used to be great forest, and, when those were chopped away, the moors appeared. When the oaks in southwestern France were cleared for farmland, droughts followed. Once there were cedars in Lebanon. Not long ago there were even cedars in what is now the Sahara Desert. Man cut and hacked and plowed, and the global landscapes changed for the worse."

"Did you support Shepard's Green Belt?"

"No, I can't say I did. It's possible to grow a redwood in the desert, but is it desirable? Is it right? There were many areas along his proposed Green Belt where trees don't grow naturally. I thought it presumptuous of him to think he knew better than nature. It reminded me of some of the literature I've read from Weyerhæuser, or Boise Cascade, or Trans-Mississippi, where they'd almost have you believe that nature's damn lucky to have them around. The Green Man seemed to be aping forest company casuistry."

"I heard a rumor that Shepard was getting cozy with Trans-Miss. Any substance to that?"

"Sounds like jealousy to me. In this movement there's a game I don't like. I call it greener than so-and-so."

"So some people liked to think they were greener than the Green Man?"

"Something like that."

"I understand Ashe O'Connor borrowed your Jeep."

Teller nodded.

"Needed a big vehicle, did she?"

The short nod again.

"What was that she was bringing to her mother?"

"I don't know."

"She didn't tell me she had family nearby."

Teller didn't comment.

"Where's her mother live?"

Tersely: "Lofield."

"With her father?"

"Stepfather."

"What's her name?"

"I don't remember."

And he didn't make any attempt to try, I noticed.

▽

12

THIS TIME TELLER didn't fall asleep, but he might as well have. He stopped answering, seemingly mesmerized by the view. The vista was nice enough, but, since we were only thirty feet up, I hardly thought we had the world at our feet. I sat with Teller for a few more minutes, then threw the stairs overboard and let myself down. As I walked away, I could hear the metal stairway being retracted.

Doc wasn't in sight when I got back to the road, either on the ground or in the trees. His motorcycle was still there, but I didn't wait around for him to reappear. I still had a little more than an hour before my rendezvous with Evans, and with that time I decided to see how the mighty are fallen.

Not far away was Scotia, and the world's largest redwood mill. Scotia was a town owned lock, stock and redwood barrel by the Pacific Lumber Company; she'd been a kept lady for over a hundred years. Once, company lumber towns were the way of life throughout the Pacific Northwest. Now there are only a few survivors. It even surprised me that there were that many. I had thought company towns had gone the way of polio and segregated water fountains. They conjure up images of West Virginia coal towns—one-store monopolies, with institutionalized repression and squalor. Mention company town and you can almost hear a bluesy voice singing: "Saint Peter, don't yah call me 'cause I can't go; I owe my soul to the company store." But Scotia wasn't like that, at least not its exterior.

The three hundred identical houses were painted a nice Tom Sawyer white. The lawns were well trimmed, and the yards immaculate. There wasn't much room for individuality, but the price was right. Maybe the residents in those immaculate houses felt a little besieged. There were a number of signs advertising NO ON 150. Also popular were placards reading THIS FAMILY SUPPORTED BY TIMBER DOLLARS and LOGGERS ARE AN ENDANGERED SPECIES.

There were also signs to the mill, but those were unnecessary. Any one of my five senses could have led me there. Smokestacks billowed, and machinery hollered. From far away, I felt the vibrations, and smelled the pulp burning, and tasted the sulfur in the back of my mouth. I had seen the mill from 101. It was immense, but anything that swallows titans would have to be.

The self-tours were complimentary. I would have been more at ease had there been a charge. Caveat emptor, especially when the price is free. I pulled up to the gate, and another sign. This one proclaimed, TO US, EVERY DAY IS EARTH DAY. I could already feel the price of admission. I was welcomed by an affable young blond woman. She handed me some informational literature, including a three-by-six-and-a-half-inch redwood directional guide. It was a nice touch, the kind of souvenir visitors would keep, but I hoped it wasn't old growth.

The huge mill seemed out of place, General Motors in the forest. The buildings were painted yellow, perhaps a shade removed from canary. You don't see many yellow buildings. You don't even see many yellow houses. They're usually about as appealing as yellow snow.

Directions were posted on yellow signs, and the guiding arrows were yellow. I was beginning to see a pattern. I followed that pattern and ended up climbing some stairs and looking out to a thirty-acre millpond. No beavers, only redwoods upon redwoods. A small placard told me that I was looking at 12 million board feet of logs. Hydraulic hoists and conveyors processed the logs along. Beyond the pond was a cogeneration plant. Another placard told me how the wood waste was turned into energy, 25 million watts a day, enough to keep the plant wheels turning and then some.

Anyone who likes quiet repose shouldn't visit an industrial redwood mill. From the observation deck, I was shaken at regular intervals. Teeth vibrating, I walked over to the barking compound. Metal jaws positioned huge redwoods. Imagine the impact of sumo wrestlers, and multiply that by a few thousand. Compared with a redwood mill, an auto-wrecking yard is a pastoral enterprise, almost genteel.

Redwoods are known for their thick ax-eating bark. Pacific Lumber solved that problem by fighting with water. A high-pressure nozzle propelled jets of water at the bark, striking it with a force of sixteen hundred pounds per square inch. In the course of a minute, twelve hundred gallons of water pounded the bark, flaying it clean. I watched the skinning of a tree behind a safety window. Every bad horror film shows blood splattering up against glass. The pulverized bark splashed my window in just such a way.

I walked along a catwalk above the goings-on of the mill. If I didn't exactly walk the plank, I walked above where the planks were being made. There was a fine mist in the air, not precipitation but sawdust. Sirens periodically went off, making me feel as if an air raid was going on. Below me, conveyor chains moved the wood along, while overhead the lumber was transported via monorail. There were edgers and trimmers, men in glass booths directing the flow and cutting of wooden traffic. Saws of all sizes and proportions buzzed and chewed and cut. Eighty-five million board feet were turned out by the mill in an average year. I watched as a battery of men sorted boards from the conveyor table. They were reminded by sign that they had worked twenty-three days without a lost-time accident.

Drying redwood boards covered some seventy-eight acres of the mill. In some places they were piled up to thirty feet high. The sight was impressive in its own right, but somehow all the pieces just didn't add up to a single standing redwood. Like a fallen Humpty-Dumpty, they couldn't be put back together again.

I came away from the mill with a respect for man's ingenuity. I left impressed by the sheer power of the place. But I didn't leave exultant, and I wasn't walking quickly. I felt a little punch-drunk, a little pummeled. My senses had been over-whelmed by all the pounding, and sounds, and movement.

But that wasn't it exactly. Inside, I felt old.

Old as the denuded hills.

Evans showed up at our rendezvous spot right on time. He asked me how Methuselah was, and I told him he was still standing. Then I mumbled something to him about how I had also "visited a slaughterhouse." Evans asked a question or two, then pretended to take umbrage.

"Slaughterhouses like that support me," he said. "About a quarter of the county's revenues are generated from timber taxes."

"And does that make the lumber companies sacred cows?" I asked.

"You're mixing your metaphors, Winter," he told me. "Slaughterhouses in one sentence, sacred cows in the next."

"Bullshit whichever way you look at it," I said. Evans looked vaguely amused.

As the crow flies, River Grove isn't far from Fortuna, but, as the car drives, it's a different story. When we got off the main road, we severely tested the car's, and our own, shock absorbers. Our conversation was limited. To talk was to bite your tongue. Evans did manage to say, though, that this was "real forest," but that no one really gave a damn, " 'specially them EverGroaners."

"Most people'll stop and snap a few pictures around the Avenue of the Giants," he said, "but that's about it. Tree huggers want to save every grove older than their grandma, but you think any of them ever bother to go out and explore those woods? No way."

With my head rapping against the top of the car, I didn't feel like giving a long answer. Instead I mimed, pointing to the surrounding forest. "Important out there," I said, then pointed to my head. "And important in here. Psychic revenue."

"Actual revenue's not such a bad thing either," he said.

"So I've been told."

The woods were thick. Real forest, as Evans had said. Most so-called nature lovers idealize the abstract. But wilderness on its own terms is intimidating. It's not there to nurture you. Most people get uneasy when they find themselves removed from the human infrastructure. For all his cynicism, perhaps Evans was more honest about the woods than I. For the sake of purity, I wanted undeveloped areas, places where RV's and concession stands couldn't intrude. Woods for their own sake. The vision was nice, the reality less than accommodating.

We weren't in the boonies. We were in the forest primeval, ancient, untouched, and old. Farther and farther, we traveled into the darkness. I looked at my watch and had to push the light option to see. It was a little after four.

"Getting near," said Evans, pointing to three redwoods growing right next to one another. "That's my landmark."

And a good example of the immortal redwood theory, I thought. The three trees were growing from the same root structure, were in some ways the same tree. In time, I supposed, one of the great shoots would be victorious, would claim the sky and crowd the others out. But how long would that take? Five hundred years? Longer? Humans play the ponies. Only the gods can bet on redwoods.

Evans pulled over into a clearing. The glade was small. It hadn't been deforested by man; it was one of those openings in the woods that naturally occur. We got out of the car, and I followed Evans. He took a few steps, planted himself, and gave me a sideways look. A retriever couldn't have pointed any better.

There wasn't anything to mark where the Green Man had died, not even a widow-maker. I looked at the towering redwood under which he had fallen, suddenly paranoid. Lightning's not supposed to strike the same place twice. But I wondered about widow-makers. I hunched my shoulders, looked around, cast some furtive looks up at the encircling giants.

Evans noticed. "Spooks you, doesn't it?"

"A bit," I admitted. "Why don't we walk? I'd feel more comfortable as a moving target."

"Where to?"

"How about Shepard's goosepen?"

Evans led the way. I've been in situations where cross hairs have sought me out. In some ways, the walk felt akin to that.

Gradually the feeling passed. There were a few widow-makers to be seen, but the path wasn't littered with them. The quietness in the woods was profound. Our footsteps made no sound.

Evans started talking, I think, to break the silence. "Cut enough trees down," he said, "and it figures that one's going to cut down a human. Wish he'd found another way to die, though. Set all sorts of tongues to talking."

"The redwoods could have picked a better target," I admitted.

"Some people would argue with you," he said.

"Politics notwithstanding," I said, "there's still not much justice in a tree planter getting killed by a tree. A couple of years ago, a man went with his shotgun out into the Arizona desert. He decided to use a saguaro cactus as target practice. I don't know if you've ever seen a saguaro. They're usually used in the artistic desert photos, the sun rising through their upraised arms. This man wasn't content with just shooting the saguaro, he wanted to gut it. He shot off a number of rounds. Then he got the biggest and last surprise of his life when the saguaro fell on him, and killed him."

Evans waited to see if I had anything else to add. I didn't.

"And that's justice?" he asked.

"Some feel the punishment fit the crime."

"Then maybe you should close down your investigation."

"Why's that?"

"Maybe the redwoods dealt their own justice just like that cactus."

"Killing a man who was trying to protect them?"

"That's one version of the story," said Evans.

"What are you saying?"

"Nothing. But some say your Green Man wasn't exactly the savior of the redwoods."

"What do you mean by that?"

"The way I heard it, he liked making an impact, liked planting in barren areas, and leaving a legacy of his green statues and monuments. The redwoods aren't like that. They've been here millions of years."

"But Shepard did organize some planting campaigns here," I said. "I saw the pictures of him putting redwood seedlings in the ground."

"He gave that up when he learned how well the timber industry does with their own plantings."

"That still doesn't explain how a redwood's killing him could be considered poetic justice."

"Not just any redwood," said Evans, "an old-growth redwood. There are some who say he was actually setting that cause back. Trees were trees to him. He loved them all, but I don't think it mattered to him if a tree was ten years old or a thousand years. He couldn't understand what all the old-growth fuss was about."

"Is that another rumor, or do you have verification?"

"I've heard it from a couple of people," he said.

So had I, even if I didn't want to admit it to Evans. We kept walking. I tried to orient myself. The road was already well out of sight. I was confused, felt like I had been spun around a few times. The trees made any mental mapping difficult. Skyscrapers without street signs. When Ronald Reagan was governor of California, a freeway was proposed through an old-growth forest. Supposedly Reagan uttered, "If you've seen one redwood, you've seen them all." His constituency didn't agree with him, and neither did I, even if at the moment I felt a little disconcerted about being in Brobdingnag and not knowing my way around. Being damned confused about the Green Man didn't help my orientation efforts either.

"Then why did he live out here?" I asked. "Wasn't he in River Grove as some kind of sentry? Didn't EverGreen make a statement that he was camped in these woods to make sure Trans-Miss didn't do any illegal cuts?"

Evans nodded. "That's the story."

"Then if he didn't care about old growth, why was he here?"

The big shoulders shrugged. "Maybe he was vacationing."

That wasn't out of the question, I supposed. A place away from it all. Shepard loved his trees. Maybe he needed the quiet. Or perhaps he had been seduced by the big trees. He had planted millions of trees in his lifetime, but none such as these. Then again, maybe he wanted the solitude for other things: his ceremonies, his lover.

In the quiet woods, our heavy breathing became all the more pronounced. I noticed that we were following a slight trail, an indentation along the forest floor. Whether it had been made by the Green Man, or the curious, I didn't know. The path led to a hollowed tree, the Green Man's goosepen. The little boy in me was impressed. In every heart there is buried a Robinson Crusoe. In some of us, it's not buried very deep. I tapped around the interior of the tree.

"Buying a used car?" asked Evans.

I didn't respond, just scrutinized the goosepen like a prospective tenant.

"He had a kind of curtain which he dropped over the opening," said Evans. "Made it look real homey."

"All you'd need is running water," I said.

The long arm of the law pointed southeast. "Stream about a hundred yards thataway."

I stuck my head into the goosepen. I stand six foot three, and I didn't have to duck. There was a shelf above me. Man-made. I reached up and felt around.

"That was his storage room," said Evans.

"What did you find?"

"A bedroll and some blankets. Some food. A lantern. Batteries. A few books, and a few changes of clothes. Guess he didn't need too many outfits if he was walking around naked the whole time."

I lay down. With some padding, it could almost be cozy. I didn't quite fit, but Shepard had been half a head smaller.

"Be it ever so humble," Evans said.

"It added to his legend," I said, getting up. "I'm finding that was very important to him. His tree planting, and much of what he did, was derivative."

Evans stretched the word out. "De-riv-a-tive," he said, giving his best impression of a yokel. "Is that a five-dollar word for copycat?"

"Yeah," I said, "but if you buy me a drink I'll call us even."

"Don't know many five-dollar words," he said. "But I do know your Green Man wasn't the first to live in a goosepen."

Evans had my interest. He was more than aware of that, and he played with me a little. "But there ain't nothing new under the sun. Guess you know that too."

"Acquaint me with the old, then," I said.

"His name was Don McLellan," he said. "He moved into

a spot not far from here in nineteen fifty-eight. Near Jordan Creek. Made himself a three-story home out of a goosepen, kitchen on the first floor, bedroom on the second, and storage on the third."

"Was he destitute?" I asked.

"Des-ti-tute?" asked Evans, again mocking my word choice. "No, he was an eccentric. My father went out and visited with him a couple of times. He told my old man he worked in the timber industry most of his life. And what he liked to do best was climb the redwoods and look out at the world. He was hell on chains, my father said, could scuttle up with his climbing rig faster than a monkey."

"How long did he live in his goosepen?"

"Over a year. Like most of the eccentrics I've known, he had a grand dream. He wanted the nineteen-sixty world summit meeting to be held among the redwoods. McLellan thought that the world leaders should camp out together in goosepens. He was sure the ancient groves would work their magic and would bring everyone together."

"He *was* a dreamer," I said.

"One that wasn't afraid of advertising his dream either," said Evans. "He hung the Stars and Stripes and California's Golden Bear from the highest redwoods, had himself the grandest flagpoles on the planet, I hear. His huge flags waved and flapped to everyone who traveled along 101."

I imagined the sight, wished I could have seen it.

"It got him attention," Evans said, "but it didn't get him his convention. When it was announced that the world conference would be held in Paris, McLellan took down his flags and went back to his home state of Washington."

"And there moved in with the Old Lady Who Lived in a Shoe?"

Evans was amused, but not that amused. "Maybe he sounds funnier than he really was," he said. "Like I told you, McLellan was an eccentric, but he wasn't crazy. My dad took some pictures of him. So did other people. And in all those pictures, McLellan was wearing a silver hard hat. He knew about widow-makers. If your Green Man had been as cautious, he'd probably still be alive."

"Probably," I said. But I had my doubts.

$\triangledown$

13

Evans DROPPED ME OFF with Rocinante. I offered him drinks and dinner but learned he had two kids, and a wife who liked him home on time for supper. I told Evans I'd be traveling south and asked where to dine. He said his wife always insisted upon the Scotia Inn. I had passed the place on the way to the redwood mill and been taken by its looks. Within such inns, history lurks. So, usually, does twelve-year-old single-malt Scotch.

I got off the freeway at Rio Dell, a town just north of Scotia. The two towns share a border, but not much else. In Rio Dell is the anarchy of most little towns, hodgepodge housing and pell-mell businesses; one yard growing flowers, the next, rusted bikes and junked cars. The demarcation line between the two towns was almost palpable.

You don't expect elegance in a company town, but the Scotia Inn was just that. I was glad it didn't have the interference of valet parking, and a doorman, and a concierge. I walked in, and looked around, and got a feel for the place without being asked for my papers.

Its interior was a hybrid Gothic that played well with the two stories of burnished redwood. There were lots of comfortable sofas and chairs, and a grand piano awaiting anyone who felt like tickling its ivories. If my repertoire had included anything besides "Chopsticks," I might have been tempted.

The front desk was small, looked neither computerized

nor dehumanized. The clerk wasn't busy and appeared glad to see me. She was about twenty and apparently hadn't yet been given a course on the dynamics of garnering the walk-in trade. "Hello," she said, as if she didn't expect an immediate return on investment. "Hello," I said. She smiled, and I smiled. Then she went back to what she was doing, and I did the same.

It took me less than five minutes to nose around most of the lobby's corners. There were blowups of old photographs, turn-of-the-century pictures of proud lumberjacks standing atop mountainous stumps of their own creation or, more accurately, destruction. The loggers had that big-game-hunter pose, their feet on top of their kill, the veni, vidi, vici, look in their eyes. At the inn there were no bear heads on display, but there was plenty of redwood.

The restaurant was to the south of the lobby. I took a look at the menu, and the dining room, and came away impressed by both. There was a classic elegance, a setting that could compare favorably with any big-city grand dining spot. It had the antique chandeliers, and the polish, and the fine linen, and the real redwood paneling, not veneer. All this in the northern woods, the hinterlands. Perfect for Mrs. Evans. But it was about the last place in the world I wanted to dine alone.

Downstairs was the bar. That's where most good bars are located. Drinking dens need an illicit air, a speakeasy atmosphere. The grandeur of the inn surrendered at ground level, didn't try to put on airs where they didn't belong. Management genius. Pretension breeds abstention.

The bartender gave me a warm greeting. He was about forty, with a full head of thick, curly hair, a whiskey voice, and a beer gut. He must have been sensitive about his weight. In the first minute of our acquaintance, he found reason to bemoan his burgeoning stomach. The extra pounds were recent he said, the result of his having injured his knee. I was glad he didn't claim his voice was the result of a slow metabolism.

I was thankful that the bartender knew how to talk and pour at the same time. He identified himself as "Dan the barman." Normally I wouldn't have thought much of his introduction, but he punctuated it with about a six-count pour of Glenfiddich. Dan the generous barman.

Only one other bar stool was occupied, and the lessee looked comatose, except for a right arm that came to life now and again. He was an old man who'd left his choppers at home. Maybe he didn't want his false teeth to get in the way of a drink. I had a feeling his pulse was as slow as his reach, which wasn't fast, but it was regular enough.

The bar menu was a lot easier to read than the one upstairs, with all the aigus and umlauts. Most of the items carried one less digit, also. Dan told me everything came out of the same kitchen, and everything was good. I told him to make a medium-rare assault on my arteries.

Conversation came with the drinks and dinner. Dan was content to talk about anything. It didn't take much to get him going on the Green Man and Sequoia Summer. In the gospel according to Dan, "every damn fool" knew that the Green Man had died of natural causes.

"Environmentalists like to paint these woods as the Garden of Eden," he said. "Well, they're not, and never were. You think if a widow-maker had skewered me, anyone would have gotten excited?"

He stood in front of me, shaking his head from side to side. I got the hint and did the same.

"Damn right," he said. "Those EverGroaners are just trying to make something of his death for political reasons. They figure they can get people to buy into their conspiracy theory."

Not that Dan didn't find fault with "the other side." He dismissed the Reverend Mr. Sawyer as an "extremist," said he "kind of expected preachers to make noise on Sunday" but thought that for them to holler on any other day "was bad taste, 'ceptin' funerals, of course."

Dan did concede, however, that it was "right Christian of Sawyer to want to bury the Green Man in the Ferndale cemetery."

I asked about that, and Dan happily elaborated. "Surprised everyone," he said. "Guess it's easier being charitable to a dead man, though. Sawyer even offered to supply a tombstone, since Mr. Green Man died a pauper."

According to Dan, Sawyer's offer had been turned down by a Sequoia Summer committee. In refusing the plot and gravestone, they explained that trees would be the only proper monuments for the Green Man. Thousands of living memorials, they said, would far surpass one cold marker. His funeral, it was decided, would be a celebration of life and not a concession to death.

Some say preachers come to their calling because they would rather preach than be preached to. Sawyer did not appreciate being rebuffed, and the finger pointing resumed right after the funeral.

"Sawyer called the Green Man's funeral a pagan ritual," said Dan, "full of chanting, and voodoo, and evil poetry."

"Was he in attendance?" I asked.

Dan shrugged.

I wondered what constituted evil poetry. Sawyer probably would have categorized anything other than psalms as obscene.

"What poetry?"

Dan shrugged again. "Don't rightly know. But I guess one in particular got his dander up. Something about communion with nature. Sawyer said Shepard would have been much better served had he taken his communion with Christ."

Which poem? The verse, and the answer, came unexpectedly. The old man awakened from his stupor, and spoke.

"To him who in the love of Nature holds
Communion with her visible forms, she speaks
A various language."

His oration wasn't the best, his words dulled by alcohol, and lack of teeth, but his dramatic entrance commanded the floor. He attended to his drink before us. When he finished sipping, he accepted my questioning glance. He had very blue eyes, or maybe they looked that way because there was more red than white to his pupils. His face was concave, the lack of teeth giving his lips a puckered look, like an old roué.

"William Cullen Bryant," he said, overmouthing the words. " 'Thanatopsis.' "

Dan said, "That's mighty pretty." But he didn't mean it.

He was embarrassed, as if the old man had broken one of the rules of the bar. He was supposed to be an oddity, a fixture like the colored plastic lamp shades or the bordello red vinyl, part of the atmosphere, the ancient rummy without teeth.

"How did you remember that?" I asked.

"Miss Lundy," he said. "In the sixth grade. She was one for poetry, made us read and memorize it. Some of the townsfolk thought she was too much a freethinker. She went out with a Wobbly, was the story."

"That was the poem recited at the Green Man's funeral?"

He nodded, long and exaggerated.

"Were you there?"

"Course."

"Why?"

"Biggest funeral this county's ever seen. Couldn't miss that. Got to pretend everyone was there for me."

I left, but not without buying him another drink, and not without telling him that Miss Lundy would have been proud of him.

Outside I found a pay phone and called Miss Tuntland. I promised that I'd give her a real call later, but in the meantime I needed to know if she'd had time to research Ashe O'Connor's comings to and goings from Humboldt County.

"I did," she said.

"And?"

"Your Green Goddess has visited Humboldt County at least a dozen times in the last three months. Typically her stays run two to three days."

"Any explanation for her trips?"

"A few, yes. She traveled there once to dedicate a grove and went another time for some publicity shots. And, of course, she attended the Green Man's memorial service."

"Was she visiting when he died?"

"Yes."

"She has a mother up here." My words sounded defensive, as if I was excusing her many visits and, in particular, her having been around when the Green Man died.

"Interesting," said Miss Tuntland.

"Why?"

"The genealogies of the gods are always enlightening."

"She didn't ask for her nickname."

"But does it fit, Mr. Winter? That's the important question."

The sun had already set, and the sky was getting darker. "I have to run," I said. "I'll call you later tonight."

"What's your rush?" asked Miss Tuntland.

"On my way to a campfire," I said, as if that should explain everything. "Wish me luck."

"Knock wood," she said.

$\triangledown$

14

I PARKED ROCINANTE ON the outskirts of camp so as not to disturb the Circle in process, then quietly made my way forward. Teller was finishing up his talk. He was perspiring and had an impassioned expression. I wondered what I had missed.

"I'd like to conclude with a thought from nature writer John Hay," he said. "He wrote, 'Trees stand deep within a kind of knowing that surpasses human knowledge. We are running too fast to absorb it.' "

For a minute or two Teller let his audience deliberate on Hay's words; then he left the Circle. His spell kept everyone else from moving. I think I was the first to stir. Undisturbed redwoods have the luxury of longevity. Their thoughts can traffic through the æons. I didn't have the option of staying rooted for a few centuries to puzzle out how the Green Man had died.

My first impulse was to follow Teller, but there were others I wanted to talk to as well. Ashe O'Connor was one of my intended interviews, but her ear was already being hotly pursued by a few of the campers. Josh wasn't so occupied.

"Let's talk," I said.

He was surprised to see me and didn't look altogether happy. "What about?"

"Midnight ceremonies," I said.

"What are you talking about?"

He asked the question, I noticed, while leading me away from anyone who might hear us.

"I'm talking about rituals in the woods," I said, "what the Green Man called a return to the sacred."

Josh let out a long breath. "There were—plays in the woods," he said softly, evasively.

"We're not talking about *A Midsummer Night's Dream*, are we?"

The setting was right, and I was beginning to suspect there was something in the Green Man very much like Puck, but I knew the plays Josh was alluding to were older than Shakespeare.

He shook his head.

"You were there."

"A few times." A pause. "Most of the times."

"How would you describe these plays? Tree worship? Sexual ceremonies?"

"You're misinterpreting," whispered Josh. "You're making it sound like orgies were conducted."

"Weren't they?"

"What happened," he said carefully, "was real and right. Shepard reminded us of the history, and of the correctness, of nature. We participated in some of the old ways. We acted out the same ceremonies that the Greeks, and the Italians, and the Indians, and the Africans did. He showed us how the ancients celebrated, and taught us holy days and holy ways that have been forgotten."

"I understand clothes weren't a big part of these holy ways."

Josh looked around, wanted an excuse to escape. "It wasn't prurient," he said. "As we became educated, we realized that clothes were barriers to the world we wanted to get closer to."

"And the Green Man was your educator?"

"No," said Josh. "Nature was. He just showed us possibilities." Strong sibilance. A loud snake in a garden. "He showed us the woods were alive, and vital. If he awakened the human spirit, was that such a sin?"

"I'm not judging," I said. "I'm investigating."

"But you make everything sound so insidious. It wasn't that way. It was beautiful."

"How often were these beautiful ceremonies held?"

"On those nights when the moon was full."

"Where did they take place?"

"In spots deep in the woods."

"River Grove?"

"A few times."

"Was a ceremony held the night he died?"

"No." Josh answered quickly, harshly.

"How is it that you now remember that night so well, whereas before you didn't?"

Josh's mouth tightened, but he didn't answer. I wondered what else had happened that night.

"How many people usually attended?"

"Between forty and fifty."

"I don't imagine the ceremony times and sites were posted in the window of the Safeway."

Josh didn't comment.

"How'd you know when and where to go, Josh?"

"Christopher would tell one of us, and the word would be circulated."

"Did outsiders ever take notice of these gatherings?"

"No. We met where our seclusion was complete."

"Did only campers participate?"

"Yes."

"No one else?"

"No one else."

"Always the same people?"

"Pretty much."

"Circles within circles."

"We weren't exclusionary."

"But I imagine these ceremonies might have shocked some first-timers?"

Josh shrugged.

"Didn't they?"

"I heard a few campers got upset. They didn't understand."

"That's not surprising, is it? Didn't these get-togethers degenerate?"

Josh shook his head fervently. "They just evolved."

"From what to what?"

"It was like an educational series," he said. The man was a genius, Stuart. Do you have any idea how difficult it is to get people excited about trees? He was able to show us how trees were sacred and wonderful, even sensual."

"Try as I might," I said, "I can't quite find trees sexy."

"That's because we've made our world outside of nature," said Josh. "We've insulated ourselves. The Green Man wasn't afraid to show us how to intermingle with the inhabitants of the forest. Over time, he taught us how to approach trees, and touch them, and hug them, and caress them."

"How long did it take him to teach all of you forest foreplay?"

I could feel Josh's discomfiture, and growing anger.

"We learned to appreciate the many wonders of the woods over a period of months."

"Did he do this tree hugging clothed?"

"At first . . ."

"But in the end he wasn't wearing clothes, right?"

Josh nodded.

"And the kids did as he did."

Another nod.

"What then?"

"Eventually, he encouraged couples to explore the trees together."

Couples who weren't wearing clothes. Couples who were probably tired of exploring bark. I wondered what the guru got out of encouraging such things.

"Did the Green Man take any lovers? Anoint some of his followers as wood nymphs?"

"No."

"No? The man was satisfied rutting with a tree?"

"He was a teacher, not an exploiter. If you weren't so jaded, you'd be able to see that."

"What did he do? Watch? Cheer?"

"He just—stood."

"Stood? That's all?"

Josh nodded.

"Funny. I heard he exhibited himself like a satyr in rut."

"That's not true," said Josh. "That's what sick minds would think."

"Explain it better, then."

"Sometimes when he hugged the trees he became—aroused."

"Brought a whole new meaning to nature loving, didn't he?"

Instead of answering, Josh stormed away.

He wasn't the only one who was angry. I decided to cool my anger by walking down to the river. I knew the way this time, didn't need the smoke from Teller's marijuana to guide me, but it was there anyway.

"I missed your talk tonight," I said.

"You didn't miss much," he said, inhaling on his joint.

I found myself mimicking his deep breaths. There was enough smoke around that I probably risked getting a contact high. But the breaths made me calmer. We practiced our different forms of breathing for a while; then Teller spoke.

"I talked about the Arrow Tree," he said.

"I'm not familiar with that variety."

"That's because there was only one. It was a redwood that stood about six miles east of Arcata. When white men first noticed it in the eighteen hundreds, they described it as a porcupine tree, full of quills.

"The Chilulas and Wiyots had warred, and they made their peace under that great redwood. They marked the holy spot with an arrow in that tree. Later, whenever anyone from one of the tribes passed by the sacred tree, they symbolized their passage, and the lasting peace, by shooting an arrow into it. Many years passed, and the redwood filled with arrows. The Indians planted them in that sequoia, instead of in each other. Would that we were so wise. I told everyone that the Arrow Tree was the best tree-spiking story I have ever heard."

I laughed. As he pulled on his joint, I could see Teller was also smiling. I didn't let him keep it for long.

"Was the Green Man the modern metaphor for the Arrow Tree?"

Suck, think, speak: "Perhaps unconsciously."

"In life, he copied the examples of others. Do you think he could have done the same in death?"

"You mean did he choose to be a martyr?"

"He was big into ceremony. I talked with the cop who

found him. He couldn't rule out the possibility of a ritual death."

Teller shook his head. "No," he said.

"You don't think he willingly became the Arrow Tree?"

He shook his head again.

"It would have been nice for me," I said. "I admired him once. Maybe if he had sacrificed himself, I could have forgiven him for all the things I'm finding out. It's hard to lose a hero."

"Find another."

"They're in short supply."

"I'll loan you one: David Douglas."

"Douglas?"

"You might know him from the Douglas fir and Douglas squirrel. He was an explorer who didn't care about gold, or fur, or any of the usual exploitations. His interest was in the northwest flora. It took some time for the Indians of the lower Columbia River to understand this man. He was very different from other white men. Over a period of years, the Indians watched him very carefully. They saw him collecting specimens, poking about in the meadows, and the prairies, and the woods. Eventually, the Indians decided there was no harm in him and gave Douglas the name Man of Grass. It was a nickname of which he was very proud."

He sucked at his joint, gave a deprecating laugh, and said, "Behold, the new man of grass."

"Have any other heroes?"

"John Muir, of course. He loved his sequoias with a passion, and fought for them too. A hundred years ago he called upon the U.S. Cavalry to patrol the parks so as to protect the redwoods from stockmen and timber thieves. I spoke about that tonight. I wanted the campers to understand how long the forest battles have been going on, and how their defenders have stood as large as the redwoods. The Sempervirens Club and the Save-the-Redwoods League didn't just happen. I told them they could not fail those heroic deeds of the past. It's their responsibility to keep the battles going into the twenty-first century and beyond."

"Sure tonight's speech wasn't a swan song?"

Teller didn't comment, save by taking another hit off his

116

joint. I watched him in his loneliness. The way his shoulders sloped, and his coat hung on his frame, he looked like a bear. Smokey the Bear.

"How do you pick your topics?"

"They pick me," he said.

"Do you remember your Circle talk the night the Green Man did?"

Teller hesitated a moment. "I have enough trouble remembering last night's talk," he said.

"He died the night of the big summer storm."

Teller was silent again. "There was no Circle that night," he finally said. "Before the rain struck, there was a windstorm, and that prevented us from gathering."

"You had the tree watch duty that night," I said. "Methuselah was your charge from eleven to seven. It must have been uncomfortable in the rain."

"It must have been," he said, repeating my words.

"Do you remember the rain?"

"Yes. I remember holding my arms up, and wanting to be washed clean."

"Sounds baptismal. Religious."

"I don't have time for religion. Only for God."

"Did the rains clean you?"

"No. But I didn't get a cold either."

▽

15

T ELLER ANNOUNCED THAT he was tired and asked if I wouldn't mind letting him contemplate his navel in solitude. That wasn't the kind of old growth I was interested in, so I walked back to camp. Ashe O'Connor was waiting at the head of the path, but not for me. "Where's Thomas?" she asked.

"Exploring some old roots," I said. "Why?"

"My car's at the cabin," she said. "He told me he'd give me a ride."

"Let me."

She hesitated. "It's out of your way."

"All the better," I said, "for talking."

"And what if I don't feel like talking?"

"I suppose we can always neck."

She didn't comment or even bother to smile, just tromped ahead of me and made it a point to get into Rocinante without any assistance. We drove north on the Mattole Road, up the Lost Coast. It was dark, and the going was twisty. We were the only vehicle on the road, but it wasn't the kind of route that invites speeding. There were too many curves, too many unknowns. Just like my investigation. The headlights picked up some reflected light, and I braked sharply. Three deer stood in the road. They didn't scurry away, just stared into the light.

"Why aren't they running?" asked Ashe.

"They're confused," I said. "The light's disoriented them. That's why poachers take lanterns out with them at night. They blind their prey that way."

Ashe lowered her window. "Shoo," she said loudly, trying to drive the deer into the safety of the brush. "Shoo."

The deer didn't respond. I turned off the engine, and the lights. A moment later, they ran off.

It was dark outside, but not so dark that we couldn't see each other. Ashe was excited by the encounter. She looked flushed and happy. Then she realized that she was smiling, and that I was staring at her.

"Why aren't we moving?" she asked.

"Because I don't want to run into the deer."

"Is that any reason not to put your lights back on?"

"A calming tactic," I said. "One that apparently works only on deer."

I could feel her bristling and decided a better explanation was in order. "Your shooing was as likely to drive the deer into the truck as away from it," I said. "I'm just giving them a little more time to get away and get oriented."

She decided an explanation was in order also. "I was worried about another car running into us."

"I'd say the odds of that happening on this road, at this hour, are about the same as one's chances of being killed by a widow-maker.

"Interesting analogy," said Ashe.

"Is that your only comment?"

"No," she said, suddenly angry. "How's this? Start the damn truck up."

"I don't 'shoo' very well either," I said.

She was close to opening the door and walking, not more than a word away. I didn't challenge her any further, just looked ahead to the black road and let my words hang there.

"I would prefer to be questioned," she said at last, "in the safety of my cabin, instead of sitting here in the darkness waiting for death to overtake us."

I started Rocinante's engine, put her in gear, and drove. In the five minutes it took to get to the cabin, we only broke the silence out of directional need.

The cabin was off a dirt road. It was lit courtesy of a

generator that sounded with a persistent putter. The edifice looked like a hybrid legacy of Abraham Lincoln and Buckminster Fuller, a log cabin that had once had pretensions of being a geodesic dome. Someone had run short of money, or blueprints, or vision, or maybe all three.

Parked out front was a car, a faded red Honda about a decade off the docks. Cars like that don't usually have personalized license plates, but this one did: YES ON 150. Dangerous message to be touting in this neck of the woods. But then Ashe hadn't been driving her own car around all day.

The cabin was sparsely furnished. There was a slant to the floor that made me feel like I was on a listing boat. The lights constantly flickered, as if the generator was tapping out. The ceiling was full of cobwebs, and the floor was covered with grit, which crunched under our feet. Ashe apologized for the state the place was in. "Sorry about the mess," she said. "The great outdoors is beginning to come inside through holes in the ceiling, and I'm afraid that I've been rushing around so that I've only had time to clean the bedroom."

"Rushing around?"

"Yes," she said, an answer that told me nothing. "Do you want a drink? There's some cheap jug wine that was in the fridge when I arrived. And there's some beer."

I asked for a beer, and she brought one for herself also. There were two chairs in the living room. They weren't far apart, and, after we sat down in them, neither were we. We drank our beers in silence, and it wasn't long before Ashe collected the empties and brought refills.

"You wanted to talk," she said.

I nodded. It was clear Ashe was comfortable being in control. I wanted to deny her that accustomed position.

"I'd like you to explain what you're doing here."

The question annoyed her. "What do you mean?"

"Same observation I made yesterday: there's an election going on. Why aren't you in Sacramento trying to grease some legislative skids, or in Los Angeles doing a fund-raiser?"

"I'm here because this is what the issue's about," Ashe said. "These forests."

"I thought the issue was about getting votes to save these forests."

120

She tried to dismiss the question. "I can assure you I've spent quite a bit of time in Sacramento, and Los Angeles, and every major city in this state."

"That still doesn't tell me why you're here."

On her cheekbones, her high and pronounced cheekbones, two angry red circles appeared. But she still managed to control her voice.

"Maybe I need to recharge my batteries," she said. "Maybe I need to see what I'm fighting for, and rally those who are here."

"A lot of maybes," I said. "Can you start a sentence without that word?"

"Maybe."

"You've visited here over a dozen times in the last three months. For someone with such pressing concerns, you're spending an awful lot of time in the backwaters."

She decided sarcasm was her best evasion. "So you think I've got some deep, dark secret," she said. "Figured it out?"

"Not yet."

There wasn't anything to indicate that Ashe was relieved. But it was something I sensed. I allowed her to feel secure for a few moments, then spoke a little too casually.

"But I suspect it might have something to do with your mother."

Again, there were no physical giveaways, but my antennæ picked up something. My remark had struck home.

"My mother?"

I nodded, then remembered Miss Tuntland's remark about the genealogies of the gods. "What more appropriate setting to look at family trees," I said.

"You know?"

I nodded, not knowing what else to do.

"He's not my father," she emphasized. "He's my stepfather."

I nodded again.

"Neither one of us talks about the relationship. I wonder which one of us is more embarrassed: Bull or me?"

Bull. The name was familiar. "Must be tough on your mother."

"Right now she has more important concerns," Ashe said. "She has cancer."

"I'm sorry."

"It's the one thing my stepfather and I have ever agreed upon," she said. "We didn't want the media to know about my mother. They would have taken what was very personal and put it on the front pages."

"What's your mother's prognosis?"

"Not good."

"Has her condition heightened the tensions between you and your stepfather?"

"Mind-sets like yours are another reason for maintaining privacy in this matter. I am not acting out of antipathy towards him. Trans-Mississippi is just one of several big lumber companies in this county. My fight is for old growth, not a personal vendetta."

I finally figured out the connection. Harold "Bull" Dozier was the CEO of Trans-Mississippi, and a favorite target of the environmentalists. I was surprised their relationship hadn't been written about, but then there wasn't a blood connection between the two of them. Or was there?

"Let's talk about young growth for once," I said.

"What do you mean?"

"How old were you when your mother remarried?"

"I was thirteen."

I looked at her and tried to guess how many years ago that was. "I'm thirty-three," she said, saving me from asking.

"Have you been close to your mother for the last twenty years?"

"Not particularly. She made her choice a long time ago to be Bull Dozier's wife rather than be my mother. After their marriage, I was put in boarding school."

"Did that make you bitter?"

"At first," she said. "In time I came to know it as a blessing."

"How so?"

"Familial bonds are supportive but at the same time restrictive. I learned how to get my self-worth outside of the family. She who travels farthest, travels alone. I have."

"Yet you've been doing a lot of detouring lately."

"My mother's dying. Is that a good enough reason for you?"

122

I didn't answer. "Who else have you told about your mother's condition?"

"Only Teller," she said.

I put my beer bottle on the floor, steadied it so it wouldn't fall on the uneven wood. "How well did you know Christopher Shepard?"

"Well enough," she said. "We were lovers."

I didn't try to hide my surprise. Or was that consternation?

"Once upon a time he gave me a great gift, but that was a long time ago."

"Sounds like a fairy tale."

She laughed a little, and that changed the tone of our conversation, made us less adversarial. I fetched two more beers out of the refrigerator and handed her one.

"Just in case we need to cry in our beer," I said.

"I won't have that need," said Ashe, but she took the beer anyway.

"Love stories sometimes do me in," I said.

"Christopher and I were not a love story."

"Oh?"

"For me, our relationship was more an education, an awakening. I think that was why he was attracted to me. Not physically. But emotionally. He sensed I was needy."

"I don't understand," I said.

Ashe blushed. She proved she could do that too. "I was twenty-six when I first met him," she said. "I wasn't a virgin. I had had my share of boyfriends, but I didn't know there was anything to sex besides watching a man exercise on top of me.

"I think Christopher was attracted to sexually repressed women. Over the years I've come to the conclusion that his love life was an extension of his tree planting. It was growth that fascinated him. I think he probably got the same thrill from personal growth as he did tree growth."

"Did he use the same manure for both?"

She ignored me. "I think," Ashe said pointedly, "that he helped to liberate me."

"Excuse the vernacular," I said, "but you don't exactly strike me as a mercy fuck."

"Why are you being so harsh?" she asked.

It was a good question. I answered as best I could. "I took

this case because a man I admired died. I believed his PR, believed in this man-myth who cared only about planting trees and working for a better world. But now the Gilbert and Sullivan line keeps playing through my head: 'Things are seldom what they seem,/Skim milk masquerades as cream.' The more I hear about Shepard, the less I like him."

"You wouldn't have said that had you known him," she said.

I didn't spare the sarcasm. "To know him was to love him?"

"Something like that. Christopher was an innocent."

There was a wistful tone to her voice, the kind you envy, the kind you wish had been reserved for you.

Disbelievingly: "Innocent?"

"Yes."

"From what I've heard, he was a wanna-be cult leader."

Ashe shook her head. "Christopher was charismatic, but he wasn't a megalomaniac. His cause was what mattered to him."

"He conducted services in the woods," I said. "He initiated rites."

Ashe sighed. "I heard the stories," she said, indicating by her tone that they were negligible. "You have to understand, that was Christopher. He was a little boy."

"Your little boy acted like a Druid priest," I said. "Your little boy liked exposing his tumescent self."

"Of course," she said. "He was primal. He was show and tell. He didn't have a great philosophy, at least not in a conventional sense. In a seed, he saw all the answers of the world. Water it, tend to it, and nurture it, and you'll find salvation."

"You underestimated him."

"No, Stuart," she said. By using my first name, Ashe allowed us a familiarity we did not have before. "It was in his simplicity that Christopher was so very strong. He did so much. What other mortal could have planted millions of trees? I always think of the saying 'When all's said and done, a lot more is said than done.' Christopher was the opposite of that. He might have had only one idea, but he succeeded where a thousand deep thinkers could not."

"You say he wasn't complex. How is it that he always had some quote handy? How is it that he seemed so wise?"

"Anything that had to do with trees," she said, "he remembered."

"If this elephant of the trees was so simple," I said, "why were you his lover?"

Ashe thought about that. "Maybe I needed something uncomplicated back then," she said.

"That's the first time I've ever heard that sex simplifies matters."

"With Christopher," she said, "it was almost that way. I think he viewed sex as an extension of nature. Something that was fun. Something that shouldn't have any hang-ups."

"The birds and the bees and the trees. That about covers him, right?"

"Yes," she said, raising her chin to my skepticism. "Rhythms, growing seasons, and fertility. He knew those things very well."

"And where did you come in?"

"I needed pruning," she said. "I was carrying the wrong kind of baggage, growing crookedly. When it came to trees, Christopher could always tell right away if something was wrong, could explain why they were stunted or growing funny. Intuitively, I think he had that same kind of understanding of women. It wasn't that he thought he was God's gift to us, just that he thought things should grow right."

I made a disparaging sound. "The all women need is a good lay theory, huh?"

She hook her head. "It wasn't a macho thing with Christopher," she said. "It was more like a healing. Sex without being sexual, if that's not too much of an oxymoron. Pleasure schooling."

"You sound nostalgic," I said. There was a little tightness to my voice.

"I probably am," she said. "You know how I think he seduced me? His story. Just a stupid little story, really.

"I met him in southern California. We were planting coast live oaks along the Kern River, trying to restore the riparian habitat as it once was. I had heard of the Green Man, of course. You know how it's always an anticlimax to meet a famous person? It wasn't that way with him. By his own example, we were all encouraged to work twice as hard. Everyone loved him, and everyone shared his vision.

"One day he approached me when I was by myself. And he said I reminded him of a beautiful statue. And then he asked me whether I wanted to hear a story about two statues. I told him that I did.

"One of the statues was a male," he said, "and the other a female. They were locked in a close embrace, twined together over the years. To those that looked upon them in the park setting, they were passion and dispassion, stone by nature, but clearly flesh in disposition.

"One day a good spirit passed over that park and looked upon those statues, and the spirit saw the unfairness of their positions, and was moved to melt the stone to flesh.

"The former rock lovers suddenly faced one another, he, strong and comely, and she, voluptuous, and desirable. In a twinkling, they knew what had to be. Hand in hand, they ran into the bushes. And there the spirit heard rustling, and laughing, and great communion.

"Before leaving, the spirit decided to take a peek at their bliss. Just a peek, mind you. And when that spirit peered through the shrubbery, he found the man and woman madly relieving themselves on every pigeon they could find."

I started laughing, and Ashe laughed too. "I expected something dirty," she said, "something tawdry. Back then I didn't care for jokes, didn't like laughing. I felt that left me too exposed. But he made me laugh. He lightened my spirit. And over time I learned it was all right to have passions that weren't only politically or environmentally oriented. When I was with him, I learned how to be free."

She stopped talking, did a little remembering, but it wasn't all serious. Every few seconds one or the other of us laughed. We only had to say "pigeons," or flutter our hands like birds trying to escape a flood, to start us laughing again. A few times I looked at her and wondered what had happened to the woman who had been so stern and humorless, so like a woman of stone. She looked warm now, and soft.

In the middle of a laugh we touched. And then there were no more laughs. We came together and started kissing, and feeling. She began to make little sounds, which built to groans and sighs. The friction increased, human sticks rubbing. Our clothes came off, not in orderly progression, but in jerks and spurts, in spasms of activity and exploration.

We were down to socks and sounds, our lips, and tongues, and hands, making mad dashes at each other. We rolled on our discarded clothes, the grit from the unswept floor cracking beneath us.

I felt along her thighs, and she slowly spread them for me. For us. She made sounds in the language of passion, but at a telling moment she remembered English and said, "No."

I retreated slightly, hoped I hadn't heard correctly, but my denial didn't help. She stood up and took a step back. I got to my feet also and wondered what to say. I thought of reassurances, words to rekindle the fire, but in the end I mutely obeyed the stop signs.

Naked, we stood facing each other. I saw a statue again, finely chiseled, flawless, but I would rather have seen human imperfections, and human desire.

"I'm sorry," she finally said.

"Who were you with?" I asked. "Christopher or me?"

"Both of you," she said.

Only half insulted, I thought. Or half lied to.

I picked up my clothes and started walking toward the door. It would be easier, I decided, to dress in the truck.

"Leaving?" she asked.

"Looking for pigeons," I said.

$\triangledown$

16

I KNEW A GOOD place to look. I had a gutful of mean and knew where I wanted to take it out. I drove to Bayshore.

There wasn't much wind left to the Blow Hole. Four tipplers were hanging on at the bar. One of them was Red. Tina must not have liked the look on my face. She didn't wave, just moved her thin arm under the bar, probably atop the ax handle.

I sat next to Red. The bar got quiet. I think I was remembered. Red's eyes were mostly closed. He hadn't bothered to look my way yet.

"Beer," I said.

Two of the men said their good nights. They weren't in the mood for a hangover and didn't seem keen on protecting Red's virtue. The third was snoring. That left Red and me and Tina.

She put the beer in front of me, looked like she was about to deliver it with some advice, then decided not to.

Overloud, I announced, "I'm back, Red."

He blinked his eyes a few times.

"Figure you owe me some answers."

He looked around. I don't think he liked what he saw. "Got to drain the monster," he mumbled.

"There an exit from the bathrooms?"

Tina shook her head.

"Go on," I said. "I'll wait."

Red stumbled off. Tina and I exchanged glances. After half a minute of that, she volunteered some words. "Course there is a phone back there," she said.

Which meant I could probably count on Cincy and Coop showing up any minute. "Thanks," I said.

"Figured you'd come back," she said.

"Why?"

"Because men are stupid."

"I'm not quite stupid enough to argue."

"That's a first for your species."

"Red talk about the Green Man after I left?"

"Nope. Talked mostly about how he was going to kill you if you came back."

I didn't say anything, but Tina must not have liked what she saw. "Oh, God," she said. "He's got his 'here I am' expression. What brought that on? Woman trouble? Bruised ego?"

Her needling took a little of the Neanderthal posturing off my face. "So he still does have a brain," said Tina. "Better remember that, Stu."

Red walked back into the room, made a point of zipping up his zipper just as he arrived at the bar. "So the faggot's back," he said.

I didn't say anything.

"You like fairies?" Red asked.

I nodded. "The tooth fairy especially. Even though he's not very smart."

Red looked genuinely confused. "What the hell are you talking about?"

"The stupid tooth fairy. You see, I keep getting into situations where I have to knock out the teeth of some asshole. And I collect those teeth and put them under my pillow. And that fairy keeps paying out."

Red announced, "You're full of shit." But he was leaning away from me when he said it.

I shrugged. "You're the one who wanted the fairy tale."

"What I want is another fucking drink. For the road. That's where we'll talk."

Tina poured him his drink. Wild Turkey, of course. Red didn't make any move to pay. I threw some bills on the counter. With my money came another long-neck bottle of beer and a cluing look from Tina. The beer arrived capped. I slipped it into my coat pocket.

"You tip the little lady well, Mr. Private Dickhead? Because she does give good service. Oh my, doesn't she give good service."

Red gulped down his drink, took off his cap for a moment, and ran his hand through a shock of curly red hair. His eyes were almost as red as his hair. He rose a little unsteadily, made his boisterous farewell to Tina, then attempted a drunken insouciance. He had the drunken part down real well. He led me away from the river and took me down an alley, where he said he knew just the place to talk.

The alley boxed us in. On one side was an old, crumbling warehouse, on the other a rotting plywood wall. Some of the lights along the warehouse were still operational, but most were not, leaving patches of gray amid the darkness. I tried to figure out where the ambush would come. Walking away would have been the smart thing to do, but I had already done that once. The alley was piled with trash and lined with old truck tires. I was watching Red, waiting for him to react. He was looking intently from side to side. I slipped the beer bottle from my pocket just before they jumped me.

Coop had a baseball bat. He tried to pull my head into left field but should have gone with the pitch. I ducked under his swing, moved inside his batting range to try a swing of my own. The beer bottle slammed into his face. In the movies, the glass would have shattered. In real life it remained intact. But I couldn't say the same thing about his face.

He was screaming, but he wasn't the only one. I was doing my banshee imitation. I was scared as hell, and I wanted everyone else to be. I made a move for Red. He was a knife man, but his reactions were a night of drinking slow. I feinted, and he brought his arm down in what was supposed to be a slashing motion. I kicked out, caught the fleshy underpart of his forearm, and watched the knife go airborne. Then I grabbed him by his hair and swung his head into the wooden wall. There were still a few solid boards left after the impact, but a few less than there had been.

Behind me a voice screamed, "Stop! I'll shoot! I will!"

130

I didn't turn around, at least not immediately. I raised one arm, the one with the bottle. It probably looked like surrender. The other arm I still had wrapped around Red's head. I didn't move quickly, instead acted in a very deliberate manner. Cincy's voice had sounded desperate, and I wasn't anxious to see how desperate. I broke the bottle I was holding and positioned it in the same steady motion. When I turned, I had the jagged edge in Red's neck. I pinked him a little, and he squealed nicely.

Cincy wasn't holding the gun very steadily. And this time he wasn't laughing.

"Your call," I said. "A philosophical question: Better Red than dead?"

Red managed to spit out a tooth with minimal facial movement. Then, through clenched teeth, he cursed Cincy. The muted profanity sounded a little odd, but, with the glass pressed up against Red's neck, there wasn't much room for his jaw to operate. The upshot of his speech was for Cincy to drop his gun, which he did. I retrieved it. With the gun in hand, I offered a few other suggestions, and Red was quick to whisper his agreement with them. Among my recommendations was that Red and I needed to be alone for a little chat. No one argued.

After Cincy and Coop left, I pushed Red to the ground. Without a shard muzzle, he wasn't quite so pleasant. "I already gave to your fucking tooth fairy," he said, "so what more do you want?"

"Maybe a few more donations."

I showed Red my teeth, displaying more than smiling. He weighed his options. "We wasn't going to kill you," he said. "We just brought the gun along for insurance."

Insurance. I suppose that's how we justify nuclear stockpiling. I let him get a good look at his insurance, casually kept the gun aimed at him. He started sweating, his body odor adding to a number of other bad smells in the alley, including dry rot, and wet rot, and urine, and garbage. I breathed through my mouth. Occasionally a light river breeze passed by, and I took to snapping at its freshness like a dog at flies. Red had to endure my mad dog act, as well the darkness and dankness of his dunce corner. He started talking even before I got around to asking him any questions.

"I got a call," he said, "and this guy asks me whether I want to make some money. Good way to get your attention, right? Man says we don't do something against them Ever-Groaners, none of us will be working. So I says I got no argument there.

"To make a long story short, I got money, and I got instructions. I had them Green Man posters made up, and me and my friends posted them. And that's about all."

I hardly thought so, and made that apparent with a look. Red started talking again, said he didn't know how he had been singled out. He had never met with the caller, said he only talked with him twice by phone. Red was advised that other jobs would be forthcoming if he could keep his mouth shut, which he did, at least for a time. He was sent seven bills, all hundreds. That provided him with a little extra spending money for a few weeks and also gave him the idea he was a lieutenant in a secret campaign. When no other calls came, Red decided to pursue some mischief of his own. Without a bankroll behind him, his pranks had been minor, just as Tina had guessed. The biggest boast he could come up with was the night he and his friends had snuck around the Sweetwater camp collapsing tents while the campers slept.

I didn't look impressed, so Red decided to give me the grand finale. He said that he and his friends had done some surveillance on the "Green machine" and were privy to a lot of their secrets. Someone should have coached him on a better beginning than "It was a dark and stormy night." But his story quickly got better.

"It was a bitch of a night," he said, "windy, you know? You could tell the sky was about to piss buckets, but me and Cincy and Coop figured it was as good a time as any to get us a look-see at what was going on at River Grove. Spy time on the Green Man.

"Thing is, what we saw mostly was his green ass. It was doing plenty of moving up and down. He was a seed planter all right. He was putting it to some slut right outside that tree of his."

Red spoke lower, more confidentially: "I've had some pieces of ass in my time that set the walls to shaking, but this one beat all. She had lungs in her that wouldn't quit. Had the words to match her screams too."

Red told me the words. Nothing original but a few creative combinations.

"She was screaming to wake the dead," he said, "and doing a hell of a job on the living, if you know what I mean. We got us closer and closer, but they was in their own world, going at it like dogs."

"How long before you awarded best of show?"

"Huh?"

"How long did they make love?"

"I don't know. They were still going strong when we left."

That didn't sound right. Not those three. "Why?"

A shrug that attempted indifference. "It got old."

Same question, as if I hadn't heard the first answer. "Why?"

Red didn't say anything, but his eyes did. He'd lost that gleam. Now, he almost looked worried. Remembering about a wild woman was one thing, but there was another memory he wasn't as fond of. Finally, half to himself, he said, "We saw something."

"What?"

"It was dark."

He had just finished giving me details a gynecologist couldn't have known; now he claimed it was dark.

"And?"

"And we left after we saw it."

"It?"

Mumbled, out of the corner of his mouth: "Bigfoot. Maybe."

It wasn't an answer I had expected, and not one he wanted to talk about. I pressed him. They saw something, Red said, that stood "seven, eight feet tall and was dark." According to him the creature packed quite a wallop; it had managed to get their attention by pounding its huge fist against a tree.

"Made a fucking redwood shiver," he said.

Red wasn't far from a shiver himself. That was probably why I believed him. His reluctance to tell the story was another reason.

"We left the bar shit-faced," he said, "and we did us some sipping and smoking on the way. We figured it'd be better not to say anything. They'da just called us liars or drunks.

We figure we'll do our talking when we go back and hunt Bigfoot down."

I was willing to bet that wouldn't be any time soon. Red wasn't able to give me a better description of the Sasquatch or of the woman. He couldn't tell me her age or her hair color. He imagined plenty but knew nothing beyond her passionate screams and colorful vocabulary. Cinderella testing was clearly out.

For another half hour, I plied him with questions. He and his friends had arrived at River Grove around ten o'clock. The location of the Green Man's goosepen was no secret, but, drunk as they were, it had taken them awhile to reach it from the road. Their return trip, according to Red, "only took about thirty seconds." He hadn't noticed any other parked cars but said in those woods a division of Mack trucks could easily be hidden away.

"We did see another car, though," he commented offhandedly, "just as we were about to leave."

I made a circular motion with the gun, encouraging him to provide the details of the sighting.

"We figured it was the cops for sure. There we was, out of breath from running, not more than a second or two inside my car, when we saw these lights a-coming up the road. But the car must have made a U-ey, 'cause the lights suddenly disappeared."

"What kind of car?"

"Couldn't see."

"Do you think the driver saw you?"

"No way. I got a Bronco, and my buck was pulled pretty far off the road."

They had left spooked, or, as Red described it, "in a rush." But they never caught up with the car they had seen.

I had Red go over his story several times. He started to sober up, which didn't help the telling. He began to whine, said that his mouth hurt and that he was bleeding. His lost tooth became a drama of epic proportions. He wanted compensation, he told me, before he said another word. I reached down among the alley's garbage, found what I was looking for, and tossed him his tooth.

"Ask the tooth fairy," I said.

▽

17

I GOT ON 101 and started driving north. Earlier in the day I had admired the open space of the area and been glad for the paucity of restaurants and motels, but now I was tired and wanted the convenience of a bed. The dilemma of the human race: wanting it both ways.

I didn't figure Red and his friends would be looking for me, but, just to be sure, I passed a few exits before seeking a place to sleep for the night. I chose a turnoff that advertised lodging and was directed along by a faded billboard that seconded that promise, but, after driving in the darkness for several minutes, I wondered if it was only a seasonal offering.

The light at the end of the tunnel wasn't much more than candlelight. There was a vacancy sign that flickered desultorily. By all indications, the resort's hibernation time was near. Some of the cottages had already been boarded up. Of about forty cabins, only two had cars in front of them. The inn wasn't expecting anybody and wasn't dressed up for visitors. The area probably exuded a rustic charm during the summer, with kids running around, wienies being roasted, and Ma and Pa sitting outside in lawn chairs, but summer seemed a long way off.

What the hell, I thought. I'm here.

There was a reception area outside the manager's cottage, but it was locked. Through the window I could see the flickering light of a television. Handwritten instructions told me to BUZZ FOR MANAGER. I tried. The buzzer didn't work. My hand did.

Strong rapping didn't bring the manager. There was probably a car chase scene on the tube. My fist went to work again, sounding like a precursor to a huffing, and puffing, and blowing the house down scene. That roused someone. He didn't look like a graduate of the Cornell School of Hospitality. He was about five foot five inches tall, and about that wide. I think his T-shirt was clean, but it was hard to tell with all the holes in it.

"Your buzzer's broken," I said.

He had thick, black glasses on, the kind Clark Kent used to wear. But even Clark never wore a nose guard.

"I know," he said.

"Are you open?"

He nodded.

"Your cottages wouldn't come with phones, would they?"

Silly question. He shook his head, pointed to a triangle island just off the driveway that was a bit darker than the rest of the area. A pay phone. Without lights, of course.

"Does it work?"

"Did this morning."

I knew better than to ask to see a cottage before checking in. I might have lost my nerve.

I was assigned to a cabin just one down from the manager's unit. The focal point of the room was an old mirror hanging above a ramshackle chest of drawers. The glass had been imperfect to begin with, its edges giving off fun-house kinds of distortions. Not helping the reflection were at least twenty-one years of bad luck, three cracks running through it. But you can't always blame the mirror. I was a mess. My hair looked like a gridiron contest had been held on it, and there was blood on my face. I tested it with my tongue, found a tender spot on my lip, and wondered if it was a result of the passion or the fight. I didn't feel particularly good about either.

I took a shower, mostly to wash away the blood. It was cool enough to help me forget about passion too. The bath towels were about the size and thickness of washcloths, but, when you're next to godliness, you're forgiving. I put on some fresh clothes, slicked back my hair, and faced the mirror again. It didn't announce I was the fairest one of all, but neither did another crack appear.

Some people have teddy bears they go to bed with, and others have rituals of warm milk, or reading a chapter in a book, or going to sleep depressed after the late-night news. I have Miss Tuntland. I grabbed a flashlight from Rocinante's cab, and with that beam I challenged the darkness, and a cold telephone, and a cold operator, and calling card numbers that could be more easily brailled than read.

In one impassioned breath, I explained to Miss Tuntland where I was, and how cold the telephone receiver was on my ear, and how I was risking pneumonia just for her, and maybe gangrene too. Was she impressed?

"Too cheap to get a room with a phone?" she asked.

"Not many phones in this neck of the woods," I said.

"What neck brought you to that neck of the woods?" she asked.

"Speaking of necks," I pleaded, "isn't it a little early in this conversation to be going for my jugular?"

"Avoiding the question won't help, Mr. Winter."

"How about if I ease into it?"

She let me do my telling in my own way. There was a lot of ground to cover. I recapitulated my day, and Miss Tuntland took notes. I finished with the revelations of what had happened at River Grove the night the Green Man died.

"Hardly sounds like a remote spot," said Miss Tuntland. "Just think how many people were there that night: Red and friends, the Green Man, the woman, and that mysterious car which pulled up at the end."

"Don't forget Bigfoot," I said.

"That's right," she said. "Sasquatch. Are you going to add him to your suspect list, Mr. Winter?"

"Why not? He can join the telephone book."

Miss Tuntland doesn't like it when I pity myself. "I can't reach my violin," she said.

"That's not appropriate forest music anyway."

"What is?"

"A power saw."

I didn't digress for long. Miss Tuntland didn't let me. We

went over the case, tried to figure out what we knew and what we didn't.

"Shepard would have been walking his lover back to the logging road," said Miss Tuntland. "Her car would have been parked there. That's why he was naked, and away from his goosepen. That's why he was out in the wind."

"The wind wasn't the only thing that was up that night," I said.

"How do you know?"

"Josh is hiding something. Everyone is."

"Why do you say that?"

"On different occasions when I asked him about events of that night, he went from amnesia to total recall. There's something nagging at me, but I can't quite place it. Something . . ."

"Yes?"

"Something that involves Sasquatch."

This time she didn't laugh. "It will come to you," she said.

"Maybe if I hit my head like Red said he hit the tree."

"Don't push," said Miss Tuntland. "What else isn't right?"

"The relationship between the Sawyers. Something's wrong there. I'd like to know where they met and how long they've been together. I'd like to know about him, and I'd like to know about her."

"I can find that out," said Miss Tuntland.

Between the frontiers of her modem, her many contacts, and her unsurpassed phone techniques, Miss Tuntland invariably learned more with her dialing finger than I did with my legwork.

"Strangely enough, I'm also curious about a Don McLellan," I said. "It's probably a childish curiosity, some mental urge of mine to get away from it all like he did. McLellan was a hermit of sorts who lived in these woods in the late nineteen fifties. Lived in the goosepen of a redwood, if you can believe it."

"If my landlord keeps raising my rent," she said, "I might consider that option myself."

Miss Tuntland asked me to stop talking for a minute so she could write some things down. She took my musing seriously, more seriously than I usually did.

"Questions everywhere, Miss Tuntland. Who was the money behind the posters? I haven't even answered that yet. And is Ashe O'Connor only being the dutiful daughter, or is there another reason for her visits? Then, of course, there's the relationship between Ashe and her stepfather. That bears exploration. Bull Dozier's been silently influencing a lot of goings-on around here. There are even rumors about Shepard and Trans-Miss. I'll have to look into those."

I sighed. "He's everywhere, Miss Tuntland, The Green Man. He keeps playing peekaboo among the redwoods. I hear his laughter, but he doesn't show himself. Why did he read from the Song of Solomon? He certainly wasn't religious in any conventional sense."

Another sigh. "I can't even tell if he cared about the red-woods, or whether his only motivation was the Green Belt. He had this compulsion to plant, a drive as strong as anything I have ever heard of. Almost sexual, I'd say. That makes it difficult to judge whether he was an innocent or diabolical."

Miss Tuntland let me ramble some more, even challenged me a few times to think aloud. When I finished with most of my questions and doubts, I tried to conclude our conversation with more pleasurable recollections, tried to tell Miss Tuntland about the great and mighty groves I had visited. I saved the best for last but thought my description fell short—short by a redwood, which is a very large verbal miss. Miss Tuntland was glad at my attempt anyway. She hadn't yet visited the redwoods but said that it was on her life list of things to do.

"I empathize with trees," she said. "I've often thought, if there was such a thing as reincarnation, that's what I'd like to come back as. I'd enjoy having birds nest in my ears, and squirrels racing along my arms, and me just observing the world and setting down deep roots."

"Redwoods don't have deep roots," I said.

"No?"

"That surprised me too," I said.

I considered that odd pairing for a few moments, all that height and no depth, and what eventually resulted from it.

"Are you still there?" asked Miss Tuntland.

"I was thinking about how redwoods die." I had already

told her about Scotia, and the mill. But that wasn't a natural death. That was man's taking the trees before their time. On their own terms, redwoods die in an unusual way, different from other trees.

"You've probably heard that trees die from the top down," I said. "But that's not the way with redwoods. They die when they fall over. Usually, right up until the day they fall, redwoods appear healthy and vital. Most scientists say that they topple over because their root system isn't extensive enough to support them."

It was her turn to be quiet. Then she asked, "Were you really thinking about redwoods?"

The woman was too wise. "No," I said. "I was wondering how the Green Man died. Was it like other trees? Did he age, and weaken, and become corrupt? Did he decline from the top down? Or did he just topple like a redwood?"

Unsaid between us was the same muse: or did someone chop him down?

Miss Tuntland knows how I get obsessed with cases, knows I start living and breathing them, sometimes to my detriment. "It's late," she said. "Time for you to count some sheep."

I promised her that I would try. But, when I did my counting that night, it wasn't sheep. It was tree rings.

▽

18

For a while, "Do you dream in color?" ranked right there with "What's your sign?" and "Don't I know you from somewhere?" as a pickup line. It would seem a pretty straightforward question, but it wasn't one I had ever been able to answer definitively. My dreams aren't like films or television shows. They're otherworldly, feelings more than colors. But when morning came I could finally answer it without an explanation, could honestly say, "Yes, I dream in color."

Or at least one color. Green.

What I like best about dreams is that you can be mad as a hatter for all the while you sleep and not have anyone lock you away. Sometimes I travel through a lot of Daliesque landscapes. Problem is, often the view doesn't change when I awake.

I didn't mull over my green dream for very long. It answered a question, but I had more pressing concerns. In the morning light, the resort looked and felt more benign, a destination for grown-up Scouts. I went to the pay phone again, got a number for the Trans-Mississippi administrative offices in Lofield, and made a call. I didn't expect it would be easy to get through to Bull Dozier, and it wasn't. I was transferred from a receptionist to a secretary to an administrative assistant. None of them wanted to take the responsibility of hanging up on a serious voice whose favorite refrain was "It's

141

important." I was pressed for details but didn't reveal much other than that I had conferred with his stepdaughter and needed to speak to him on "matters of significance."

Dozier must have tired of his underlings interrupting him. I was listening to some very pleasant hold music, Vivaldi I think, when an extremely annoyed voice suddenly broke into my musical reverie and said, "This is Dozier. What do you want?"

I explained who I was, and who I was representing. And then I asked him for fifteen minutes of his time.

"Why should I give you that?" he asked.

"Because the Green Man died on land your company owns," I said.

Silence. Not even Vivaldi.

"Because I'm supposed to get answers back to those who hired me," I said, "and, if I can't find any tangible evidence that he was murdered, then maybe there will be less finger pointing your way, and fewer people saying the lumber companies were somehow involved in his death."

"Talk to our public relations department."

"Last night I spoke with your daughter," I said.

"Stepdaughter," he said, his correction quick.

"She didn't like the questions I was asking about the Green Man," I said.

"So what?"

"So I'm an equal opportunity alienator, and a persistent one."

"And that's supposed to recommend you?"

"Reassure you, maybe. My dogma won't get in the way of your dogwoods, or redwoods for that matter. I'm not looking for information to match a prearranged answer. I'm just looking for information."

He taunted: "The last honest man."

"Does that scare you?"

"Be here at ten-thirty," he said, and hung up.

Lofield was about ten miles northeast of Eureka, a familiar word to most Californians because, *"Eureka"* is the state's motto. When Archimedes discovered how to determine the purity of a gold object, he shouted *"heurēka,"* which translates "I have found it." Two thousand years after Archimedes, the gleeful cry was still going strong, was in fact the catchword of early Californians seeking that big vein of gold. But Eureka's naming wasn't solely related to the gold fever that swept the state. It was more the result of Captain James T. Ryan's stepping ashore on the mud flats of Humboldt Bay in 1850 and shouting, "Eureka!" Ryan rediscovered an elusive bay that had been found and lost several times over a forty-year period. His exclamation presaged the naming of the city.

I didn't know if the city of Eureka was still something to shout about, but Lofield clearly wasn't. Although Lofield wasn't officially a company town like Scotia, it was dominated by the Trans-Mississippi Lumber Company. Their mill didn't offer tours. It was closed to the public, fenced off like a military post or a castle. It didn't take much imagination to envision towers, and turrets, and moats, and pennons, even though the reality was cranes, and holding ponds, and flagged lumber. The gate guard didn't ask me "Who goes there?" but it took a few minutes for me to get passed through. My name was apparently not the password of the day.

The administrative offices were in a compound away from the noise of the mill. Almost as much attention had been paid to their insulation as to the interior decoration. The offices compared with the toniest San Francisco business addresses, with black leather, and white-white paint, and chrome, and flashy paintings with big price tags and small messages.

I was about two minutes early, and that was how long Harold "Bull" Dozier made me wait. He wasn't what I expected. Men with the nicknames Bull or Bear are usually big and brawny. Bull was neither. He was natty, and trim, and of medium height. Someone named Bull should drool a little, and have a permanent case of pinkeye. This Bull had a white handkerchief in his suit pocket and unsullied blue eyes. He wasn't exactly effete, probably didn't ask for a lime with his beer, but he wasn't the kind to drink it out of a bottle either. Bull Dozier. Bulldozer. He probably didn't like his nickname, but, when it fits, you wear it. Or you level it.

We shook hands, and he asked me to sit. Then he tapped a large microphone, made sure it was operational, and asked, "Do you mind if I tape our conversation?"

The question was apparently moot, because he had already turned on the recorder. "No," I said, "but I should warn you that I might break out into song. Microphones do that to me."

Bull didn't smile, merely announced his name, and then mine, and the date and time the recording was taking place. Then he looked at me expectantly. I had half a mind to lean over and thank the Academy, but now and again I do show restraint.

"Do you tape most of your conversations?" I asked.

"Some of them."

"Do you have the Green Man on tape?"

He acted surprised. "What do you mean?"

"Isn't the question self-explanatory?"

If it was, he didn't answer it.

"I'll clarify," I said. "I understand the Green Man visited here. I heard it wasn't too long before his death. Is that true?"

Dozier picked up a pen on his desk, looked at it. "I would prefer not discussing that subject."

"Ah," I said. "Something you have in common with the conservationists. They don't want to talk about the Green Man's visit here either. It's sort of the same relationship you have with your daughter . . ."

He looked at me, and I corrected myself. ". . . Your stepdaughter. Neither one of you is keen on having anyone aware of your relationship."

"Let's say for argument," he said, "that the Green Man did visit here."

Interesting, I thought, that he prefers talking about a controversial dead man to discussing his own familial circumstances.

"When did this hypothetical visit take place?"

"Let's say the last week of August."

"How did arrangements for . . . this mythical meeting . . . occur?"

"They didn't. It was unexpected. Unannounced. He just showed up."

Dozier had put a quit to the fantasy guising, and I was only too happy to follow suit. "What did he want?"

"Our tree-planting expertise."

144

"I would have thought him expert enough."

"Not on a massive scale. Last year about five million redwood seedings were planted in Humboldt county, many by our company. He was quite interested in large-scale planting operations."

"Did you oblige his curiosity?"

"We gave him a tour."

"What did he think?"

"He was impressed."

"Can you elaborate?"

"He was very impressed."

"Did you personally give him the tour?"

"Yes."

"And how long did it last?"

"Half a day."

"Is that the only time you saw him?"

Dozier hesitated. His eyes moved slightly, rested for a moment on the tape recorder. "He only visited here that one time."

"And did you tape that conversation?"

"At first."

"But you stopped?"

"Yes."

"Why?"

"When I realized he wasn't a Trojan horse, wasn't a plant, I didn't see the need. He was sincere, and that surprised me."

"Did he tell you why he was interested in your operation?"

"Yes. Apparently he had a dream for something called the Green Belt . . ."

"I'm familiar with his impossible dream," I said, "with his forest circling the world."

I was surprised when Dozier came to his defense. "Not so impossible," he said. "In this country alone, close to three billion seedlings are planted every year, most by the timber industry."

"Trying to do better than Mother Nature?"

"In some ways succeeding. Our trees grow faster, and larger. We develop healthy woods, and tend to our tree gardens carefully, because we know they are our lifeblood. We are quite aware that as we sow, so shall we reap."

"You didn't sow the old growth. And what you call reaping, others call raping."

"There is a higher percentage of redwoods preserved than any other commercially harvested species," Dozier said, "and there are more redwoods around today than when man first started harvesting them."

"Most of them young redwoods," I said, "second and third growth. While our remaining old growth is being swept away at a rate of three percent a year."

Dozier shook his head sadly. "Figures lie, and liars figure," he said. "I would have thought that your profession would have made you skeptical of statistics, Mr. Winter."

"It's done even better than that," I said. "It's made me suspicious of everything."

"Then you shouldn't get caught up in their big lie. Redwoods don't automatically become as old as the hills, nor do most grow to be thirty-story giants. The Green Man was smart enough not to be fixated on old growth. He knew that having an abundance of trees is more important than having a few groves with antique pedigrees."

Dozier stopped talking, cleared his throat.

"Go on," I said.

"I'm finished."

"Did Shepard tell you that? About the relative importance of old growth?"

Dozier exhaled, then nodded.

"I don't get it."

"What?"

"Why you're not broadcasting his sentiments from the rafters. Why you're not harpooning the whole *Yes on 150* campaign with those revelations."

"We had plans . . ."

Another statement started, then stopped again.

"But they were curtailed when he died?"

He nodded.

"You must regret having shut off your tape recorder that time he visited."

Dozier gave me a studied look, then offered a slight tilt to his head. I suddenly realized how many head nods I'd been getting. He'd been all too aware of the tape recorder, had been

146

unwilling to commit himself while it was on. As if thinking those same thoughts, he reached over and shut it off. That made me wonder what had really prompted him to stop recording his conversation with Shepard.

"Without proof," he said, "we knew it wouldn't be in our best interests to reveal Shepard's change of mind."

"And he just decided all of this out of the blue? Came to this conversion in front of you?"

"As I told you, he was impressed with our tree-planting operation. He knew we were good stewards and didn't think it a crime that we were protecting our own interests. He also didn't think that caring for trees and getting a return on investment were mutually exclusive endeavors. Would that other environmentalists were so pragmatic."

"Did you press him to speak out? Did he plan to make some sort of announcement?"

"At this point, such speculation would be moot. It was quite evident, however, that he was more concerned with the Green Belt than he was with old growth."

"How did you react when you heard that Shepard had died in River Grove?"

"Naturally, I was disappointed. And suspicious."

"Suspicious of whom?"

"The environmentalists. I know they were afraid of having one of their own offer a voice of reason. That might have helped stop their agenda of destroying an industry, and putting more lumber workers out of their jobs."

The figures I had read suggested that the mills were doing a good enough job of laying off workers through automating and shipping the jobs overseas, but I didn't want to cloud the issue.

"Do you think some renegade greens killed him?"

"I wouldn't rule out that possibility. I had our investigators look over the death site very carefully. I personally oversaw the operation."

"When did you go out there?"

"Right after they found him."

Dozier looked at his watch, a gold Rolex. The gesture and the timepiece were a reminder to me how precious his time was. "Have we concluded?"

147

"No," I said. "I still have some more questions about trees."

The topic didn't appear to bother him. Until I clarified. "Family trees."

Dozier looked decidedly uneasy.

"Your stepdaughter has been in the area quite a bit lately because of your wife's illness."

Dozier nodded.

"Where do you live?"

"On the outskirts of town."

"Does Ashe ever stay in your house?"

"She has not availed herself of that opportunity."

"How often does she see your wife?"

"I really couldn't tell you. We have a tacit understanding. I work Monday through Friday, from eight o'clock in the morning until five-thirty in the afternoon. If she visits during those hours, she's reasonably sure of not seeing me."

"Does your wife tell you when Ashe is in town?"

"She doesn't have to. If I come home, and Anne's upset, I know her daughter has visited."

"Why the ill feelings between you two?"

"She was spoiled. She thought I stole Anne's love. Before I married her mother, Ashe announced that she couldn't tolerate living with me, and that if we went ahead with our plans she would go to boarding school. I said she was welcome to make herself an exile, and she did."

"What happened to Ashe's father?"

"He died in a car accident when she was six."

"You and Ashe both love the same woman," I said. "That's something in common."

"There's something else we have in common," he said.

"What's that?"

"We hate each other."

▽

19

WHEN VOICED VEHEMENTLY, there's no stronger four-letter word than *hate*. Dozier hadn't qualified the emotion, had given it a profane emphasis. But he didn't allow me to pursue it further. Our talk was interrupted by his secretary, who reminded him of another appointment. I tried to wangle a few extra minutes, but he tapped at the crystal of his Rolex.

I got on the road and was trying to think, but my stomach was sending a lot of interference to my brain. The billboards weren't helping. Like Oscar Wilde I can resist everything but temptation. One in particular intrigued me. The Samoa Cookhouse was advertised as the last logging camp cookhouse in existence. That piqued my historical interest. The heaping displays of food played to a more primal need. I had a Paul Bunyan appetite and a gleam in my eye that probably would have set Babe to running.

Cookhouses were once a part of every logging camp. The appetites of loggers were legendary, with many of the lumberjacks selecting where they worked not on the basis of pay but on the victuals they were served.

The Samoa Cookhouse was an unprepossessing structure. It almost looked like a military barracks, and not a compound from a recent war but one from around the time of the war to end all wars. The restaurant was situated on a rise, with is parking lot overlooking the Louisiana-Pacific lumber mill. The cookhouse itself bore the ubiquitous L-P logo, but the restaurant was only leased from the mother company, which meant it no longer had to feed hungry loggers three times a day. Now its obligation was to the public. I wondered which was worse.

I arrived just as the cookhouse opened. The room was lined with picnic tables that were covered with red-and-white-checkered oilcloth. I was directed to a table which soon filled up. No one stayed a stranger long, what with all the passing around of food and the companionship of satisfied stomachs.

The cookhouse wasn't the kind of dining establishment where you mentioned the *C* words, like cholesterol, or carbohydrates, or calories. The service was casual but efficient, more like your Aunt Betty passing you food, and plenty of it, than a manikin telling you her name was Monique and the special of the day was ahi served with a sauce of papaya and lime and sprinkled with macadamia nut shavings. In short order I was offered salad, and soup, and homemade bread. Then the real eating began. I was told the cookhouse changed its menu every day, but today there was ham, and fried chicken, and all the fixings. I didn't aspire to gluttony but succeeded in spite of myself. When I thought I couldn't eat any more, they offered their homemade pie. And I found I could eat a little more.

The kitchen wasn't separated from the dining area, and the diners got to rubberneck the preparation and the platters of food coming out. Antique cooking utensils lined the wall, ladles and skillets and cutlery. The dining room chairs were anything but uniform; I counted four versions of four legs, and the wooden floors, though well varnished, looked like they had seen hordes of calk boots walking through. The napkins were housed in Farmer Brothers coffee cans, and the flatware was about as consistent as in most households, mismatched but serviceable.

I got the feeling things hadn't changed much at the cookhouse for the better part of a century, felt I had taken part in a lumberjack tradition. For the amount and quality of food serviced, the bill was ridiculously low. I loosened a notch on my belt, leaned back, and gave a contented sigh. My waitress kept coming back and offering me more food, which was my incentive to leave. Nothing like being killed by kindness.

Before waddling outside, I wandered through the restaurant's logging relics room. The minimuseum featured a collection of tools dating back to the age of muscle, the likes of which I had never seen, including drag saws and branding hammers, pickeral bars and chain binders, timber augers and splitting mills. The contest of man versus tree was more even in the old days, the payment for wood made with flesh, and blood, and sweat, and tears. Tall trees, and the men who dared to challenge them, had once been the stuff of tall tales. But it wasn't that way anymore.

One of the display cases featured climbing gear and pictures of the brave toppers hundreds of feet in the air, supported only by their climbing belts. The equipment didn't look too different from Teller's old harness, the one Doc had been using. I had seen in Teller's expression an almost fatherly pride when I had told him about Doc's climbing. I suspected Teller's tree climbing tutelage was much more than that, a stage that allowed him to show Doc how to pull himself up by his own bootstraps.

I walked outside and was confronted by the effluent rising from the smokestacks of the L-P mill. The spewing towers were constant backdrops to the immense Samoa operation. The mill could handle everything Bunyan could, and more, but it wasn't the grist of legends.

A full stomach doesn't necessarily make you think better, but with one you feel a lot more confident about taking on the world. I walked up to a phone booth and, instead of calling dial-a-prayer, I dialed a minister.

The Reverend Reginald Sawyer wasn't glad to hear from me. He told me that I had upset his wife, said that, "like her sex," she was delicate and nervous. I thought the notion of women as the weaker sex had gone out with the Victorians. Sawyer did everything but assert that she suffered from the vapors. He resisted the idea of a face to face until I hinted that perhaps his wife could answer my questions. Reluctantly, he invited me over.

Sawyer was waiting for me in the vestry. He had chosen a table away from the door, away from prying ears. Directly behind him was the mosaic. Whether by coincidence or not,

Sawyer had positioned himself in the same seat as Christ. That, or he purposely had his back to him.

He was scribbling when I came in, put his pen down as I took a seat. "I won't waste much of your time," I said.

Sawyer looked grateful for that. He appeared subdued. In my presence he hadn't talked much about man's dominion over old growth. The only thing that had gotten him excited was the Green Man, and even then I had had to push him.

"You vied against Shepard when he was alive," I said. "You thought him an enemy of your faith."

Without fervor, he gave me an imperceptible nod.

"Then how come, when he died, you were concerned enough to offer a plot and a headstone?"

"Christian charity."

"Why?"

"Love your enemy. Forgive trespassers. Turn the other cheek. There are many examples in the Good Book."

"How come you're so selective when it comes to practicing those examples?"

"I'm not perfect."

"You didn't like Shepard while he lived. You said he corrupted youths. You said he led them into evil practices. Why would you care about his burial arrangements?"

Sawyer didn't say anything at first, just looked off into space. "Maybe it was time to bury the ax."

"That's not what you're known for, Reverend. You're known for brandishing that ax."

"In the heat of an issue, rhetoric sometimes escalates."

"Sometimes, it's more than rhetoric that escalates."

He didn't comment.

"Shepard's death didn't change how you felt about him. You're not the type to bury the ax, or bury Shepard either. From your reputation, that's out of character for you."

"I hope my reputation is only that of a man of God," said Sawyer.

"Since the Green Man is now dead, who's the new enemy?"

Sawyer looked puzzled. "What do you mean?"

"It's easier to square off against a person than it is an issue. The Third Day gained renown when you attacked the Green Man. You personified the evil."

"He did that himself. I only asserted God-given truths."

"Strange how those assertions benefited some very powerful interests."

"It was mankind that they benefited."

"What about nature?"

"You speak like a pantheist. Worshiping nature is an affront to God."

"Why did God make the forests then? Because on the third day he was bored silly? Because it seemed like a good thing at the time?"

"He provided us resources for man's use."

"Then is it so wrong to want to leave some ancient vestiges of his handiwork?"

Reverend Sawyer didn't argue any further. I wondered what had happened to his renowned head of steam.

"Where does The Third Day get most of its funding?"

"Friends."

It was common knowledge who those friends were. "Lumber interests, I understand."

He shrugged.

"Does the dog wag the tail, or vice versa?"

"I don't understand."

"Do they call your editorial shots?"

"The Lord is my master."

"Have you gotten the word to attack the Green Goddess?"

"She presumes much with her blasphemous title."

"It wasn't a title she selected."

"But one she aspires to, that or the Great Whore of Babylon."

I had come to make him angry, but he was doing a better job of that on me. "The tough thing about making enemies is that they don't always stay that way," I said. "But I suppose you know that. Did you get the word to stop putting the heat on the Green Man? Did they tell you right before he died that he was really a friend? Is that why after his death you offered the plot and the headstone? Or were there other reasons?"

"I might consider making the same offer for you," he said.

"Is that a threat? Or just wishful thinking?"

"I'm a busy man, Mr. Winter, and I don't enjoy word games nearly as much as you do."

"Did it confuse you when they changed the Green Man's status from bad guy to good guy? And in your heart were you able to go along with that decision?"

"I'll leave you to your idle speculating, Mr. Winter."

I let myself out and walked along the sidewalk. I was deep in what Sawyer had more accurately than not called idle speculating when I heard the sound of clippers at work. Ruth Sawyer was doing some pruning in the middle of her rose garden. She was wearing a panama hat and had on a white dress. In the garden setting she almost looked comfortable, less nervous and harried.

She handled the garden shears expertly, didn't hack uncertainly like most weekend gardeners I know. Acknowledging my presence with a little smile, she continued her work. I watched her prune for a minute, and that didn't seem to bother her. "Another vanity?" I asked.

She remembered her reference and blushed a little. "I suppose," she said, wistfully touching one of the remaining flowers. "You should have seen these roses a month ago. They were in full bloom then. They were bright and vibrant and full of life. Now there's not much life to them."

I leaned over and smelled the wilted blossom. There was still a sweet reminder of life. "They say a rose forgives better than all things," I said, "offering a fragrant scent even to the heel that steps on it."

"I hope you can be as forgiving for my outburst yesterday."

"As forgiving as a rose."

She smiled a little, then started cutting into another branch. White petals dropped to the ground. I picked up a few of the tears and said frivolously, "She loves me, she loves me not."

Ruth moved on to another rosebush. I knew she wasn't through talking, but I wanted her to speak in her own way and time. When she was finally satisfied with the cut, she did her own examination of the fallen petals. This bush was shedding pink. She picked up some petals and held them outstretched in one hand. She didn't talk of love, as I had. "He died in a strange and terrible way, didn't he?"

"Yes."

She let the petals drop from her hand. "I think that was proof of God's judgment."

"That presumes much."

"My husband thinks God's hand is in everything."

"He didn't think it was in Shepard's death."

She nodded uncertainly, as if that didn't make sense, as if there should be no exception to his rules. Then, as if seeking an escape from thinking, she picked up the shears again and started on another bush, began to cut into it vigorously. Her target was more overgrown than the others, and she attacked it with a ferocity she hadn't shown before. Branches, and petals, and leaves fell. Then, unexpectedly, the shears themselves dropped.

"Oh," she said. "Oh."

I looked to see what was the matter. At first I thought she had cut herself badly. She was mewling in pain and misery, hugging herself while shivering violently. Then I saw what had upset her. A mouse was impaled upon a large thorn.

"Oh," she said, her hurt sounding very deep. "Oh."

Her trimming had opened a window she didn't want to look through. I reached out and held her, and tried to explain about shrikes, told her how I had seen one in the field just the day before. I talked through her despair, and, when I ran short of words, I made soothing sounds.

The mouse was a couple of days removed from being cute. It was hooked from its neck. Shrikes hang their prey that way. They like to feed from the head down. I suppose shrikes think they've found a better mousetrap, but it's not one the world is going to beat a path to buy.

Gradually Ruth's cries became less frequent, and her sobs more hiccups than anything else. Her shivering lessened, and I released her from my arms. She didn't say anything, just walked away from me toward the parsonage.

I pulled the mouse from the thorn, then tossed it into some shrubbery. I hoped that shrike would forgive me for getting between him and his larder. In some ways I felt as if I had stolen his meal. I owed him for the food for thought, if nothing else.

▽

20

THE SWEETWATER CAMP looked almost deserted, with only a few of the campers moving languidly about. I intercepted a young man on his way down to the river and asked him where everyone was.

"Siesta time for some," he said, scratching his unshaven chin and stretching, "berry time for most."

"Berry time?"

"Blackberries, man. Harvest time."

He started to walk away when I stopped him again. "Is Sasha here?" I asked.

"Think so," he said. "Look for the tent with flowers."

I walked around the campground. On my nightly visits I hadn't noticed that some of the tents were decorated. There was an abundance of artistic efforts, most suggesting there is something to be said for not having too much spare time.

The tents were painted with trees, and slogans, and peace symbols, Peter Max colors and flowers. There were so many artistic bouquets that I despaired of finding Sasha's quarters. Then I saw what had to be her tent. The flowers were planted, not painted. She had beds of geraniums and mums. The cheery plantings created a homey atmosphere. There was even a welcome mat in front of her tent.

"Hello," I said. "Anybody home?"

There was a rustling from inside. I could hear Sasha's bracelets clanging. The tent flap rose; then she gave me a big smile. "Hello, Stuart!" she said. My pasta server looked glad to see me. She held out her hand, just as she had at my first Circle, and welcomed me inside. "Come on in."

Her tent wasn't exactly spacious, but it was protection from the wind that had picked up outside. Sasha sat down easily, planted her legs under her tail, and immediately looked comfortable. It took me about a minute to get considerably less than comfortable.

"Want a drink?" she asked.

I raised an eyebrow.

"Kool-Aid," she explained. "I've got cherry, grape, or orange."

I passed. Sasha decided on grape. She poured the contents into a pint container filled with water, then shook it up.

"You decided to pass on the blackberry expedition?" I asked.

She nodded, took a swig of her grape drink and puckered her lips appreciatively. "A couple of people have already asked me about making cobbler," she said. "I told them that with the solar oven we'd just have to see. The thing's not exactly a convection oven."

"Are you the cook?"

"Someone's got to be," she said, "otherwise we wouldn't eat. Amazing how everyone's willing to eat the food, and complain about it, but no one's willing to help with the work."

"Must be tough cooking for so many."

"Not really. It's not like there's much variety to the menu. We don't have the money, so we're big into the starches."

She patted her thighs dubiously. "You'd think I would have lost a few pounds while being up here, but no way."

"Where's home?"

"Pasadena."

"What do your folks think about your being here?"

"They're not crazy about it. They see those snippets on TV, the ones where Humboldt looks like an armed camp, and the movement seems like it's advocating revolution, and they think I'm involved with a bunch of dangerous kooks and that all sorts of things are going on. What they don't understand is that most days are like this: quiet and no marching."

"But not all days?"

She considered that for a moment. "No, not all days."

"How long have you been here?"

"Since June the third."

Four months. "What do your friends say?"

Sasha shrugged. "A couple still write. They're mostly involved with school and boyfriends. I don't think they understand why I'm up here."

"Why did you stay when most of the others left? Camp was supposed to close on Labor Day. Certainly no one could have blamed you for leaving."

She shook her head. "It's not that," she said. "I just couldn't leave. It wouldn't have seemed right just sitting in some class at my JC. After what happened, I wasn't ready to leave."

"What did you think of the Green Man?"

"I thought he was a great man."

"Did everybody?"

She rubbed her hand along her plump cheek. "No."

"Why not?"

"You can't please all of the people all of the time," she said.

"That's an answer I'd expect from someone sitting in some class at a JC," I said, "not from a savvy member of the movement."

My teasing got Sasha to blush a little but didn't gain me a better answer.

"I noticed your name on the tree-sitting list," I said.

Sasha shrugged. "Everybody gets Methuselah duty."

"How does that work?"

"You just sign up."

"You tree-sat on September second."

"So what?"

"Does anything about that day stand out in your mind?"

"Should it?"

I could feel Sasha being evasive again. But that didn't bring me any closer to figuring out what had happened that day.

"You relieved someone named Barry. He had the seven-to-three shift. You got the three-to-eleven watch. It must have been windy."

158

"It wasn't bad to begin with," she said. "But toward the end it was really beginning to blow."

"When did it pick up?"

"Eight o'clock. Maybe nine o'clock."

"Odd," I said.

"What?"

"There wasn't any Circle that night. Everyone said it was too windy. If the wind picked up that late, it shouldn't have affected Circle."

Sasha spoke too quickly. "It probably started earlier."

"Was Teller on time that night?"

She didn't immediately answer, looked as if she was stuck for what to say.

"Teller had the graveyard shift," I said, "didn't he?"

"No," she said.

"No?"

"Teller didn't feel well that night. Doc replaced him."

"Doc? Had he ever tree-sat before?"

Sasha smiled. The thought seemed to amuse her. "No. He was just doing Teller a favor."

"What's so funny?"

"The idea of Doc tree-sitting. He's always trying to be so scientific."

"Does he hang around camp much?"

"Only during mealtimes." Then Sasha smiled again. "And when Jane was here."

I feigned ignorance. "Who was Jane?"

"His summer romance. Everybody around here seems to have had one." She looked at me, perhaps a bit hopefully. "Maybe I'll luck out in the fall."

"Did Jane leave around Labor Day?"

Sasha thought for a few seconds. "Before that. End of July, I think."

"Why?"

"Who can figure it? Maybe some people just don't take to no running water, outhouses, mosquitoes, and a lot of baked beans."

"Was that it?"

Sasha avoided my gaze. "It wasn't like I knew her that well," she said.

159

"You're not your sister's keeper?"

"Exactly."

"Come on, Sasha," I said. "Give."

"It doesn't sound right," she said. "You're an outsider. You wouldn't understand."

"Try me."

"Jane wasn't—hip," Sasha said, not sure how to begin her story, or end it.

How had Doc described her? He said she liked to go around reciting Joyce Kilmer poetry. Definitely not hip.

"And she got pretty upset at some of the things that were going on."

"Things?"

"I can't explain."

I could feel Sasha's dilemma, wanting to tell me, yet not wanting to betray those around her. But why her embarrassment? Then I remembered.

"Did she go to one of the Green Man's ceremonies?"

Sasha looked relieved. She didn't know I had known. "Yes," she said. "She was disgusted."

"Disgusted that the Green Man was walking around without clothes, and invoking the spirits of the woods, and conducting rituals?"

"Disgusted with everything. She freaked out. We told her it was all in fun, that it was just a way of remembering the forests, and how they were once holy, but she didn't want to hear that. She thought it was perverted and decided to leave. Jane was twenty going on twelve. It's usually the other way around."

"Did you ever attend any of the ceremonies?" I asked.

Sasha shook her head. "I was curious," she said, "but I didn't. I guess I like my clothes on." Then in a little voice she added, "Most of the time."

I couldn't tell whether she was making a pass at me or not, so I did as I had been taught in the woods: I offered her my hand.

We held hands for a few minutes, listened to the wind whistling against her tent. It wasn't a summer romance, but it felt good anyway.

▽

21

I GOT INTO ROCINANTE, and we started to drive. I didn't have any preconceived notion of where we were traveling, left it up to my steed. When the road signs started popping up showing the mileage to San Francisco, I should have been surprised. Part of me thought it was a big mistake to be leaving Humboldt County, but I knew I needed a day or two to think. I had to get away from the redwoods or I'd never be able to see the forest for the trees.

The puzzles played over and over in my mind. There was plenty to piece out, considerations that left room for collusion and conspiracies. I thought about the gaps, and who the Green Man's death would have benefited most, and why he had had to die.

I don't think I noticed the WELCOME TO SAN FRANCISCO sign, and I would swear that I didn't have any conscious thoughts about visiting Golden Gate Park, but somehow I found myself there. Bewildered, I looked around. This wasn't any time to be traipsing around a park. But maybe that's what I need, I thought. A day away. I got out and started walking. My legs knew where to go.

The Golden Gate Park is situated on over a thousand acres and features museums, cultural exhibits, and open space. There is a Japanese tea garden, an aquarium, a planetarium, and an arboretum. I didn't go to any of those places. I went to the John McLaren Rhododendron Dell.

McLaren had moved from Scotland to California in 1870. When he saw the redwoods, he fell in love. He said he wanted to plant trees, especially redwoods. McLaren didn't think small. He announced that during his lifetime he hoped to plant one million trees. By the time he died in 1943, at age ninety-seven, he had planted his one million and then some.

In many ways the Golden Gate Park is McLaren's legacy. When he became the park's chief gardener in 1887, its area consisted mostly of sand dunes. Through his ingenuity in building walls and pumping water and creating landscapes, McLaren sculpted one of the great parks of the world.

San Francisco's own Green Man was not without his quirks. He was fanatical about some things. McLaren hated statues, thought the true monuments should be his trees and plants. Whenever the City put statues in his park ("stookies," he called them), the dour Scotsman tried to hide them with his plantings.

McLaren would not have approved of the stookie erected to him at the rhododendron dell, but he would have loved the twenty acres and over 140 varieties of rhododendrons his statue overlooked. In his lifetime he had seen to the planting of over five thousand species in the park, had created life out of dust.

And what of youthful vows? McLaren had never forgotten his intention to grow redwoods. I went to admire the grove he had raised from seed. His father had often told McLaren that, if he had nothing to do, he should always go out and plant a tree, because it would grow even while he slept. Mc-Laren had put his redwood seeds in the Golden Gate's ground when he was eighty years old. When he died seventeen years later, his redwoods stood thirty feet high. In his long sleep since, they have grown much higher.

I sat in the park for a few hours and thought about McLaren and the redwoods. McLaren hadn't wanted his park to be merely a showpiece, a place that people couldn't enjoy. One of his demands when he took the job was that there were to be no KEEP OFF THE GRASS signs in his park. Around me Frisbees were flying, and babies were crawling, and people were reading, and lovers were kissing. No one was keeping off the grass.

With the sun setting, I decided to go home. There are about fifty hills in San Francisco, give or take a couple. The figure is contested, because residents of the city like to make mountains out of their molehills. In the early days of San Francisco, no one wanted to live on a hill. A slope that you had to trudge up wasn't anybody's idea of a prime location. The poor were relegated to the nosebleed seats until mechanization made the ascents easier and the nabobs discovered the views, realized how nice it was to look down on the world from their castles in the sky. Like Jack and Jill, the poor were eventually sent tumbling down the hills. Or at least most of them.

I live in a rental on Potrero Hill, a subdivided frame house on Carolina Street. When giving directions to my place, I always instruct visitors to look for the thorn between two roses. My house is nestled between two Victorians, but that's not to say the area is a museum piece; the Potrero district hasn't gentrified nearly as much as most of the other hills. It's a polyglot working neighborhood, at least for now. I keep watching for extensive renovations, for telltale signs of encroaching espresso roosts, or bubble-bath dens. Luckily, I'm not the only one. The Neighborhood Watch isn't only for criminals; I think most of us are on the watch for developers.

I took a suspicious look around my neighborhood and didn't see any new construction, so I decided I could enjoy the view. Swiveling my head around in Linda Blair fashion, I saw the bay to the east, the city to the north, and Twin Peaks to the west. Then, I took a deep breath. The aroma was courtesy of Hills Bros. Coffee. They do their roasting down the hill. Whenever I sniff for very long, I can always pick up some of their wafting scent. My senses told me I was home. My mind wasn't as accommodating. The case stayed with me.

The telephone awakened me from a reverie that had me back in Humboldt County. Like Archimedes, I kept looking for the opportunity to shout "Eureka." Norman Cohen was a welcome interruption. Norman's a psychoanalyst. Most of his patients have too much time, and too much money. As I often remind him, he's not afraid to help them waste both.

Norman wanted to know what I was up to, and whether

I was busy for dinner. I briefly told him about the case, which prompted him to pick our dining spot: Greens.

The vegetarian restaurant is at Fort Mason. Norman was waiting for me inside. Greens' association with San Francisco's Zen Center might also have entered into Norman's decision for us to dine there. A few weeks earlier he had announced, in typically dramatic fashion, that he was becoming a Zen Buddhist. Norman was always becoming something or other.

As usual, Greens was full. Most people remember the food at Greens, and the wall of windows that look out to the berthed boats, San Francisco Bay, the Golden Gate Bridge, and the Marin headlands. I had forgotten about the huge redwood burl that divided the restaurant and the waiting area. The natural sculpture had been burnished to a brilliant burnt sienna. I got to admire it up close, because we were seated next to it. Redwood country, and the case, kept following me.

We stuck our noses in the menus and had to do some deep stomach searching. One of the problems with Greens is that there are too many choices, but we were hungry enough to do plenty of ordering. I had the jicama-orange salad, and Norman had the lentil salad with mint, roasted peppers, and feta cheese. We both ordered a cup of black bean chili with olive oil bread, and for my main course I settled on the rosemary linguine with caramelized onions and walnuts, and Norman had the eggplant gratin with saffron custard.

Norman started talking about all the inner discoveries he was making through Buddhism. I figured the similarities between Norman and Buddha started and finished at their waistlines—Buddha is usually portrayed with an ample belly. But while Buddha's stomach would have evolved from sedentary thinking, Norman's came from a love of eating. I didn't see him with a begging bowl and robe any time soon.

We talked about my case. My hand kept unconsciously reaching out to the redwood. Norman thought I had done the right thing to come back to San Francisco. "Your mind will sort things out here," he said. "Give it a little time. Examine your dreams."

His birthday was the next week, so I gave him an early

present. I told him about my green dream. That seemed to make him happy.

Then it was his turn to talk. Usually, I'm a better listener. I vaguely heard him go on about his ashram and some of the wonderful things he was learning. He turned philosophical, talked about his zazen training, and then, with a dramatic whisper, asked me one of those ancient Buddhist unanswerables: "If a tree falls in a forest, and no one is there to hear it fall, does it make a noise?"

My preoccupation showed through. I had my own deep thinking to do, but it didn't involve falling trees so much as falling branches. "If a man falls in a forest and never gets up," I countered, "and no one was there to see him fall, was he murdered?"

Norman didn't like his philosophical toes stepped on. He asked for the check from our green-aproned server.

Later that night, I called Miss Tuntland. I started the conversation by saying, "I keep thinking I'm barking up the wrong tree."

She laughed, and I felt better. I wondered if she looked forward to my voice as much as I did hers. Miss Tuntland is a year older than I, and maybe a few decades wiser. The month before she had turned thirty-nine, and, as she was quick to point out, that "wasn't a Jack Benny thirty-nine." Guile wasn't in Miss Tuntland's nature. She had once told me she had a Norwegian face, a French bosom, an Italian backside, and, above all, a Yankee sensibility. I knew about the last but couldn't help but be beguiled by the rest of her United Nations description. For two people as close as we were, it was damn strange we'd never seen each other. We both knew that, but both of us were also afraid of a face to face. I wondered if it was easier for me to accept her as a ghost, a vibrant voice in my ear, rather than as a person.

"Maybe I can offer you a few more trees," she said.

"Woof."

"Ruth Sawyer," she said, pretending she hadn't heard, "isn't a local girl. In fact, two years ago she came straight from Mombasa to Ferndale and married the Reverend Reginald Sawyer. Her parents are missionaries, and, from what

I could gather, they arranged her marriage. They were old friends of Sawyer, having served with him in an African mission about a dozen years ago."

"An arranged marriage," I mused. "Not exactly a modern practice."

"Ruth was apparently quite willing. Mombasa didn't offer much in the way of marriage material."

I'd heard the same thing said about San Francisco, but I didn't see that many single women jumping to marry men twenty years their senior. But it wasn't the age factor that bothered me so much as something else, something I still couldn't pin down.

Miss Tuntland assumed my quiet was a desire to hear more, so she briefed me on Reverend Sawyer. His background surprised me. She said he had never been an activist until the past year, had toiled quietly in the fields of the Lord throughout his ministry. Even his first few years at Ferndale had been quiet. But that had changed. He had started speaking out from the pulpit, warning against the evils of pantheism and tree worship. Less than a year ago he had formed The Third Day. Miss Tuntland said there were no public documents on 3-D's funding, but it was commonly assumed that it was "generously supported by lumber money." Harold Dozier, in particular, was a prominent attendee at many of their functions.

Don McLellan was Miss Tuntland's final subject. I had forgotten that I had asked her about him and couldn't even remember why I had thought him important to the case. She said that McLellan hadn't always stayed in his woods. He had enjoyed bicycling and often rode as far as Eureka. Although he didn't wear his silver hard hat while he cycled, McLellan was easily identified by the long black coat he wore. It flapped as he rode, a banner almost as identifiable as his flags. The hermit apparently hadn't liked living in the open as much as the Green Man had. Miss Tuntland said McLellan had installed thick redwood doors in his goosepens and locked those doors with steel padlocks.

"One time he took a bicycle trip," she said, "and stopped in Scotia, where he demanded to see the head of the Pacific Lumber Company. No underling would do. When the executive presented himself, McLellan handed him the keys to his goosepens and said he was entrusting him to hold them until his return."

He had probably been good for a lot of laughs, I thought. The local eccentric in the woods handing over his keys to the forest. But something sounded a little off.

"Keys?"

"Three of them" said Miss Tuntland. "One for each of his three goosepens."

"Does Goldilocks enter somewhere into this story?"

"The goosepens served different functions," she said. "He lived in one, kept his bicycle and his climbing equipment in another, and the third one he used as a smokehouse."

The Green Man had only had one goosepen, I thought. But then McLellan had lived in the woods for more than a year, and Shepard had only been there during the temperate summer.

"I even did a little research on giant Leucænas," said Miss Tuntland, "today's miracle trees."

"And here I've only heard of the burning bush."

"You're behind the times, as usual. In the tropics, a giant Leucæna can grow more than twenty feet in its first year. Its seedpods are excellent nutrition for people, and the leaves are exceptional fodder for livestock. Even its roots fertilize the soil. And Leucæna wood is as good for furniture and building as it is for burning."

I thought about that. Then I said, "Tell me, Miss Tuntland. Does it make a good cross?"

▽

22

I WAS UP BEFORE the sun and on the road a little before 5:00 A.M. I pushed Rocinante well over the speed limit and made it to Ashe's cabin in about four hours. I hadn't shaved, hadn't slept much, and looked like hell. There was a sharpness to my rapping, an impatience. She came to the door dressed up, ready to leave. She also came with a .22 in her hand.

"When I left your place here the other night," I said, "someone else pulled a gun on me."

"The other night was a mistake, Stuart."

"But holding a gun on me isn't?"

She remembered the firepiece and tucked it discreetly into her purse.

"Worried about something?"

"There have been a few death threats," she said. "I don't carry a pistol because of its designer look."

"Since you feel you're in danger, why don't you stay in a safer spot?"

"Because I like it here. Because I don't like having my lifestyle dictated to me. Because it's convenient to Sweetwater."

"And it's far enough from Lofield and your stepfather."

She didn't comment. We sat in the same chairs as we had on my previous visit. I wasn't the only one thinking that. We leaned away from each other, afraid to be close, afraid to remember.

"Shepard was seeing a woman," I said. "She was visiting him in River Grove the night he died."

I told her about his babe in the woods. Ashe was a good listener. When I finished, we looked at each other for a long time.

"You have questions, I suppose," she said.

I nodded.

"Your story doesn't surprise me. Christopher was that way. As far as I know, he only made love out of doors."

"That was your experience?"

She nodded. "He said that walls were constraining, that they kept emotions in check. Outside, in the groves, he said you were free."

"I thought you told me he was attracted to inhibited women."

"I did."

"By description, this woman was about as quiet as a heavy-metal concert."

Ashe blushed. "Maybe she was partially that way—for him."

"What do you mean?"

"Christopher's desire was for emancipation of the spirit. If he could get a woman to say things, and do things, and experience things, that she had never done before, then he was excited. The exhilaration of freedom, of breaking out, can be quite heady. Christopher would have been cheering her on, encouraging her."

"So you're saying she was screaming for herself, and for him?"

She nodded. The silence between us grew. Abruptly, she kicked the dirty hardwood floor.

"Ask the question," she demanded.

I did. "Were you his lover that night?"

"No." she said. "Disappointed?"

As an investigator, or as a potential lover? "I'll live. Shepard didn't."

"That doesn't mean he was murdered either."

"You can't have it both ways, Ashe. You can't privately tell me he was done in by a widow-maker and publicly associate with groups who all but say the lumber interests killed him."

"And you can't say the timber industry is innocent, even

if they didn't actually kill him. They're the killers of nature."

"That's not the case I'm working on. I was hired to try to find out how a man—or should I say a myth?—died."

"If you're not part of the solution, you're part of the problem."

"That was trite even back in the sixties."

"Do you like snooping in dirty doorways, or do you like taking a stand?"

"I like bringing murderers to justice."

"Is that what this is? Murder?"

"I think so."

"Why?"

"Too many people have too many secrets."

"That hardly qualifies as a smoking gun."

"No. But I find it more interesting than the smoking limb theory."

"Am I a suspect?"

"Shepard has proved more valuable dead than alive to your cause. He was a liability while he was alive. What you described as naiveté could have been interpreted by others as something much more insidious. Then there was the matter of his meeting with your stepfather in late August and getting a personal tour of the Trans-Mississippi tree-planting operation. The word is that Shepard might have been soft on the old-growth issue. Or more than soft."

Almost imperceptibly, Ashe nodded.

"You and your stepfather have a virulent dislike for each other," I said. "Your attitudes go beyond familial discord. I'd like to know why you hate him."

Ashe didn't immediately answer. "Maybe because I think he's a murderer," she said.

"Of the Green Man?"

"No. Of my mother."

"Explain."

"My mother has ovarian cancer." Ashe made the statement like it should explain everything.

"I can sympathize, but I still don't see—"

"Have you heard of the drug taxol?"

"No."

"To make a kilogram of taxol, you need twenty thousand

pounds of yew bark. My stepfather's company, all logging companies, have long considered the Pacific yew a waste tree, a weed if you will. It grows in the old forests from the south of Alaska to northern California. It's an understory tree, not the kind of tree people ever even notice. The yew isn't a fast-growing tree. It has a thin, purplish bark. It takes time to get substantial amounts of bark, hundreds of years. Logging companies don't have that kind of patience—for either trees or humans."

A tear ran down her face. She struggled to keep talking. "Clinical trials have shown that taxol reduces melanoma tumors. There have been promising results, especially with ovarian cancer. But the doctors don't even have enough taxol to continue these studies. And they don't have enough taxol to give to my mother."

I wanted to wipe away Ashe's tear. I wanted to comfort her. But I guess I wanted answers more.

"Does your mother blame him?"

"No. But he thinks she does. She pressed him on the yews, and the taxol. It made him angry. He couldn't lash out at a sick woman, though, so he blamed the messenger. He blamed me."

"That's why he hates you?"

She nodded. "He's a control freak. My mother always toed his line before, and now, in the end, she's become her own woman. She's questioning things. He doesn't like that."

"What's she questioning?"

"Everything. Tin gods can't stand losing their true believers. He can't tell her to have faith in him and everything will be all right."

It was all very neat. It explained why daughter and stepfather couldn't stand each other. But I didn't think it explained enough.

"I'm late," said Ashe. "I'm supposed to be in Sacramento by one o'clock."

We both got up from our chairs at the same time, touched by accident, and felt the electricity spark up once more between us. Again, she stepped back, either afraid of me or afraid of herself.

"When you think of flailing limbs," I asked, "do you only think of trees?"

$\triangledown$

23

ASHE DIDN'T ANSWER the question. She drove one way, and I drove the other. I had the feeling she wouldn't have approved of where I was going.

Harold Dozier's address was listed in the Humboldt County telephone book. It was a solitary entry. Not Harold and Anne Dozier, just Harold. I wonder about married men who list their names alone, and I wonder about the women who let them.

The Doziers' home was a five-minute drive from Lofield's Trans-Miss plant. The house was set well back from the street, in the middle of several acres. Most Lofield residences used indigenous trees and plants in their landscaping: redwoods, and oaks, and madrones, and scrub. Dozier, or his gardener, preferred the imports: Japanese maples, pink dogwoods, cider gum eucalyptus, and shrubbery dominated by lilacs and gardenias.

I walked up the long path and rang the doorbell. I expected a servant or a nurse to answer, but Anne Dozier surprised me by opening the door herself. I saw hints of Ashe in her, but only hints. It's difficult finding resemblances between the very sick and the very healthy. Mrs. Dozier had a consumptive thinness and a pallid complexion. Her funereal appearance contrasted with her dress, a pastel floral pattern. Mind and body were clearly not yet in accord.

I identified myself, said I had been hired to look into the

death of Christopher Shepard, and offered her my business card. For a few seconds the card and my hand hung in the air. But Mrs. Dozier wasn't interested in the card. She stared at me, finally nodded, and motioned for me to enter.

"You're in luck, Mr. Winter. I actually dressed and got out of bed today, and told Marian to go shopping. Otherwise I wouldn't have answered the door, and she wouldn't have let you see me. Our timing was right. I consider that an omen. I'm considering lots of things omens these days."

I followed her down the hall. We progressed slowly toward the living room, Mrs. Dozier making sure of each step. "Would you care for coffee?" she asked, not bothering to turn her head, or not daring the effort.

"No, thank you."

"Thank God. It probably would have taken me half an hour to walk to the kitchen. I woke up stiff today. I'm not sure whether it's the illness or the medication. Between one and the other, I have my symptoms du jour."

She seated herself on a black leather chair with a grateful sigh. I found a place on the matching sofa. The living room was made up of contrasting blacks and whites, almost a checkerboard motif: black baby grand Steinway piano atop thick, white carpeting; white porcelain lamps resting on black inlaid art deco tables; black wrought-iron sculptures bookending a white marble fireplace.

Mrs. Dozier looked at me expectantly. My eyes are gray—not in keeping with the decor. That might have been why she noticed them.

"You have unusual eyes, Mr. Winter. Not quite hazel, and not quite green."

"Gray," I said.

"An uncommon color."

"For eyes, maybe."

"They become you. But I imagine they change color in different lights."

"Just like people."

She half-laughed and half-coughed behind her hand. "Cynical."

"No, curious. Right now I'm trying to find out if the Green Man changed colors."

"You're direct. I like that. I can especially appreciate that nowadays."

She didn't appreciate it enough, though, to comment any further. "You know I have cancer?"

"I've heard about it from your daughter, and your husband."

"Same cancer," she said, with that coughing laugh of hers. "I don't know if they'd agree."

"They wouldn't. The only thing they would agree on is that I shouldn't be talking with you."

"But you're talking with me anyway."

"Why not? Illness offers you the opportunity to act with impunity. It's brought me a freedom I never had before. Isn't that strange?"

I nodded.

"We're both investigating death, aren't we, Mr. Winter?"

I didn't say anything, wasn't sure how I should respond. She didn't want pity, and I didn't want to give her the kind of honesty she demanded. Investigating a death is easy. Investigating the living is where most of us stumble.

"My husband and daughter treat my illness very differently. Harold thinks that if neither one of us talks about it, my cancer doesn't exist. Ashe is just the opposite. She wants to talk everything through, thinks that together we can lick it. She's big on the holistic and homeopathic approaches, and is always bringing me some new age healing process, everything from visualization to extracts of yarrow and foxglove. You name it, she's suggested it."

"Taxol."

She sighed. "Yes. But miracles don't come easily, do they? It was difficult accepting that there weren't enough old yews. I pressed my husband to help me get my magic potion. It was a difficult time. I was in my denial and anger stages then."

"I still am."

She gave me a little smile, then drifted away to other thoughts, spoke more to herself than to me. "I used to say it over and over again like an incantation: Yew. Harold must have thought me mad."

I didn't interrupt her reverie. "Yew," she said again. "It

wasn't a word, or a tree, with which I was familiar. But then someone reminded me that Robin Hood's bow was made of yew."

She looked at me, remembered my presence. "Your Green Man wasn't an archer, was he?"

"Not that I know."

"I keep thinking it was an arrow they found in his head, but it wasn't, was it?"

"No. It was a branch."

"That's right. A widow-maker."

She had brought up his name again, so I brought up my surmise. "Did he meet with your husband here?"

"I don't know if I'm quite ready to give you my deathbed confession, Mr. Winter. Let's wait a few minutes, shall we? But do be clever in the meantime, and tell me why you suspect what you do."

She closed her eyes. I didn't have a bedtime story. I didn't even have very much in the way of cleverness. "Your husband was very careful to tell me that the Green Man only visited his office one time," I said. "Later, I thought about what he had, and hadn't said. I call it listening for echoes. He implied they hadn't met in other places at other times, but he didn't preclude that possibility.

"Your husband also mentioned that Ashe knew what hours he worked at the office, and that if she visited during them she could be *reasonably* sure of not seeing him. He qualified his statement with that one word, but I didn't pick up on it at the time. He didn't say he never saw her, just made it clear that they tried to avoid each other.

"And finally, though neither your husband nor your daughter tried to hide how each felt about the other, I'm not satisfied with either's reasons. I think something escalated their feelings, something recent, and something that I suspect involved the Green Man."

She opened her eyes, turned them in my direction. "So who are you asking me to betray, Mr. Winter, my husband or my daughter?"

"Maybe neither. Maybe both."

"That's a lot to consider," she said, "and there's already so much to think about."

Mrs. Dozier closed her eyes again. For a minute I thought she had gone to sleep. When she finally started talking, her eyes were still closed.

"Lately, Mr. Winter, I've had to think of what comes before alpha, and after omega. You'll think me odd, no doubt, when I tell you that I've started to imagine myself as a seed almost ready to be planted. I know that with the right rain, and the right earth, I'll bloom again. Maybe not in the same form. Maybe not as anything recognizable. But I feel as if I'm now going through a great metamorphosis.

"I think of nature's examples of rebirth, of frogs that bury themselves in the ground for many years awaiting a little rain, and seventeen-year cicadas, and the unseen life that exists in the dryness of a vernal pool. I think of tardigrades that can lie dormant for so long, and the seeds left with mummies for millennia, seeds still ready to germinate. And I think of myself, and know there's a vibrant part of me that's alive, that's full of secrets. No one sees that part anymore. They see a worn vessel that's not really me. I know that something else, something greater, is waiting to come out. Can you understand that?"

"Yes."

She opened her eyes again, looked at me to see if I really did understand, and was apparently satisfied by what she saw.

"I don't know what's right or wrong anymore, Mr. Winter. I'm not sensible like I once was. I think that's what upsets Harold the most. I say things that he doesn't understand. And I do things that make him angry. Or will make him angry. Like talking with you."

"And giving me answers?"

"Offering a few seeds, perhaps."

"Did the Green Man visit this house?"

She breathed, and decided. "Yes."

"Did you meet him?"

"No. I was in bed dozing and awakened to voices. One of them was Harold's. I called to him, and he came upstairs and told me he was meeting with a business client."

"How long did they talk?"

"An hour or two. I'm not sure."

"Did you hear what they said?"

"No."

"So how did you know your husband was talking to the Green Man?"

"It was Ashe who announced that to the world. When she walked in on them, she screamed, 'Christopher!' And after that a lot more screaming ensued."

"Whose?"

"Ashe's mostly."

"How long did the shouting go on?"

"For five or ten minutes."

"Did you hear what was said?"

"I heard the tone of what was being said. It wasn't pretty. It never is when Harold and Ashe get together, but this was worse than I'd ever heard them before."

"Did you hear the Green Man speak?"

"I heard him try and speak a few times. But Ashe was beside herself. She wouldn't let him."

"Did you come downstairs?"

"No."

"Why not?"

"Getting between a dog and a cat usually only gets you scratched or bitten."

"But eventually you got an explanation?"

"Two explanations."

"I'd like to hear them."

"After the confrontation, Ashe came upstairs. She said that Christopher had sold her out."

"Do you know what she was talking about?"

"No."

"What else did Ashe say?"

"She didn't stay very long. She was upset. She said he was a traitor. She said that thirty pieces were still thirty pieces, no matter how the counting, and how the justifying, was done. And then she left."

"When did you get your husband's version?"

"Not until later. He had gone back to his office. When he came home, he wasn't very inclined to talk about what had happened. He just said that part of business was cutting corners, and saving money where you could."

Two explanations. But I was still short the Green Man's.

▽

24

I STOPPED AT a diner in town and ordered the Lumberjack's Breakfast, which consisted of three eggs, hash browns, three pancakes, and three links of sausage. While cutting up the pancakes and sausage, I looked for spikes but didn't find any. A few of the pieces were starting to come together. Finally. I tried to line my dominoes up in place. Ecotage was on my mind. There had been much made of EverGreen's participation in Sequoia Summer. They had agreed to forsake their guerrilla activities for passive resistance. I suspected that as the summer passed and the old trees continued to fall, it had become more difficult for the EverGreeners to bridle their passions and exercise restraint. Among them were those who were adept at taking out heavy logging equipment with salt, or dry rice, or Super Glue, who knew how to make logging roads impassable with spikes, and metal punji stakes, and caltrops.

I believed a clandestine ecotage campaign had been organized on the night the Green Man died. None of the campers wanted to talk about what had gone on that night, or they conveniently couldn't remember. There had been no Circle planned. There were also the matters of Bigfoot and the clay.

When I had first walked into the Sweetwater camp, the potter's wheel, and the clay, and the propane kiln, hadn't made much of an impression on me. Only in my subconscious had I recognized them as something not quite as innocent as a Coleman stove, something just a little out of place. You expect campers, especially young campers, to play with mud and clay, and most of those participating in Sequoia Summer were only a few years removed from their summer camp days. I should have noticed that there were no misshapen mugs or droopy vases sitting around, should have wondered why I never saw any artisans hunched over the potter's wheel. But then it's easy to overlook clay. It's benign. It's earthy. Fire it up, though, and you can make ceramic pieces that rival the firmness of metal.

Over the last decade, the threat of tree spiking has prompted many sawmills to examine their logs for metal debris. Some even go so far as to routinely scan the wood with metal-detecting equipment, making the old sabotaging standards of sixty penny nails and bridge timber spikes ineffective. To counter such measures, ecoteurs began crafting ceramic pins. In addition to being undetectable, the bits are durable enough to turn most saws and blades into scrap. With a cordless drill, an adept ecoteur can insert hundreds of ceramic pins into hundreds of trees in just a few hours.

I had read enough accounts of ecoteurs going out on night missions to know that they often darkened their faces, or disguised themselves with ski masks or watch caps. Loose, dark trench coats were said to be the garb of choice, because they could conceal both figures and equipment. Three drunken men had seen Bigfoot smashing his hand into a tree. I suspected what they had really seen was a coated ecoteur wearing gloves and wielding a three-pound hammer. Or perhaps what they had really seen was a murderer.

Before Rocinante and I got on the road, I walked over to Lofield Hardware and bought a thirty-foot extension ladder. Ecoteurs like to conduct their spikings above eye level, the theory being that the higher the spike, the less likely it is to be discovered. With the ladder, I could better look for the holes in the theory.

When I turned on to the logging road, the trees blotted out the sky. It was just the forest and me. Rocinante pushed along the rough road, her motor straining. There were no other vehicles, nothing but ancient woods. To my untrained eye, there was a sameness to the forest. Without any man-made landmarks, I had difficulty getting my bearings. I stopped half a dozen times, thinking that I had arrived, or that I had gone too far. Then I saw the trinity of trees that Evans had pointed out, that signaled the Green Man's shrine.

I took a deep breath. The stillness around me was overwhelming. The great trees were all-encompassing, and shrouding. I felt like Adam, alone in his Garden.

I thought of the ancients who had gone out to the groves and asked questions of the oracles who lived among the trees. They had asked questions and gotten answers. It was time for me to do the same.

The sibyls didn't immediately speak up. Nothing about the redwood under which the Green Man had died appeared out of the ordinary. But I wanted to go the whole nine yards—literally. I grabbed the extension ladder and set it up. Fully extended, the ladder barely tickled the feet of the giant. It struck me that looking for signs of a spiking in a redwood would be much like looking for the proverbial needle in a haystack. There was so much area to cover, and so much to look for, that the task was daunting. The immense girth of the tree was such that I figured it might take as many as half a dozen positionings of the ladder just to fully scout around its circumference, but I started my search anyway.

As I moved up the rungs, I paused every few steps to examine the tree. Nothing stood out. I went higher, and kept looking, searching with fingers as well as eyes. Still nothing. I ascended to the top of the ladder, scanned fruitlessly, then descended. When I reached the ground, I repositioned the ladder and went up a second time.

Spikers say that Mother Nature is on their side, that within a few months she covers up their handiwork. I found my first hole at about the twenty-foot mark. It was mostly masked, growth already healing the scar. I pushed my pinkie inside the hole, and it bumped against something that wasn't an acorn. I pulled out a pocketknife and started poking and probing and carving. Eventually I worked out a ceramic bit. It wasn't alone. As I moved up the ladder, I found more holes and more ceramic bits. I couldn't dig some of them out. They had been inserted deep into the heart of the tree, were waiting mines to a band saw. The tree spiker had meant business. But was it only trees that had been spiked? Twenty-five feet up doesn't sound very high unless you're the body up there. I looked down for the first time, measured the drop. I thought of possibilities. I thought of Humpty-Dumpty.

I spent the next hour examining other redwoods near the logging road and found two more trees that had been spiked. The oracles had spoken, but I wondered if they had anything else to say. I started down the barely visible path toward the Green Man's roost. Red and his friends had walked the same way, and I tried to follow his memory lane. When the goosepen came into sight, I started scrutinizing the redwoods not too far off the path. I was looking for Bigfoot's mark.

About sixty yards west of the goosepen, I found the redwood. The bark was flattened and splayed, had stood up to a pounding. If it was truly Bigfoot that Red and his friends had seen on that dark night, then the creature had taken up with the radical environmental movement. Some three-penny nails had been hammered into the tree.

Other trees nearby had been spiked as well, but they didn't show the telltale destruction of bark. The nails had been driven in at about the seven-foot level. I went back to the Sasquatch tree again. To get the attention of Red and company, the spiker had probably used his hammer like a mallet. I made a hammering motion at the tree, tried to gauge the spiker's height. The indentations ranged from the eight- to the eight-and-a-half-foot level.

More ideas were beginning to rattle around in my head. The Green Man's goosepen drew me forward. I looked inside it again, poked around its interior for a second time. I couldn't shake the feeling that I was overlooking something. But how many others had already done that same kind of scrutinizing? Deputy Evans. The detectives. Even Bull Dozier. Everyone had looked. As before, I found nothing. Not even a goose feather.

I stepped back, started examining the area around the goosepen tree. I did my surveying in ever widening concentric circles, did tree rings around tree rings. The three redwoods nearest the goosepen had been spiked, but I couldn't find anything else out of the ordinary. My circles grew wider and wider. To identify the territory covered, I took to marking trees. At the end of an hour, I stumbled upon a second goose-pen tree.

Another cave within a tree, another hole to explore. I stuck my head inside the redwood. It was dark, and I hadn't brought along a flashlight. I reached inside, suddenly felt some fluttering and heard some high-pitched squeals. Startled, I jumped back, tripped on a root, and fell.

The bats, and my clumsiness, saved my life.

It took me a second to figure out what was happening. Half a dozen bats were flying out of the goosepen. Two things had disturbed them: my intrusion, and the bullets that were chewing into their home.

The gunfire was muted by the forest. In an alleyway, the percussion of a gun can sound like a bomb, whereas in the great woods there wasn't much more than a popping. I rolled behind the tree, stifled the impulse to flee. The redwood was thick enough to protect me from bullets. I sneaked a few looks but didn't see anything or anyone. The shots had been fired at close range. I suspected my assailant had gone hunting with a handgun. I peeked again, tried to make sure no one was sneaking up on me, but there were enough redwoods around to afford the sniper plenty of cover. I was safe only as long as I had the tree between me and the shooter. Half a minute passed, and I started imagining footsteps. How long, I wondered, would the sniper stay in place? How long before the advance?

I looked for my best escape route. Less than ten yards behind me was another redwood. There was heavy brush around it, enough ferns and sorrel to allow for limited cover. I took a deep breath, then made a dash for the tree, covered about eight of those ten yards without being shot at. At the sound of gunfire, I dove and belly flopped behind the tree. The wind was momentarily knocked out of me, but I was still bullet free.

I tried not to hyperventilate, tried not to panic. Hunted deer often suffer heart attacks. I could understand why. I chanced some more glances but still couldn't see anyone. Slowly, silently, I started backing away from the tree. I used its cover to retreat into the scrub. There I moved low to the ground. I darted at quick angles, dashed from one tree to another without drawing any more fire, and finally took up behind the fort of a great, thick redwood.

For a few minutes, only my eyes moved, but I didn't see any sign of the sniper. The wise thing would have been to stay where I was, but I no longer felt like one of the hunted. Intuitively, I sensed that my assailant was withdrawing. I wasn't willing to bet my life on my gut feeling, though. When I left my position, I did so cautiously. My advance was circuitous; I moved backward before beginning on a long curved route toward the road, my progression a series of starts and stops from tree to tree.

The sniper made it to the road well ahead of me. I heard the distant sound of an engine. Without the need for caution, I sprinted to Rocinante. Any hopes of a car chase disappeared when I saw her four slashed tires.

I sat down in Rocinante's cab and did a little sweating, a little shaking, and little swearing. Then I tried to figure what the hell had just happened, and why.

After a few minutes of thought, I was certain of one thing: I wasn't scared of widow-makers anymore.

▽

25

IT WAS A LONG walk to a telephone. The hours hoofing it gave me that much more time to consider what to do next. There was a circle of silence surrounding the Green Man's death. I was convinced the muzzles were in place for a number of reasons, not all of them having specifically to do with Shepard.

When I called for a tow, the road service dispatcher wasn't concerned that Rocinante was on a private logging road. His only worry was that I would have enough "cash money" to pay the driver. I assured him I was solvent. It took an hour for succor to arrive. My knight was about twenty years old, had long hair and a Fu Manchu mustache. Our conversation consisted of him asking me if he could play some "tunes." It proved to be a long, loud drive.

I had some tires installed at a service station, then got on the road to Ferndale. The parking lot of the Truth Evangelical Church was more than half full, but it appeared the congregation hadn't come to have their souls saved so much as their stomachs filled. A church supper was going on in the vestry. I was tempted to join the food line but decided to go to church instead.

Reverend Sawyer must have had to play his collection plates like tambourines to pay the monthly electrical bills. Floodlights played on the church from all angles. But it was all exterior lighting. I couldn't see any illumination from within.

A credit card gained me entrance through the locked doors. Would that heaven's portals were so easy to enter. I was surprised at how the church looked at night, or at least that night. The wind had picked up and pushed at the stand of pines that stood between the spotlights and the stained glass. The shifting trees caused a kaleidoscope effect. I walked down an aisle of dancing colors, was led forward by rainbow Tinker Bells. Rather than hunt down votive candles, I dispersed the demons by turning on the lights. If a city on a hill couldn't be hid, then maybe the truth couldn't be either.

I poked around, curious about what kind of preaching had been going on for the last month. I searched through hymnals and prayer books, the usual depositories for Sunday programs. This congregation wasn't different from any other. I found a few old programs, and a few new thoughts. The turn of a lock made me look up.

She gasped when she saw me. The shrike had returned for his prey.

"Please sit down," I said.

"The lights . . . ," she said, explaining her presence, as if she were the one who didn't belong. "The Reverend told me to check on them."

For a few moments Ruth Sawyer stood there uncertainly, then she did as I asked, even if she did keep a row of prayer books between us.

I used a Freudian gambit. "Tell me about your parents," I said.

"My parents?"

I nodded.

"They're missionaries," she said.

"Where?"

"In Mombasa. That's in Kenya."

"So that's where you met him."

"No. I met the Reverend in Togo. He and his wife, and my parents, were assigned to a mission . . ."

"I was talking about the Green Man."

At hearing his name, she started.

Miss Tuntland had documented the Green Man's tree plantings, but I had been slow to make the connection that he and Ruth had been in Kenya at the same time.

"He was part of a mining restoration project in Mombasa," I said. "He planted thousands of trees and worked tirelessly to bring back some ravaged quarry land. I suspect he worked as tirelessly at winning your affections."

She opened her mouth, then shut it.

"The two of you were lovers."

She bit her lip very hard. She didn't wear lipstick, so, when the droplet of blood emerged, it stood out on her pale lips.

"Not long after the Green Man came to Humboldt County, he participated in a forum with your husband, and there he read from the Song of Solomon. That was his declaration of lust and love. He did it because you were there. He captured you with those sensual words, broke down all your bonds of resolve not to see him."

Mrs. Sawyer couldn't deny it.

"He was calling you again, calling you to his grove. Your husband knew that."

Again, I waited for a denial. But it wasn't voiced.

"Your husband must have known the two of you were lovers in the past, must have feared the Green Man's coming to Humboldt."

She slowly nodded her head. "He had heard I was—with child in Kenya," she whispered, "and knew it was Christopher's."

"What happened to the child?"

"I miscarried."

"How far along were you?"

"Late. Much later than usual. Five months."

She nodded, communicated her shame with her red face and martyr's posture. Ruth Sawyer didn't carry a scarlet letter. It was more the green variety.

"Your parents weren't understanding, were they?"

"I sinned," she said.

"What did Shepard say about the child?"

"He had already left by the time I learned."

"Where had he gone?"

"China. He went to do a planting along the Yellow River."

"Did you ever tell him?"

"No."

"Were you relieved when you miscarried?"

"My parents said it was God's will."

I wondered about that, wondered if it hadn't been the will of some tribal remedy, and whether that had subsequently added to her guilt.

"Was it God's will that you marry Reverend Sawyer?"

For a moment Ruth Sawyer looked troubled, then she firmed her face. "The Lord works in mysterious ways. Just after my—difficulty—was resolved, my parents received a letter from the Reverend. His wife had passed away, and he said it was difficult doing the Lord's work alone. He said he was lonely."

Ruth's parents would have read between the lines. At the time they were probably frightened. There's nothing like a pregnancy to make parents realize they don't have a little girl anymore. They'd probably been afraid that their daughter might get into trouble again.

"And when they wrote back to Sawyer, they didn't spare the details of your so-called fall."

"They didn't."

"Enlightened of them," I said.

Ruth was determined to blame herself for everything. "It was only right."

"But Sawyer was still willing to forgive you, and marry you?"

"Yes."

"What about you?"

She looked up for a moment. "What do you mean?"

"Did you ever forgive yourself?"

She bit hard enough into her lip to start the blood running again. "I needed to atone for my sins."

She had accepted the hair shirt of her loveless marriage, had married a man over two decades her senior. Everything might have been all right if he hadn't made the mistake of falling in love with her, and if she hadn't continued to carry a torch for Shepard.

"You tried to be a good wife to your husband," I said, "but

it was a union that didn't bring you any happiness. You still loved Shepard. He was different from everyone else. He gave you freedom. He encouraged you to throw off guilt, and upbringing, and fear. He gave you joy."

She lifted her head. Her eyes were wise and free once more. Beacons of affirmation. Then, the door swung open. She turned, and the lanterns of her eyes dimmed. The Reverend Sawyer stood there. He looked like an unhappy Old Testament patriarch. "Ruth," he said. She rose obediently, anticipating a command. "The flock needs tending." A moment later and Sawyer and I were alone.

He scowled at me. "I have asked you to leave my wife alone," he said. "She isn't a strong woman."

"I hadn't intended to bother her," I said. "I came to talk with you."

Habit made him walk up the aisle. He assumed his position in the pulpit, as if he was ready to lead the church into service.

"Earlier this week, I got a preview of this Sunday's sermon," I said. "You left your tape recorder here. You quoted from Mark, recited a passage where Christ is restoring a blind man's vision: 'And he looked up, and said, I see men as trees, walking.' I've studied the church programs of the last three weeks. In each, that passage has been cited."

Sawyer tried to bluster. "The miracles of the Lord should not be forgotten."

"I see men as trees, walking," I said, repeating the words. "Is that what you saw?"

"What are you talking about?"

"I'm trying to reason out a death. I think that subconsciously you are too."

The Reverend Sawyer started turning the pages of his large Bible. His paper rustling was overloud. "The Gospels recount forty-seven parables of Christ—"

"I only have one parable to recount," I said. "And I'm afraid it's not written in any holy book."

The pages stopped turning.

"Mohammed said that if you hear that a mountain has moved, believe; but if you hear that a man has changed his character, believe it not.

"In the past year, everyone says you've changed quite a bit. I don't think that's true. I think only one thing changed: you were in love, and you were desperate for that love to be reciprocated. It wasn't. That made you insecure. You fought with a phantom that you labeled a devil. And then that phantom took form.

"About a year ago, the Green Man announced his intention to come to Humboldt County. His declaration corresponded with your so-called change. You prepared for your devil by starting The Third Day. You raised your voice and attracted a new, rabid following. You showed your wife vigor and resolve, and drew the lines of good and evil.

"You became a man you weren't. You defined God and the godless. You made the Green Man, and what he stood for, forbidden. You tried to make your wife have to choose between God and the Green Man. You thought you could keep her that way. But she couldn't deny her heart. She went for the forbidden fruit. She went to his garden.

"You knew about that garden. You spied on the Green Man regularly, knew about the ceremonies, knew about his goosepen. The Green Man lived in River Grove not because he was protecting three thousand acres of old growth but because it was so close to your wife."

What had Sawyer thought, standing out in the darkness, listening to her screams of passion? I wondered if he had been sickened. I wondered if he had felt shortchanged, saddened that she could never offer that vitality to him, that she couldn't give that side of herself. I wondered if he had been excited by this woman he didn't know, or whether the mænad in her frightened him.

He suddenly looked bent, and old, and sick. His feistiness was gone. He had been defensive not for himself but for her. "I prayed for a miracle," he whispered, "not once, but many times. I prayed in those woods. And my prayers were finally answered."

Had he prayed loudly enough to drown out her cries of pleasure? Had he thought that by turning his back and bending his knees he could live with being cuckolded? He had convinced himself that his prayers had been answered, that an angel had come, but in his heart of hearts he knew that

189

it wasn't divine intervention he had witnessed. Like the blind man, he had seen men walking as trees.

He thought that by citing the Bible he could assure me, and reassure himself. "In Genesis we read that angels are God's providence to man, and can also be the instruments of his punishment. Do you not remember the angels destroying Sodom?"

"Tell me about your angel," I said.

"He dropped from the sky and fell on the worshiper of Baal. In Judges six, verse twenty-five, God tells us that the Israelites planted groves in Baal's honor, and an angel was sent to Gideon and told him to cast down the altar of Baal and cut down his groves. And Gideon went and did as Jehovah asked."

"What did your angel do?"

"He struck down the idolater."

"And what did your angel look like?"

"Ethereal. There was a nimbus around his head, a celestial light surrounding his flowing mane and beard."

"And what happened to this angel?"

"After he dropped from the sky he stood over the body of the forest devil. I was too afraid to look anymore. I just prayed."

"What about later? Did you go and examine Shepard's body?"

He shook his head.

"Did the angel ever see you, or acknowledge you?"

"No."

"And besides your wife, and Shepard, and the angel, did you see anyone, or anything else, that night?"

He could no longer look in my direction. His hands covered his eyes. I watched him shake his head. I felt sorry for Reverend Sawyer. He had had to confront his own tree of the knowledge of good and evil, had faced the double bind of God and love, and right and wrong. The Green Man hadn't been the only casualty in the woods.

I left the church and went to call upon an angel.

▽

26

I PULLED OFF THE dirt road but parked well away from the camp. With the moon to guide me, I walked forward. Circle was long concluded, but there were still sounds from the camp, some laughter, the strumming of a guitar, the drowsy chant of voices.

From the outside, I looked in. I felt like an animal, a predator. A familiar voice caught my attention, and I came in from the darkness. Josh knew my shadow and didn't want to have anything to do with it. He turned from those he was talking with and walked away. I followed him to his tent, but by the time I got there he had zipped the entrance closed behind him. I've had thousands of doors shut on me, but never a tent. I knocked on the fabric. That made for a little rustling and not much else. It was like trying to push into Jell-O.

"Josh?"

No answer. I started kicking the tent poles, and that got him out. Maybe his tent had been one of those Red had uprooted. He was mad, and he wanted me to know it.

"The last time we talked, Stuart, I vowed I'd have nothing more to say to you as long as you persisted in a line of questioning antithetical to the pursuits of this organization. Lone wolf doesn't make it out here. We have collective goals."

"I need you to tell me about the spiking, Josh."

For a strong advocate of free speech, Josh was never too happy to have our discussions aired in public. He motioned for me to follow him. He didn't stop walking until we were away from the lights of the camp.

"It was a very emotional issue," Josh said by way of a whispered explanation. The Sequoia Summer campers had transgressed their word. "We were divided as to whether we should do the spiking. But we finally agreed that, by not acting, we were breaking the greater trust of letting holy shrines fall."

"How many of you went spiking that night?"

"About thirty of us."

I asked Josh where they had spiked, and he named the spots, virgin groves throughout the county. He said the ecoteurs had worked in teams. Ecotage is like scuba diving. You're not supposed to do it alone.

"Everyone had a partner?"

Josh hesitated before answering. "Yes."

"You didn't mention spiking River Grove."

"We skipped that area."

"Why?"

"For the Green Man's sake. If the spiking was discovered, we didn't want him to get blamed."

"Whose decision was that?"

Truculently: "All of ours."

"Shepard took precedence over an old-growth forest?"

Josh shook his head. "We just changed our time frame. A few of us put dibs on it for this fall."

"How did you know Shepard wouldn't be around in the fall?"

"We knew about his plans. Some of us intended to be a part of them, to be a part of history."

"His Green Belt?"

"He said you'd be able to see it from the moon," said Josh, "from out in space. He described how it was going to go across the entire earth, circle it, you know? He figured it would take about ten billion trees. When he talked about it, you got goose bumps. It was like the earth was a painting, something we could improve upon."

"Why haven't you spiked River Grove since his death?"

Josh shrugged. "Political considerations. Maybe, because of his death, we won't have to."

"Meaning it wouldn't be very good PR if just before the election a logger or sawmill worker was injured or killed by one of your spikes."

"There are those who would tell you that the logging companies have done their own spiking, and caused their own accidents, to get publicity."

"It wasn't loggers that went out spiking last month," I said.

"Like I told you, we spiked as a last resort. The lumber companies love to scream to the media how we're irresponsible and don't have any conscience. They like to say we endanger the lives of so-called innocent workers. But do you know how many mill injuries have occurred from our spikings over the years? A handful. It's a psychological threat more than anything else."

"I seem to remember a mill worker who was almost decapitated a couple of years ago."

"That wasn't one of our spikes."

"But the next one might be."

"We intend to warn the logging companies before they begin any cutting in the areas we chose to protect. That's the purpose of spiking, you know. Prevention. We don't want people to get hurt. We just want to save some trees. We've found the timber industry doesn't care much about their workers, though. If they did, they wouldn't be shipping all their lumber jobs to Mexico and overseas. It's not the thought of injuries that bothers them. What hurts them most is when something cuts into their profits. Blades are damn expensive, and so is downtime. It's easier to replace a man than a blade. That's their mind-set."

Sometimes, to get answers, you have to put up with sermons. "Who went out on the spiking expedition?"

Josh shook his head. "No way."

I worked on getting the answer another way. "Did you rendezvous afterward? Did all of you meet somewhere?"

"No. We drifted back into camp at different times."

"So you took separate cars?"

"Not all of us. Like I told you, we spiked in tandem. And since some teams were spiking groves near to one another, we rode along together."

Carpooling to a spiking. But not everyone, I imagined. "There was one among you who spiked alone, wasn't there?" I tried to read Josh's face in the dim light. His facial contortions told me I had hit the spike on the head. But his expression was more forthcoming than his answer. "Don't ask for specifics, Stuart. You've played that game with me before. I only have one answer for you: the majority ruled." "I wonder if you ruled for murder," I said.

The scent of cannabis didn't guide me this time. It was their voices. From the top of the path I could hear Doc and Teller talking. I didn't actively eavesdrop, just stood around listening to the sounds of their words more than the words themselves. Their conversation was lazily lobbed back and forth. There were some soft sighs, and some light laughter, and some unhurried talk. There was no speech making, just balloons of thoughts set sailing from one to the other. There is a certain pleasure in listening to friends ramble, and not having to discern double meanings or undercurrents. Friends can speak aloud to each other and not worry about whether they're making absolute sense, or verbal points.

The big man and the little man were sitting on rocks looking out over the river. I made enough noise so that they heard my approach.

"Roll up a rock," said Doc. "Or, in your line of work, do you usually crawl out from under one?"

I didn't laugh, and neither did Teller. Doc suddenly got the idea that I hadn't come to socialize. In the lengthening silence, he also sensed his presence wasn't wanted. He faked a yawn, and, when he announced that he had to leave, no one voiced any objections.

I took his place on the rock. I pulled my coat to my frame and rubbed my hands. Teller waited for me to talk. In the interim, he pulled out a joint and lit it. We didn't face each other but looked out to the river instead.

"Did you go there to kill him?"

"That's a good question."

"Do I get a good answer?"

"Why don't you tell me?" he said, then toked on his joint. I knew how long his lungs could hold things in, so I went ahead with the talking. "Ashe came to you," I said. "She told you that the Green Man was selling out. She was upset and didn't know what to do. You told her that you would take care of everything.

"She didn't arrive at a good time. You were all ready to go out spiking. I suspect Doc was going to be your partner. It would have been a chance for the two of you to use the climbing gear. But you told him that he couldn't go spiking with you that night. I don't know what area the two of you had been assigned, but you ended up at River Grove. When you arrived there, you didn't immediately find Shepard. The area was supposed to be off-limits to spiking, but you decided to make use of your time. You spiked some trees near his goosepen, using the traditional hammer-and-nail method.

"Eventually, Shepard showed up, but he wasn't alone. He was preoccupied with his company, which allowed you to slip unnoticed into the woods.

"You didn't leave, though. You spiked a few more trees. They never even heard you over their lovemaking. You were determined to try and reason with Shepard. You were desperate. If the Green Man came out against Proposition One-fifty, you knew that all you had worked for was in jeopardy."

Teller nodded. His agreeing didn't make him look any happier.

"I have four witnesses," I said, "who can place you near the scene of the murder at about the time it took place. Three men saw you in the woods, or, more accurately, they saw what they thought was Bigfoot. They were drunk, and it was dark, and you were wearing a heavy coat, and gloves, and a ski mask, and chose to communicate with them by pounding on a redwood with a hammer.

"You scared the hell out of them. They fled, and you followed them to the logging road. There, you decided to wait for Shepard. You didn't do your waiting in the normal way. You decided to while away your time by spiking the redwoods nearest the logging road.

"You were more careful with those trees, thought it more prudent to hide your activities. You pulled your climbing rig out of the Jeep and scaled some of the big trees, peppering them with ceramic bits. But you hadn't come to River Grove just to spike, or at least not just to spike trees. When Shepard returned from walking his lover back to her car, he passed under one of the trees you were spiking. It was then that you dropped from the tree and struck him."

Teller responded unemotionally. "How do you know that?"

"My fourth witness. With your white hair and beard, he thought you were an angel."

"Devil would have been closer to the mark." Teller reacted calmly, as if he had resigned himself to this moment long ago.

"It was the third tree I scaled that night," he said, "and each had proved more difficult than the last. I'm a stubborn son of a bitch. Or a stupid one. I guess I don't know how to give up."

He flicked the last of his joint out to the river. The water subdued the spark. It didn't even utter a last gasp.

"My limbs had stopped obeying me. It had been too long since I last used a climbing rig. I had forgotten the rhythm, and I didn't have the upper-body strength anymore. I was weighted down. The tools of the tree-protecting trade are many, and heavy.

"I felt stupid up there. The belt supported my weight. I hung there, fat, and old, and useless. For what seemed the longest time, I couldn't move. I was too tired to get down, too tired to even think anymore.

"The wind picked up. It was wind enough to move the big tree, wind enough to blow an old fool around like a leaf.

"The lovers passed beneath my tree while I was being blown around. They never noticed me. He was naked, and she was clothed, and they had their arms around one another. Her car was parked several hundred feet away. I prepared for his return, for our confrontation.

"I tried to get my hands and legs to obey me, but my body had gone numb. My tree was shaking, and so was I. The gusts continued to get worse. I could see Shepard coming back, and I called to him, but the wind snatched my voice. I worked on loosening my rig.

"I remember pulling at a catch and beginning to shimmy down. That's when I lost control of my descent. I fell. He never knew what hit him."

Teller's voice caught a little and he stopped talking. Like the wind, I pushed at him.

"And you figured no one would believe a freak accident like that could have happened?"

He nodded.

"So you pulled a widow-maker out of the ground, and tried to disguise the way he really died?"

Teller shook his head. "I panicked," he admitted. "I was disoriented. I hurt all over. All I could think of was that I had to get up and leave. And that's what I did."

"You never examined Shepard?"

"Just for a moment. I saw some blood. That was enough."

"But you came back later?"

He nodded. "The next morning."

"How do you explain the widow-maker?"

Teller shook his head, then he sucked on his index finger and chewed hard on his lip. His cannabis hadn't proved to be lotus leaf enough. "I've thought about that quite a bit," he said. "I've had to.

"I figured it was possible he hadn't died but had broken a leg, or an arm, and might need my help. So much for wishful thinking. Hit and run in the middle of the forest. By the time I came back, it was too late.

"I've seen his death in my mind a thousand times. He might have been alive—hurt, not moving. If I had just moved him from that spot, just helped him, the widow-maker would never have struck him."

Teller answered incriminating questions that I didn't ask. He had been trying to exorcise his demons for the past month and still hadn't found the words. Or the explanation.

"You ask me why I didn't go to the police. Selfishness. Not personal selfishness, at least that's what I tell myself, but selfishness for the sake of the old trees."

Teller looked at me. Challenged me to challenge him. "I was going to confess after the election," he said.

He stroked his long and knotted beard. His face was gray. He looked like one of the old trees in Longfellow's primeval forest, bearded with moss.

"What time did you return from River Grove?"

"Around ten-thirty. Doc was waiting for me in camp. I had

left him without much of an explanation. I went off upset, and returned much worse. Doc reminded me about Methuselah duty. We had planned not to be out very late because of it. I asked him to take my place."

"Did you tell him why?"

"No. Ashe and I were the only ones who knew about the Green Man and her father. She had begged to go with me, but I wouldn't let her."

"Where did she do her begging?"

"Right here. On this spot."

"Afterwards, did you tell her what happened?"

"No. I didn't want to implicate her in any way. I only told her not to ask me any questions, and to avoid talking about that night."

"When did you see Ashe to tell her that?"

"The next day. After I returned from River Grove."

I considered all that he had told me. Teller must have thought me crazy when I announced, "Eureka!"

▽

27

DEPUTY EVANS AND I drove in darkness. I had called him late the night before and extorted an early-morning ride. I had brought along a flashlight and a gun, and examined both. The deputy wasn't too impressed with my Saturday night special.

"You call that a gun?"

"Not much of one," I admitted, "but I didn't have the foresight to bring a piece along. The triumph of hope over experience. I took this one off of some of your good old boys."

Evans raised an eyebrow, and I told him the story. It wasn't the first tale he had heard from me that morning. "You've been a busy boy," he said.

I shrugged, and we didn't say much else, just took in what scenery we could. On my previous visits to River Grove, it had been dark enough even in the full light of the afternoon. Going there before dawn was a new experience. The ancient forest didn't look welcoming. The lights from the police cruiser barely penetrated the gloom. It felt like we were traveling into a nightmare.

We stopped where the Green Man had died. "You sure about this?" Evans asked.

I nodded. I didn't want any cars around, didn't want anything to make the killer suspicious. Evans was supposed to return at noon. By then, one way or another, I hoped my wild goosepen chase would be over.

"Good luck," he said.

We waved to each other; then he turned the police car around and drove away. I stood there for a minute and tried to acclimate to the darkness. Halloween in Transylvania didn't have anything on this setting. It was dark and cold, and I was more than a little afraid. The redwoods were whispering among themselves, and I felt as if I was encroaching. I buttoned my coat and took some deep breaths. Then I started walking, overcompensated for my fears by taking brisk, directed strides. It took me about half an hour to hunt down the goosepen tree where I had almost died. If I was right, there would be another goosepen, and this one wouldn't be empty. Don McLellan had used three goosepens during his stay in the woods. The Green Man would have known that but wouldn't have had need for another goosepen until late in the summer. That was why I had been shot at. The murderer had made the connection that there was a second goosepen.

I started my surveying again. In the world beyond the big trees, the sun was rising, but that light wasn't penetrating very far into these woods. I went from tree to tree, using my light and my system of circles. I looked for two hours before taking a break. What halted my investigation was a sound I first thought was a barking dog. The vocalizations continued, and I crept forward. "Whoo—whoo—hoo—hoo." The spotted owl was sitting in a canyon live oak. I had a minute's worth of rapture, then he flew off. Only then did I notice the adjacent goosepen tree.

I walked over, wondered if my luck would hold for two remarkable findings in one day, and shined my light inside the hollowed tree.

There weren't any bats this time. There was just a weathered backpack. I looked inside and found the Green Man's green.

I sat in the goosepen and watched the dark gray world turn a little less gray. I had time to kill, so I thought about the circumstances of the kill.

The Green Man had been looking for seed money for his Green Belt. Bull Dozier was a businessman, and he sensed a good opportunity. When Shepard had expressed his ambivalence about the ancient forests, and told him where his true dreams lay, Dozier had acted. The No on 150 campaign had already cost the timber industry millions of dollars. With his tape recorder off, Dozier had suggested they might be able to work together. He would have offered an unofficial contribution to the Green Man's cause. I also suspected he had proposed a deal whereby Shepard's seedlings, millions if not billions of them, could be gained from the lumber interests. The Green Belt might ultimately have proven very lucrative, very green to Dozier's business. Tree planting is a popular venture these days, with lots of groups and interests behind it. The lumber baron had been a not so unlikely believer in the Green Belt. He hadn't thought of it as a pipe dream, had gone so far as to defend it in my presence.

When the Green Man had died, Dozier had personally come out to River Grove. He had advanced a sizable amount of money to Shepard, and he wanted it back. It wouldn't have done to have had a large parcel of money found in the woods. Questions of bribery and impropriety would have been voiced. But Dozier hadn't been able to find the money.

Ashe had seen Shepard with the payoff. That explained her "thirty pieces" reference to her mother. She would have told Teller about the Green Man's selling out, but Teller wasn't the kind of man who would have gone to the woods thinking about money. That would have been the last thing on his mind. He would have been fixated on the threat to the old trees, and Ashe's state of mind. He had seen her desperation, had known that he had to act. Teller and Ashe hadn't really talked since the night the Green Man had died. Each of them had been afraid for the other. In their own way, all had been bound to silence. Not Dozier, or Teller, or Ashe could talk. They were all holding secrets. I suspected if I scratched much further I'd find other hidden deeds; Dozier's hand, I was sure, was behind the activities of Red and his friends, at least before he had become allied with the Green Man.

I sat in the golden goosepen. I couldn't even guess how much money was in the backpack, but I knew it was a lot of trees. I waited in the knowledge that greed is its own best lure.

Faintly, almost imperceptibly, I heard footsteps. A light played on the crevasse. The beam didn't touch me, but I pushed away from it anyway, stayed enfolded inside the tree. The light and the steps came closer. A head breached the opening.

I put my gun next to his head, and, when I had all of his attention, and then some, I asked, "What's up, Doc?"

▽

28

He had told me when we first met that money is "the root of all evil." I guess I should have taken that as a confession.

I motioned Doc forward with my gun. Almost immediately, he started trying to explain his actions. "There is such a thing as justifiable homicide," he said.

"I guess I'm going to hear about the science of murder," I said.

"He deserved to die," said Doc. "He was corrupt to the core."

"You didn't have much reason to like him," I admitted.

Shepard had scared his Jane away. Doc knew his science, but he didn't seem to know much about real life. Maybe Jane was his first girlfriend. She was important to him, and the Green Man's ceremonies had greatly upset her, had driven her from him. He had felt challenged, and jealous, and angry. Those feelings would have come to the fore again when Shepard defied Teller, his father image. Shepard's decision not to support old growth had threatened all of Teller's work. In short order the Green Man had hurt the two most important people in Doc's life. But that wasn't the reason Doc had killed him.

"His Green Belt was going to promote forest fascism," said Doc. "He didn't care about biodiversity or old growth. He would have planted a monoculture . . ."

"Funny how those things mean so much to you now," I said, "whereas they didn't before. I'm sure you'll get a good lawyer who will amplify on those themes and paint you as a noble defender of the earth. But spare me that speech. I was the one you tried to murder, remember?"

I held the gun on him, and he remembered.

"You were there when Ashe came storming into camp. You were ready to go spiking with Teller, not because you believed in ecotage but because you wanted to show off your climbing skills to your mentor. You watched Teller lead Ashe away, and, curious, you followed them. I know how those voices can carry up from the river. You would have heard about the money. Ashe probably made it sound like a million dollars. Manna from heaven, you must have thought. Teller told me how you weren't used to working, how you'd been a professional student your entire life. He said you inherited some money, but a stockbroker put you into some bad investments. That's another way of saying you were greedy. Stockbrokers don't make the investment decisions. You wanted a high return on your cash. The speculation didn't pan out, and suddenly you were looking at a life of toil like the rest of us. You got a little taste of that life, and you didn't like it. When your doctorate didn't immediately open the doors you thought it would, you became that much more embittered.

"When Teller came back to camp looking desperate and dazed, you knew something had happened between him and the Green Man. You agreed to tree-sit Methuselah, but, after relieving Sasha, you didn't stay in the tree house for very long.

"I don't think you went to River Grove with the idea of killing the Green Man. But when you came upon him lying prostrate in front of you, you saw your opportunity. It was windy, not a good time to be out in the woods. The widow-maker was embedded in the ground near him. The thought would have come to you that widow-makers had killed before. Everyone knew that. You pulled the branch from the ground and stood over his recumbent body. He was sleeping off Teller's fall, and his nakedness offended you, provoked you even more. You would have thought of Jane. You might even have thought of Teller. But what you thought about most was the money. You could take that money, and no one would know. It would mean not having to suffer the indignity of handouts at camp. It would allow you to be an independent man of means once again."

In my mind's eye I could see him raising his muscular arms skyward like a sacrificial priest, then driving the stake home.

"It must have shocked you when you didn't find the money in the goosepen. You would have kept looking, would have grown more and more frustrated at not being able to find the Green Man's cache. Your search was certainly interrupted by the police investigation. You didn't want to be anywhere near those woods while they were out there. Keeping a low profile would have limited your ability to rummage around. You followed me while I was doing my snooping at River Grove. At first you must have wondered what the hell I was doing going around in what would have looked like circles. But when I came across that second goosepen, when I reached inside, you suddenly thought I had found the Green Man's treasure. You weren't about to let anyone else have it. Even though you didn't kill me, you drove me away from the tree. No money again. But you left convinced that the money would be in another goosepen. No more pushing over old logs, or searching under rockpiles. The only problem was getting to it first. It made sense that the tree wouldn't be too far away from the Green Man's roost. You decided to extend the search from where I had left off. You can try to paint your motives under a noble brush, but it was money that drove you to murder. Not pure, but simple."

"No," said Doc. "That's not how it was. He was like a weed in the woods, a spreading and destructive weed. He had to be eradicated. It was in the interest of the world that I acted. I did it for the old trees. I did it for biodiversity. I did it for—"

"Money," I said. "The same reason you were willing to kill me."

Doc had justified the murder in his mind, had convinced himself that the Green Man was the Hitler of the environmental movement. He continued to make his case for what

205

he had done, and kept talking about his altruistic murder, even after Evans read him his rights.

I returned to San Francisco but found it hard to leave the woods behind me. I didn't come home empty-handed. I brought back three redwood seedlings purchased at the Humboldt Redwoods State Park. One was for Miss Tuntland, and one was for me. I was going to have Miss Tuntland's sent over to her apartment, but she told me to plant it for her.

"My gardening is limited to the window-box variety," she said. "God didn't mean for me to till the earth, so I'll entrust that chore to you."

Then she laughed and said the prospect of the planting put a tingle down her spine.

"The moment you finish," she said, "I want you to call and tell me all about it, and don't leave out one detail."

I told her where our trees were going to be planted, and she approved. John McLaren had been there before me, had even prepared the ground.

I took the three root balls and went to McLaren's redwood grove at Golden Gate Park. I followed the instructions that had come with the seedlings, dug my holes one and a half feet wide and three feet deep, mixed up some nutrients, then placed the root balls in their new home.

When I finished, I wiped the sweat from my brow and took a look at the future. It's always difficult to imagine something else, something greater. Three little seedlings, no more than five inches high, were hard to envision as monuments. I put a name on each: mine, Miss Tuntland's, and the Green Man's. I thought of him more kindly now, pictured him in the proper backdrop of more than 2 million trees. With only three to my name, I already felt as if I had conquered the world, or at least had done something to better my own universe.

I saved my words for Miss Tuntland. She wanted to know all about her tree. I described its exact location and how healthy it looked. Then she asked about my tree, and where it stood in relation to hers. I remembered the digging for her, and the planting, and how it had all felt good, and proper, and right.

"It was like Jack and the beanstalk time," I said. "If I didn't know any better, I would swear those redwoods grew even as I watched."

"Beware of giants," she said.

Or giant killers, I thought.

"My tree is going to grow and grow," Miss Tuntland predicted.

"And so is mine."

"Race you to the stars."

"You're on."